ALL
ALONG
THE
ECHO

Also by Danny Denton

The Earlie King & The Kid In Yellow

DANNY DENTON

ALL ALONG THE ECHO

atlantic · *fiction*

First published in hardback and trade paperback in Great Britain and Ireland in 2022 by Atlantic Books, an imprint of Atlantic Books Ltd.

The author is very grateful to the Arts Council of Ireland, who provided invaluable financial support in the writing of this book.

1 2 3 4 5 6 7 8 9

A CIP catalogue record for this book is available from the British Library.

Hardback ISBN: 978 1 83895 553 3
Trade paperback ISBN: 978 1 83895 554 0
E-book ISBN: 978 1 83895 555 7

Printed in Great Britain

Atlantic Books
An imprint of Atlantic Books Ltd
Ormond House
26–27 Boswell Street
London
WC1N 3JZ
www.atlantic-books.co.uk

for Rachel,
across the counter in the Royal George,
at Gougane Barra,
see you in bed x

'Let them think of what that meant, of the calling which went on every day from room to room of a house, and then think of that calling extending from pole to pole; not a noisy babble, but a call audible to him who wanted to hear and absolutely silent to him who did not, it was almost like dreamland and ghostland, not the ghostland of the heated imagination cultivated by the Psychical Society, but a real communication from a distance based on true physical laws.'

Professor W. E. Ayrton, the chairman of the Royal Society of Arts, calling for a vote of thanks to Mr. G Marconi, who had just presented his paper 'Wireless Telegraphy' (on the future of radio) to the Royal Society of Arts, in London, May 1902.

the

body

stump

SLKNSSDNSLKDNSMNEQWNQWNNNA DQWEFRMHHMSDLOOFJDFDLKWEN WWWKFDFLSDPAOOTHENAKFNGF NEISNSFDNWEW IN THE STA TIC

the first noise is the hum of electricity, radio in its own language, dreamed or not, and the first vision is the ghost of the receiver antenna, silhouetted against the night's clouds, some part or echo of it blinking red at intervals. Through the dark came once the rustling, the beam of torchlight, the slow whistle of the engineer, as he fumbled and dropped his keys, as he fished for the keys in the dark grass of the field and found them, and unlocked the bolt and pulled the chain and then yanked open the gate against the long grass. The transmitter station is two squat breezeblock huts with corrugated roofs — one for signal, one for power — and the engineer had yet again to sweep aside swathes of long grass and nettle and thistle to get to the signal hut's door and its lock, and again in the dark he found the key for that door and pulled it open, and fumbled for the light switch as his eyes clocked in the gloom the 'ON' lights and the signal lights of receivers and transmitters and servers and the signal dissipator and the hot pipes that still carry the signal back and forth, the signal that is clearest shortly before the dawndfmfmgkykyher bsbndfnfgnynuljhpkjlsjandcnvbnxcbaswejktykydnnfn ghturksamdsndnfnnununununuynuibbibibibibbsiwopdkfk kgkhmyntnanandndnntnykykululilipdmmgnsndflllglglyy fgtyuisasfgbhywjhmyntelgmyny

BROADCASTING SIMULTANEOUSLY on 5264 kHz + 1420 MHz...

playback: the pale moon was rising above the green mountain / the sun was declining beneath the blue sea...

first voice: *[static] nine... five... seven... two... [static] broadcasting to all, but to nobody in particular of course... [static] they say your life flashes before your eyes... [static] but the listener forms their own image [static] the big ear listening straight out as the world turned [static] i hear them [static] and therefore i see them [static] just like this...*

OFF-AIR, he dreamed that the car competition had already begun and he sat alone in the driver's seat of a tiny Mazda, pulled into the hard shoulder of the dual carriageway, overlooking the Mahon estuary just beyond the slip road for Rochestown. And from that weather hill he could see where the seaweed shores encrusted the land, and where the city sprawled in the distance. On the opposite riverbank, smoke rose from low blocks of nondescript facilities that might have been pharmaceuticals, or warehouses, or makers of tiny plastic cylinders. And he saw the marshland, the river, the slip roads and flyovers, the castle, the docklands, and, rising out of the city's roofstacks and steeples and aerials, the radio station's mast. The beacon. And it was all the same, but it was utterly different.

'COME ON WILL YOU, TONY!' a voice boomed, and when he turned there was the giant head of a man in the back seat. Bald and bearded, cross-eyed, gaping at him.

'I must get back to Ireland for me funeral,' the head said.

It was just a head, filling the back seat on the passenger side.

'I fucking hate London,' it said. Was its voice coming from the back seat or the radio speakers? 'I will not be buried here again!'

'But we're in Ireland,' Tony pointed out, reasonably, via the rear-view mirror. 'We're in Cork?'

In the mirror he saw, next to the head, a gaunt woman he did not know. Or did not know he knew. She was all bone and wrinkle.

'We are in my crooked eye!' the head bawled, alone on the back seat. 'DRIVE ON TA FUCK!'

But Tony didn't know how to drive. Though he pressed the accelerator with his foot, the car wouldn't budge. Just revving, just noise.

'What are these boxes next to me?' the head brusquely asked. 'They reek of age.'

Tony looked in the rear-view and saw his vinyl collection, all boxed up, collected first in London — fifty pence a record in the basement of a place in Greenwich – and added to then throughout the years. 'That's the *collected*,' he told the giant head.

'THE COLLECTED WHAT?'

'My records. I collect records. Music?'

'AH, MUSIC! The music of what happens, that's what I liked best. When I was… How long til we're back in Ireland? I fucken *CANNOT* be buried here again, and will not, and you must get me home.'

'I can't impress this upon you enough,' Tony said, slowly and clearly. 'We are on the South Ring dual carriageway in Cork. That's the slip road for Rochestown there.'

'WE ARE IN MY EYE!' the giant head bawled.

The gaunt woman grinned at him through the rear-view. 'Listen to yer man,' she said. 'Eyes!' Every wrinkle was a smile.

'Do *you* know how to drive?' he asked her, and yet he had already released the handbrake and the car began to roll slowly backwards.

'THIS,' the head boomed, 'is not my country. *This* is an abomination.'

'You're not wrong there, Eyes,' the gaunt woman said.

Hands to the wheel, Tony tried to keep the reversing car on the tarmac and off the grassy verge. Mercifully, there was no other traffic on the road. 'You might not be wrong there,' he said, and it was his radio voice that emerged.

'I asked them to take me with them. Me head. I was a good friend to them. I told them stories of old. I fucking sang to them, Tony. I fucking *sang* to them.'

'Right.' The car rolled backwards. Tony's whole being felt… *braced*.

'Me! A giant! And what'd they do? RATS! Don't open the door, I said! God knows where they are now.'

They rumbled into the verge and the box of vinyl bounced violently.

'Sorry about that,' Tony said. 'Doing my best here!'

'Get us home quick, Anthony. Before I'm fucken buried

again. EIGHTY JOYOUS YEARS ME HOLE!'

'Where is home though?' Tony asked, the radio voice again. Fuck.

'THE AULD SOD, YOU CRETIN! THE AULD FUCKEN SOD! Come on will you, you ignoramus! You *amadán*! GET US HOME!'

But no matter how hard Tony tried or how much abuse the giant head hurled at him, or how the gaunt woman smiled, they made no progress. What seemed to be the city of Cork lay in front of them, and the county seemed to lie around them, but they only revved and rolled backwards on the dual carriageway, forever, even after the point in the dream where Tony realised he was dreaming.

[static] and when he did awake, did it not for the briefest moment feel like he'd woken into someone else's dream? [static]

OFF-AIR, the night sky was a wide open space, but then the grey morning hauled itself out from underneath the distant edges and the slates of the terrace rooftops began to clarify, one deep dull colour to another. She should really have known more specific names for the colours but she didn't. The cans she had this night were POWER ORANGE and SHOCK WHITE, their brightness so far from the colour of that city, the colours of that warm dawn wind moving over cold air.

She made one last mark, the can's near empty rasp the sign of a decent night's writing; the blockygood letters of a throw-up, big and square and bright. Of course you always got a little more time on these ancient terrace lanes, where the roofs were all different heights, sort of leaning on each other, lanes watched only by cats and puddles and grates and the ghosts of the sewers. Fifteen times tonight she'd made her mark – her name – both large and small, bombs, tags and throw-ups, all around the lanes on the North Mall. Remember me, you smug fucks. You drunken fucks. You rich, moneygrabbing fucks. You snobby fucks, you fucking shits. You fucking shits with your vampire smiles. You remember my name.

A cough, someone coming. In a panic, she thrust the can into her big pocket, as if a guard might come around the corner *right then*, or some early-morning dog walker or jogger... But there was no one there on the old terrace lane, only herself. Only herself and the wind, and the damp brick walls and curtained windows, and two cats yowling at each other somewhere nearby, and bodies turning in sleep in bedrooms all around her, all around her in a city that sprawled and twitched, mossy rooftops and parked cars and cracked paving slabs and the river that split and diverged along by maltings and walkways, that ran along behind the streets of government departments and hotels and guesthouses and warehouses, the river merging again then and swinging out past the dockyards to lose itself to the harbour. And her mother, her father, her sister, all asleep in one little room in one little guesthouse in that city.

Who had coughed then? Maybe no one.

Maybe God.

But she had given up God after making her confirmation. She'd asked the Holy Spirit to let them keep the house, and to get the leccy back on, but no appearance or help from the Holy Spirit, so fuck God. It is very tricky to explain to your friends why you have no electricity in the house. You can't say it's gone all over the estate, because they live on the estate and their leccy is obviously on. Trickier again to say you're moving house but not say where you're moving to. You just sort of have to disappear, let them forget you.

No, there was no cough, nobody there; she'd see no one til she got back out onto the Mall, and she went that way now quietly, watching the first gulls come down from over the rooftops and the cranes. She would get back to the guesthouse, slip in, fit into her place. Get a couple of hours' sleep before she was supposed to go to school. Mam and Dad probably knew she was gone from the room alright. Probably. But they didn't know her name. Her *real* name. All over the city – on every wall, lamp post, bin and door…

'You off to work this early, love?'

It was that skinny alco she always saw dancing outside McDonald's. He was just sitting up on the riverside bench and looking over the water, the vague, middling tide. He yawned. His shaven head was all scars. Could he see her or was he only talking to someone imagined? 'Hah? Early to work is it?'

'Yea.' She clenched the spray cans in each pocket. Why had she stopped by him?

'Grand morning for the walk in.'

'Yea.'

'I'm an agent of thought you know…'

'Cool.'

She started to walk on, past him, but then he stood up into her path and raised his arms like wings.

'I got the milk too! He said to me, he said you better watch it. I said, watch it? You fuckin *know* me, man!'

'Yea,' she said. He was only a couple of inches taller than her, him by the bench, her by the river railing.

'It's not fuckin on me,' he suddenly spat. He was pleading – this man with bony cheeks, and bruises and scabs all over his face – but he seemed not to be seeing her. 'It's on *him*.'

'Yea,' she said. 'I'm off to work now though. See you.'

He turned as she tried to squeeze past, close enough to smell the vomit. 'Fifteen years he fuckin knows me!' he cried.

She focused on the space between his arms and the railing – walked straight through it. Left his pleading behind her, hoping he wouldn't follow. But he wasn't the worst, only another sad human in a derelict city. She hurried on towards the crossing and the bridge as a silver Mazda charged past, speeding to make it through an orange light, the puddles of yesterday's rain hissing, and then another car behind it, and suddenly there was the white noise of the morning picking up.

OFF-AIR, elsewhere, Marta came into the kitchen and went straight to check if the cat was in her bed.

Lou was hunched over a bowl of cereal before heading to the radio station. 'Still no sign of her.'

'Still no sign,' Marta sighed.

'She'll come back, love.' Lou tipped up the remains in the bowl and slurped. 'If she's not back by Friday, we'll put it on the radio.'

ON-AIR

> A VOICE
> Who's there?

TONY
Keep your ears peeled for the hourly cash call, coming up in just a few minutes' time…

> A VOICE
> **The point is, right, is that nobody's thinking of the thousands dying every day in the Middle East. They're only thinking about their own. Why haven't we been up in arms for thirty years, for all the deaths in these places with names that are hard to pronounce?**

TONY
Well, there's a thing, Declan, called *emotional proximity*?

A VOICE

Plasma cutters came into contact with some
old oil—

———

A VOICE

SWAT teams are currently storming an
Anglican church in—

———

A VOICE

Thanking you for two decades of support in
our efforts to provide the best deals in home
appliances—

———

TONY

And so how exactly are we only ten per cent
human?

A VOICE

Well, these microbes that we talked about,
Tony, that we often hear about, that live in our
body – well, studies have shown that actually
they make up a much larger portion of the
body than previously thought. In fact, close to
ninety per cent of the body is made up of these
organisms that do not originate in the body
itself. In my book, I explore this very finely
poised ecosystem... the ecosystem that each
person *is*—

———

A VOICE

And of course you're goosed then...

———

A VOICE

It's the food, Tony. We just don't know what
we're putting into our bodies anymore.

TONY
And you reckon it's some secret form of
government control?

                              A VOICE
          I do, yea. Whether we know it or not we are
                    controlled by unseen forces, Tony...
TONY
But our bodies?

                                      A VOICE
                    Sure your body *is* your mind—
                          _____

                                      A VOICE
                    The Bishop, we call him, Tony!
                          _____

                                      A VOICE
          Fix eight out of ten breakdowns right there on
                                      the road—
                          _____

                                      A VOICE
          But would these *crayturs* not have access to
          bombs of mass destruction? Could they not be
                    blowing us all away right now?
                          _____

                                      A VOICE
          See, all we really are, Tony, is transformed
                                      groceries—
                          _____

                                      A VOICE
          ... are living in fear. London is not a place you
          can go now. Every restaurant, pub, museum is a
                    target. They're coming for—
                          _____

                                      A VOICE
          ... an eighty-seventh minute substitute—
                          _____

11

                                        A VOICE
                    YOOOOUUUU'RE *TALKING TO TONY!*

TONY
Is that Eamonn Carter? Eamonn, it's Tony
Cooney here making that hourly cash call...

                                        EAMONN
                    Oh god, I missed it! Is it thirty-seven, Tony?

TONY
No, Eamonn, unfortunately it was just a little
higher; it was fifty-seven—
                    ─────

                                        A VOICE
                    ... building traffic along Collins Quay at the
                    moment, starting to look a bit congested on
                                        this Friday morning—
                    ─────

                                        A VOICE
                                        Unfold yourself—

BROADCASTING SIMULTANEOUSLY on 5264 kHz + 1420 MHz…

playback: the pale moon was rising above the green mountain / the sun was declining beneath the blue sea…

first voice: *[static]* one… one… seven… eight… *[static]* two… one… seven… seven… *[static]*

i

am

in

here

OFF-AIR, someone named Ann, dying in a hospital bed.

Would anybody come to her?

What had that man said, something about mothers?

… What?

As she stirred, she again imagined, or perhaps remembered, or had perhaps dreamt saying to Doctor Madden: I have waited my whole adult life to be told by you or someone like you that I had cancer. I knew it would happen. I didn't know which cancer it would be, or how I'd find it, but I knew this appointment would come, some day, in a room like this. And I knew my eyes would fall upon the posters as you told me, so we wouldn't need to look at each other. And I knew I would say thank you. Because I would already be seeing the world in a different light.

Or maybe she'd only described it that way to Tony that time? It was hard to remember anything when the brain was so foggy with the chemo and all the rest. You spent a lifetime trying to clarify things and it all went foggy on you anyhow.

In her weakness she could only half turn her head towards that angle of window she had, and she saw now, sort of above her, a cloudbruised sky, and the presence of a sun blanching the roof of the Wilton Shopping Centre. Water boiled somewhere, it sounded like. She coughed a bit, and it hurt in a distant way. Her head was spinning. She was dreaming. A small dog was barking somewhere; voices mumbled away behind curtains: home; a funeral. Or was it all on the radio? A time came to her: walking in rain, with wet socks, and finding a pub with a fireplace. And these chaps there all glued to the Rose of Tralee on the tele behind the bar… What was this taking place in her mind now? Memory? The pain settled into her, away from her somehow, and then there was the hospital ward again. Her in the bed, her arms by her sides again, still dying.

Open the channels.

She looked for a button to press, or a dial to turn.

14

**They are in fact reduced to a set of learned
and practised responses to a set of predictable
verbal, visual and situational stimuli. They rely
on stereotypes, Tony. They're inflexible—**

She found herself able to fiddle with the button to clear slight static, just when Tony Cooney told her that a horse broken loose on the South Ring dual carriageway was causing chaos. A brief bloom of light fell across the little plastic radio; then a cloud, and darkness with it, seemed to fall right into the hospital ward, right over her bed, as a chorus of phone-in voices beheld:

The woes of a landlord at the mercy of vicious tenants...

The release of a rapist back into the same community in which he had offended...

The inflated price of licences for farmers' market stalls...

And Keary's Hyundai again offered four-thousand-euro scrappage bonus.

And there had been a decrease in miscarriages.

And the sinking of the *Edmund Fitzgerald* was remembered nearly fifty years later.

Then it was seven minutes past ten. Phone numbers were repeated, and then a haunted caller phoned in to recount for the show how twenty minutes into the performance of *Hamlet* at the National Theatre on the South Bank in London, shooters had burst in and started firing in all directions. Some people ran for the exits and some people followed the actors exiting left to backstage, and some people, like this caller, cowered on the floor between seats and played dead, waiting to be shot in the back where they lay. And this caller did not flinch or pause or whimper as she explained that she felt lucky that she'd been there alone, and not with a friend or a partner or a family member – that she hadn't had to lie next to her dead boyfriend, or mother, while she pretended to be dead herself. She described the silence of the fallen audience as the gunmen

15

walked about the theatre, checking for survivors with their guns raised, and she explained that she could see only dust rising into the spotlights, and could hear only the crying out in pain or pleading of the ones hurt but not dead. And, after a few minutes then, the gentle murmur of many phones vibrating. And the caller said that this murmur increased into a chorus, and that she realised then, or after maybe, that already word must have been spreading to news outlets and social media, and that all the murmuring, the vibrating of phones in dead or dying people's pockets was their loved ones checking if they were okay. Well, she told Tony Cooney, they were not okay. And she was lying there all this time – who knew who else was still alive and doing the same as her – and hearing now even the odd ringtone of a phone someone had forgotten to switch to silent mode, and the odd burst of gunfire. She was lying there next to a dead person and she didn't know whether they were male or female or whatever else, because at first she'd tried to run, and she'd left her seat and ended up in another row, and the whole time she said she was just trying to breathe as quietly as possible and not move, and was waiting for something to happen – she didn't know what – and then she heard a very loud and sudden bang and things landed on her – bits of wood and dust and ragged wet material that might have been cloth or might have been... well, skin – and yet still she just lay there, in dread of being seen moving, and then moments later there was another explosion – and then

HELEN
... absolute chaos like, Tony – and that must
have been when the SWAT teams arrived and,
and, and...

`[static] there was then at least two full seconds`
`of dead air, as much as you can realistically`
`allow, timed to perfection by TONY COONEY,`

16

a DJ with thirty-five years broadcasting under his
belt [static]

TONY
In my thirty-eight years *[lies!]* as a journalist,
Helen, that is the most horrific thing I have
ever heard. I don't even know what to say
to you, Helen. I'm sitting here with tears
streaming down my face. I'm stunned. Lou
is stunned in the producer's booth. We're all
stunned—

[static] i have my doubts about whether there were
tears streaming down TONY's face. but maybe you'd
believe it. maybe it's true [static]

Helen agreed with Tony, though Tony hadn't necessarily said anything to agree with. Helen, who was from Buttevant but had been living in London twenty-two years, had never lost her accent, and her voice didn't waver; she finished the story with the matter-of-factness and defiance of someone who'd been ripped off by a car salesman. She insisted that unlike many others she wouldn't come home – that would be letting *them* win – and she said that she would never wash the clothes she had worn that night. Filthy though they were, she never wanted to forget just how close she'd come to death, and just how costly freedom in the West really was...

But then, after a few ads and jingles, they were back to rent control, and tried to decide – with callers for both sides – who was more put out, landlords or tenants. Some texts came in chastising Tony for being too harsh on an elderly caller, which texts, in fairness to him, he read out on air. The word **martyrs** was thrown around, as was the word **allocated**. Ann turned painfully and began to drift again. There were a number of first-time callers moved by Helen's story and discussion ensued about

17

all the Irish people coming home from London and where they'd go and how they'd fit back in. Rent allowance was nowhere near the rate of the average monthly rent. The rise in homelessness was something per cent in a decade, someone claimed. There was nobody living in the small towns anymore, the people said; they were referred to as **ghost towns**, as the pain subsided and the hospital tuned out, and Ann tuned into the ward briefly again, before the mind returned, at the very last, to the Rose of Tralee.

ON-AIR

TONY
So these terrorists are communicating via shortwave radios? Isn't that a very old-fashioned thing?

A VOICE
It is, Tony. But surprisingly successful. Militaries have been doing this since World War One, like. Basically, you only need a very cheap shortwave radio to tune into these frequencies from anywhere in the world.

TONY
It might be worth explaining – because this is fascinating to me – how shortwave radios actually work.

A VOICE
Well, Tony, radio is the broadcasting of radio waves out into the world. Radio waves are just another frequency on the electromagnetic spectrum, like microwaves or even visible light. And basically the shortwave radio signal is a sine-wave that undulates like the surface of an ocean, and can travel vast distances to

broadcast... well, whatever you want... Because when you direct them at the ionosphere—

TONY
What's the *ionosphere* when it's at home?

A VOICE
Basically it's the outermost layer of the earth's atmosphere, and you can bounce these shortwave signals off of it, so that they deflect back to Earth great distances away. It's called *tropospheric ducting,* which is basically bouncing the signal up to the ionosphere and back to Earth over and over until the signal is gone over the horizon. FM can't do that, but AM can you see.

TONY
Right.

A VOICE
So hence, back in World War One, spies were given number code books, and then in order to communicate with each other, the military and their spies could use shortwave to broadcast and receive these sequences of numbers, which, when checked in the code books, could be deciphered as messages. So you could be in Russia, for example, and tune into a broadcast and hear a sequence of numbers, and those numbers were a message for you, or you could relay information back to base if you had the ability to broadcast your own sequences of numbers...

TONY
Which was why they were called *numbers stations.*

A VOICE
Exactly, Tony.

TONY

And so the evil, evil people running a guerrilla war in London now are using these very old methods to organise and carry out attacks.

A VOICE

Exactly, Tony. But it's not new in today's terms either. I mean Cuban drug dealers have been using shortwave for years. See everything on the internet now is traceable, crackable, recorded, whether you're browsing incognito or not. And I suppose the levels of encryption and internet decoding now just aren't as secure as good old-fashioned—

———

TONY

Irish people are coming home in their droves – *Cork* people are coming home in their droves – but they're not all finding places to live and work. The government are thrashing out the final details of repatriation and relocation grants, as well as emergency housing—

PAT

But why can't we open our *doors* to these people, Tony?

[static] northside accent, always the kindest [static]

I mean, Tony, loads of us have spare rooms nowadays; anyone with kids gone to college or whatever. Why can't we throw open the doors to these people who need us. I for one have two beds in the spare room. The twins are gone off to college in Waterford. Any man or woman home From London is welcome to them. Pass

on my details, Tony. Do what you like. They're
our own people, Tony. And they're leaving
their jobs and their homes out of fear. They're
essentially refugees, Tony!

TONY

They are, Pat. They are. You're not wrong. If
only there were more like—

———

MARIAN

And why... these *displaced persons* you're talking
about, Tony. How are they different from the
migrants who've been flooding into Europe
from war-torn countries for decades? What's
different that we're suddenly offering up the
kids' bedrooms to them? Because they're *Irish*,
is it? Because they're *puuuare Cark*? Shouldn't we
be stuffing them into Direct Provision like so
many poor creatures before them? Or are they
exempt from that because of the colour of their
skin? Should we be giving them an allowance of
nineteen euro a week?

TONY

Well there's a thing, Marian — I've said it
before — it's called emotional proximity, and it
explains why we care more about people dying
in London or, say, during 9/11, or the Paris
attacks, than — rightly or wrongly — people
dying in the Middle East, or coming over from
distant lands...

MARIAN

Distant lands? Arra come on now, Tony, don't be
codding yourself—

———

21

TONY
… and how long are you seeing him,
Daniela?

>> **DANIELA**
>> Nine months, Tony. It's been a great nine
>> months too!

TONY
And ye met online?

>> **DANIELA**
>> We did. I wouldn't normally do that kind of
>> thing. I—

TONY
But you think nine months is too soon to move
in together?

>> **DANIELA**
>> Well, I dunno. It's a bit soon like, isn't it?

TONY
You know, Daniela, it's funny, I'm squeezing
my brain back through the years and I do
believe that the Dancing Queen and I moved
in together after nine or ten months together.
I had to snag her good and early you see – no
one else would put up with me! But… d'you
know, seriously, I think sometimes you *just know*.
You don't know in the sense of the Hollywood
movies – love at first sight and all that blather
– but you know that you trust someone enough
to open yourself up to them. And once you've
opened yourself up to them, and they to you,
then everything after that is easier. Even the
hardest stuff. I've talked on here before about
losing our son after only a few days… But yes,
once you open yourself up there are less games,
less problems… And it's easier to compromise.
There's that saying about one person *wearing the*

pants or whatever, well that's a wet auld rag too
if you ask me. The best relationships, the ones
that last, are the ones that involve compromise.
Where you wear the pants in certain things
and she wears the pants in other things. Be
they logistical things or emotional things. The
Dancing Queen, for example, she's a bit more
thrifty than me and so she handles the bills,
the internet providers, that kind of thing. But
I'm the man that knows which bins go out on
which nights... And it goes further than that.
You trust the other person to look after you.
You trust them to lead the way when you can't,
or to ease off when things are a bit manic. You
trust them to remain open with you. You put
yourself on the line and they put themselves
on the line – through grief and through joy...
It's all an ongoing... *fluid* compromise; it's
not a fixed contract or a game like the glossy
magazines would have you believe. So, Daniela,
what I'm saying... I think... is that if nine
months feels right, then maybe it's right? And if
you're not ready, you're not ready, you know?

> DANIELA
> I suppose so.

TONY
God, I remember the early days, meeting the
Dancing Queen to go to the cinema, or dancing
or what have you. I wasn't too long back from
London that time. I remember the talking. A *lot*
of talking. Good talks, good times. But they're
still good and all. The talking never stops. Never
let the talking stop. Never bottle up something
– just blast it out because if you can't say it to

your number one, who *can* you say it to? And
never go to bed mad at each other either. I'll
give you that one for free. Sure, there'll be fights
– arguments and what have you; god knows
myself and herself have had our fair share of
roaring matches – but talk it out before you
go to sleep and if you never go to bed angry
you'll be fine. I'm not gonna count up the years
now because she'll have my guts for garters for
outing her, but I will say that I put it all down
to compromise and talk and not going to bed
angry, and Lou is glaring at me here to stop
pontificating and reminiscing and get on with
the show and sher look, Daniela—

———

TONY
… the washing machine changed more lives
than the internet has—

SUSAN
Now, I wouldn't know about that, Tony, because
he does the clothes and I do the dishes. The
utility room is his *sanctuary* as he calls it. But
it's as if motherhood has been turned into a
problem. Since when did that happen?
TONY
As the previous caller said, we need to get over
ourselves.

BROADCASTING SIMULTANEOUSLY on 5264 kHz + 1420 MHz…

playback: the pale moon was rising above the green mountain / the sun was declining beneath the blue sea…

first voice: *[static] one… one… seven… eight… [static] two… one… seven… seven… [static] i hear them, and therefore i see them. i am in here.*

second voice: *so you keep saying… but what is it you're actually doing 'in here'?*

first voice: *what? who's there?*

second voice: *just me. just another disembodied voice, floating across the shortwave, listening in, trying to piece it all together, stumbling across you, rambling…*

first voice: *oh. okay. well, what am i doing? well… i hear… hmmm… imagine a room… imagine a person in that room, and all she or he has of the world outside that room is the radio. this frequency we're on. that person might listen to the radio every day, hoping for that signal. like the BIG EAR back in the day… trying to find a way to see the world beyond the room through that signal.*

second voice: *every day?*

first voice: *every day.*

second voice: *the day long?*

first voice: *the day long… seeking the company of other voices, other stories… and such a person might find a way to form a whole world from what they hear. i hear it therefore i see it [static]*

second voice: *i recognise that line from somewhere…*

first voice: *[static] radio as gospel.*

25

second voice:	has this hypothetical person you mention not heard of a TV? the internet?
first voice:	TV IS NOT THE THING!
second voice:	woh! okay! alright! [aside] jeeeesus.
first voice:	voice is the thing. story is the thing. the radio is my indochina.
second voice:	okie dokie. wait, indochina? i've heard that before too…
first voice:	i hear it and so i see it.
second voice:	aye. yes. you said that. a few times.
first voice:	i am in here.
second voice:	yes. of course. which is where exactly?
first voice:	[static] one… one… seven… eight… [static] two… one… seven… seven… [static] three… eight… five… nine… three… eight… five… nine… three… eight… five… nine… [static]
second voice:	one thing i was wondering, having listened in… would all these people really be flooding home from london? isn't terrorism just a part of city life now?
first voice:	ah, beautiful. that's a great question!
second voice:	[static]
first voice:	[static]
second voice:	and what's the answer?
first voice:	god, i don't know… hmm… maybe it's something more driving them back? everything more? the terrorism, the latest virus, coming back in waves, the sinkholes appearing, the slackening death of capitalism and that economy. the increasing lack of air and water… maybe it was that fucking guy. that prime minister. maybe it was all that. besides, there's this thing, you see, called 'emotional proximity'?

26

OFF-AIR, hunched over her desk, something so drastic and spiderlike about the height of her looming over the console in the small producer's booth off the studio, Lou realised that one of the doodles she'd drawn on the pad next to her phone looked like a weird little foetus, and there she was then thinking of the mother and child parking spaces as places she and Marta might park, with their own little person in the back seat. Mother and mother and child off across the car park, the little girl or boy swinging between Marta and herself... It was possible. It was a good thought.

And then simply by acknowledging the good thought, she let the bad thoughts back in: she'd be the worst type of parent. Dead mam: freak cancer genes. Her dad on the wine: tendency for alcoholism. Inexplicable sadness. Yadda yadda yadda.

Then Tony stuck his head in the door and said, 'Lou, can we just go over this car competition stuff one more time?'

'Of course, Tone.'

He came into the room and did that thing where he arranged himself against the furniture like one of the old movie stars, levering himself against the filing cabinet, angled so that one leg crossed the other and one scuffed black brogue was screwed into the carpet tile, *present* in the room, physical, repeating yet again: 'So we're saying that it's a nationwide competition but that Cork listeners should encourage their relations to get involved if the car is not spotted in Cork itself. Like, *We're appealing to Cork listeners to get onto their cousins, friends, and their neighbours' cousins and friends, and so on, to make Ireland smaller, to get people they know to find this car so that they can win the competition.*'

'Yea,' Lou said. 'And just remember to repeat that *anyone* home and displaced by the London attacks can enter the

27

competition, whether they're from Cork or anywhere else.'

'*The countrywide angle suits the idea of pilgrimage…*' he said, mimicking the Mazda PR guy.

'Oh, yeah.' She slipped the doodle and the inexplicable sadness under the telephone console and forced a grin. '*People love the notion of the road, even if they're not out there, because it shows them that they could be. Because, deep down, every Irish person dreams of owning a camper van for that exact reason. The road trip.* Blah blah blah.'

'Hah! Just once you know it's you doing all the driving, Lou…'

She was still grinning, now manically perhaps, at their impressions, but the potential for material with the car competition was pretty wild, to be fair. She'd already been picturing people sitting into the passenger seat of the car, hoping they'd win the car, telling their story over the airwaves from inside the car, in floods of tears as they recalled some experience or other, listeners phoning in then and sobbing and babbling like brooks as they thought of the poor fucker and her poor story. Follow-up calls then with old ladies saying, you know, 'Kathleen? It's Mary Murphy here. I knew you in the eighties, girl. We worked the switchboard together?' And all of this was happening in the car. This artefact. Not only a vehicle, but a path back to redemption, to safety, to family, to kids grown up… And they're sitting in this thing, shedding their life stories in the very fucking car that they want to win!

'I mean,' Tony was saying, 'at this rate it's a shame we couldn't run the competition in England. Have them actually driving the car back to the safety of the motherland, the auld sod.'

'Jesus, that'd be IMRO award stuff,' she replied. 'Racing down along the Thames as buildings explode… That'd be prime time.'

'You're something else, Lou!'

'Ah you know I'm only codding. But look, it'll be grand. In fairness, it is going to be massive. We've always done well out of the car competitions.'

He chucked his head up and went to leave, but paused with a hand on the doorknob. The news was almost finished. 'But, Lou, what if no one turns up?'

'...'

'For the car?'

'People will turn up, I'm sure of that. We'll build the search all morning on the particular Fridays. If we need a plant or two, so be it. I'm sure we all know someone who knows someone who's come home? Though I doubt it'll come to that.'

'Grand,' Tony sighed. 'You know, I genuinely don't know whether this is the best or the most ridiculous project we've ever worked on...'

And then he was gone from the doorway like an apparition and she was sliding out her doodle again, and sighing and thinking of her own 'young' mother, dying and then dead in the ground. And of sadness in general, explicable or not. Thing is, she was gone ten years now. It wasn't about her anymore. And then of Marta, the good thing. And then the cat of course. Thinking about the missing cat, yea, beloved Tabitha. How could you keep kids when you couldn't even hold on to a fucking cat?

ON-AIR

TONY
Now, here's something completely different. And I mean *completely* different. You're going to be wrapped up in this now for the next month. You're going to be calling every relative and friend you know. You're going to be getting in touch with people you haven't seen for years, in places you haven't even been for years. Because over the next month, someone, somewhere in this wonderful country of ours is going to win a *brand new car*. Yes! Starting next week we're

giving away, to one lucky person, courtesy of Jerry Collins Motors, a brand new Mazda 2. Incredible! How would you like a *brand new car*? But it's not that simple. Sure who said winning a car would be simple?! Jerry's been listening to us for yonks – a loyal listener but never called, he says – and he's been listening to the plight of the London Irish, the people coming home, the returned exiles, the people struggling to re-settle, to find jobs and homes and to re-establish themselves. And between Jerry and ourselves we've come up with a plan to help them. He wants to give one of them a car. To help them get back on their feet. Isn't Jerry just exactly the kind of man we need on the earth at this point in time? So myself and Lou will be travelling the length and breadth of Ireland every Friday for the next month, looking for returned exiles, and at the end of the month we'll be giving one of them the very car we've been driving. Not only that, but each week there's *a year's free petrol* to be won too, courtesy of Circle K. A year's free petrol. Look, we've a lot of our people coming home in awful circumstances at the moment, and I'm sure listeners to the show will have heard many of their stories. I've heard them. I've felt them. And I lived in London myself for a long enough time... Emigrating... or... immigrating, or re-immigrating... Coming back is hard enough, but doing it under such strain... Well, anything we can do to ease the burden... And Producer Lou's in it with me. So who can win the car, Lou?

LOU

Tony, any Irish person who's moved home
because of the chaos in London can win the
car. We'll set off every Friday and park up
somewhere, and the first person to find the
car will be the winner for that Friday, and
they immediately win a year's free petrol for
themselves. We'll have four winners by the end
of the month, and then out of those four the
winner of the car will be chosen at random.

TONY

And tell me, Lou, what are we asking Cork
people to do? Say if the car doesn't end up in
Cork on a particular Friday for example. There
are *other counties* after all, and it is a *national*
competition...

LOU

Yes, well we understand that a person living in
Cork might only have one chance to win the
car, but maybe they have a relation somewhere
else who has been displaced by the Troubles
in London. Maybe they know someone, an old
friend or colleague, and they want to help. So
maybe our listeners can spread the word once
they hear what county we're in and they can
help someone win the car. The winner doesn't
have to be a Corkonian, you know – my own
dad is from Kerry dare I say it!

TONY

Ah, we'll forgive him that I suppose... Now, our
sister radio stations in Dublin and Galway will
also be broadcasting this on our behalf, so for
a month at least, the country will be united in
its quest to find a happy owner for this brand
new Mazda 2. And I'm damn sure there are

31

Cork people living in all these counties so let's
try and make it so that we've four rebels in the
car come that final Friday. Now... where are we
going next? Oh yes...

[static] the sobering shuffle of papers; the
clearing of the throat [static]

Stage four ovarian cancer. Three years fighting
it, and she's been checking in with us from
time to time. She's some hero. But, well, she's
not had the best of time of it lately. Tell us how
you're doing, Ann?

                                            ANN
            Tony, boy... I am doing the best I can—

[static] a cracked, spirited voice, barely managing
the words through her interrupted breathing, the
making significant of the moment [static]

TONY
I understand that you're back in hospital, Ann.
Back on the rack, waiting on test results?

                                            ANN
                                        I am, boy.
TONY
And tell me, Ann, are you afraid?

                                            ANN
    I'm not, Tony, no. There is pain, yes. But no fear.
                        I know... where I'm going.
TONY
And where's that?

32

ANN

There are two adventures in life, Tony... the
adventure in love and the adventure in death.
I'm on the death adventure now. And I don't
know what will happen me... of course... no
one really does... but I know that I'm passing
through. The body is only a stump. I know that
there's something beyond this pain... I'm after
forgetting your name, but if I knew it I'd say it
to you now.

TONY

It's Tony, Ann, love. We've never met in person,
I know, but sure we know each other with years
from your phoning in to the show.

ANN

Sorry, Tony. The morphine. I do feel that we've
known each other a long time, but I can't place
you now.

TONY

Don't be silly, Ann; you're grand, girl. No
apologies necessary. We've never met as I said
but we've loads in common. We both grew up
in Passage – our parents worked together in the
Mount actually. We both have two kids. I think
we established that before?

ANN

Tony... I have never felt... so close to the
mystery... Are you there?

TONY

I am, girl. I'm here.

ANN

I'm? ... The Rose of Tralee? ... Sorry, I'm after
forgetting your name again!

TONY

It's Tony, love—

BROADCASTING SIMULTANEOUSLY on 5264 kHz + 1420 MHz…

playback: the pale moon was rising above the green mountain / the sun was declining beneath the blue sea…

first voice: *[static] four… three… eight… five… four… three… eight… five… they call it 'dead air', but silence isn't the lack of sound; it's a murmur, all sounds distant at once: wind in trees, cars on roads, planes overhead, ships in the harbour, waves rolling, facilities spewing fumes, electricity, everywhere, constant unseen fields of electromagnetism, keyboards, air-conditioning, sexual intercourse, conversation, the vibrations of myriad sine-waves, breathing, coughing, spitting, tramping — the whole of human life and earthly rumination and output percolating a murmur that denies silence, an ever-breaking wave, all the radios simultaneously broadcasting the peoples' stories, all the engines turning at once, all the chewing and the scraping and everything else. it is… happening. it is constant. how could there be silence when voices come even from the past into the present moment? when voices fill heads? [static]*

second voice: *silence? sure how could there be silence with the likes of you? 'when voices fill heads'? that's rich! ha!*

first voice: *ah, gimme a break will you. i'm trying to get it down as i see it. as i hear it.*

second voice: *as you hear it? i'll give you one thing: it is constant, this broadcast.*

YOU'RE *bloody constant. bloody hell.
'sexual intercourse', like?*

first voice: *i knew love once, brother! oh i knew
it once.*

second voice: *ah... go on away and give yourself a
break...*

[static growing fainter]

ON-AIR

                    DANNY
Tony I'm after hearing you talking to Ann there
and fair play to that woman I'll tell you. I'm
only off the ward myself and I'll tell you it's not
                                              easy.

TONY
I'm sorry to hear that, Danny – were you in
long?

                    DANNY
A week in hospital, Tony. Wait til I tell you – on
my first night in I couldn't sleep at all. It was
poxy. I lay awake long after the others on the
ward fell asleep, and they won't leave you turn
on the TV after lights out so I was listening
to the other fellas snorting and snoring and
farting... Just laying there, Tony! And well
eventually I couldn't hack it anymore so I
switched me lamp back on and started to read
an auld paper, and I hadn't even got past the
headlines when a light comes on over the way
on the ward, and this phlegmy voice goes:
Eamonn Fitzpatrick. Abbeyfeale. Eighty years of age.
So I says: *Danny McCarthy, Tralee, seventy-six.*
I was a bricklayer, he says: *here and in London. Four*
kids. Seven grandkids. One great-grandchild.

35

Merchant seaman, I says: Seven children. Thirteen
grandchildren. Two great-grandchildren.
Then he coughed a bit, and said, *In here five*
weeks. Cancer.
In just the one week, **I said.** *SAGITTARIUS!*
TONY
Jesus you're an awful man, Danny.

OFF-AIR, too late in the evening, when they'd finished prepping the next morning's show, himself and Lou walked out to the car park together.

'Do you ever miss living in London, Tony?' she asked, struggling to zip up her jacket.

'Yerra, no. Not really, Lou. London feels like a lifetime ago…'

She grimaced with the effort, small babyish teeth clenched together, and he was still able to see the gothy nineteen-year-old child that had loped up to the station on work experience all those years ago. The tall, skinny, fidgety, clambering young thing, though with an enthusiasm that was contagious, and a way of looking out at the world and all of them in it that could either be painful or joyous depending on the day.

'D'you know,' she said, when she'd finally drawn up the zip. 'London was the one foreign holiday I took with Mam. I dunno if you remember but she wouldn't get on a plane. Had a deadly fear of it.'

'I remember,' he said. 'What a lovely woman – absolutely robbed of life. I was only thinking about her when we were talking to Ann earlier…' He could see that Lou didn't know what to say to that. 'Didn't ye do the tourism – what was it?'

'Virtual tourism! Yea. God, that was in the last few months. I'd bring the laptop to the hospital and we'd go on the web and take virtual tours and print and paste the information into our scrapbooks. Didn't matter where it was, really: Paris, Rome, Bucharest.'

He remembered her now, sheepishly downloading and printing photos for the mother in the office, as if they were their own holiday snapshots. But so once they had gone to London together, on the ferry, in real life. Their only foreign holiday together. Lou pulled her hair from inside her collar now and that seemed to snag too, though she ignored it. In fact she did have that anxious look about her now alright – the eyes alert and yet adrift, as if they were vacant here but panicking elsewhere. Or as if she were about to suggest something drastic. Something profoundly serious. Something mortal. There were times he looked at her and he thought of Aaron; if Aaron had lived they'd be about the same age. What would he have been like by now? A nervy type? A confident lad? But suddenly he was thinking of something else – a car rolling?

[static] GIANT HEAD [static]

'Anyway,' Lou said, pulling out her keys while he nearly fell over the bike trying to unlock the back wheel. 'I'm off to look for this cat with Marta. I'll see you in the morning.'

'Still no sign?'

'No, Tony. I swear to god that woman loves that cat more than she loves me.'

'Hah. Same in my place. The pecking order is the kids, the animals, then me… Sure look, they always come back. Or they don't. We'll run it on the show if she's not back soon?'

'We'd better or I'll be thrown out.'

'Alright. Drive safe, girl. Maybe ask the white witch where your cat is.'

'Hah! Not seeing her for another week. I'm telling you, I'll get you live-broadcasting a reading with her if it's the last thing I do… Cycle safe, Tone.'

The rain cooled the evening's air, but he enjoyed the freshness of it once he was warmed up and out of town and on the gloomy gravel path out the old railway line in the direction of home. Out the line, all he could really see was the tunnel of light his bike cast – a tunnel of gravel and dead leaves and the fringes of undergrowth, bare trees leaning in from both sides as if to listen to his passing. It often occurred to him that once, before walkers and joggers and cyclists on the gravel, it had been the single light of the city train going up and down, steaming alongside the estuary, headed to Passage and beyond. Before the dual carriageway, before digital: just simple people and their hats looking out on the river and the fields of Blackrock, Passage, Rochestown, Monkstown, Raffeen, Carrigaline… all the way out to the Atlantic.

On the headphones he listened to the London playlist, for the night that was in it. And he was already formulating the story of listening to the London songs on the cycle home, for tomorrow's broadcast and continued discussion. *You all know that music has a way of bringing you back in time. Transporting you. Well I'm cycling home last night – yes I like to try and keep the weight off by cycling the odd night! Yes I'm as surprised as ye! – well I'm cycling home and this particular song came on my shuffle-all – we all love a shuffle-all, I know – and I wasn't cycling the line anymore, no. I was walking down Deptford High Street of a Saturday in the late eighties, with most of a week's pay in my back pocket, and I was smelling the smells of a food market and hearing the calls of the vendors and feeling that grumble in my belly that said* Saturday Morning Hangover. *I was there, guys. The music brought me there. Amazing how that happens…* Cold nights; warm ales; the tube in wet trousers after a soaking in the rain. He could bring that conversation anywhere. A bit of nostalgia for their Wednesday mornings. What had that caller said – heartbreak was a disease of repetition? Maybe nostalgia might be the salve? After that break-up with Lolly, he had listened to the same records on repeat, had he not? Had the same memories on repeat? The same words they'd said to each other on repeat, imagined conversations, again and again. He slowed now through the dodgy underpass, where the AERO tag appeared like an apparition in his bicycle lights. He could use that tomorrow too. Great link there, from

London to the graffiti issue. His cycle home could be the thread for the whole three-hour show!

And soon he was huffing and puffing over the footbridge, looking down on the long queues of traffic both ways on the South Ring, the sequences of lights quite magical. He paused a moment to take it in, and to catch his breath that bloomed on the growing dark. The cycling was alright once you got into it; good for the lungs if a bit raw on the knuckles. Then, suddenly, with a strange beep, the music stopped – Nuala was ringing – and he heard the traffic and the horn-blasting of the evening before he answered.

'Hello, my love.'

'I heard you were talking about me on the radio again?'

'Ah sure, any excuse to tell the county about my Dancing Queen.'

'And does all that blather about *compromise* mean we can have a proper talk with Sadie tonight so? The three of us? The school have been on to me again.'

'Ah Jesus… Look, yea fine. I'm just halfway home now…'

And so while he spoke to her he hastened on down the other side of the footbridge, onto the line again, and the wind and Nuala's voice filled his ears like a bloodrush, and there was the dark woody rustle of bare trees too, and the creak of the saddle towards home, and he was thinking down the side of all that noise: how will I get out of this one?

OFF-AIR, later that night, Lou was watching the tele on the couch with Marta when her mobile rang.

'Hi Dad, everything okay?'

'Why wouldn't I be?'

'Oh. You're just calling very late?'

'Oh, fuck, sorry love, were you in bed?'

'Well, no. I just. It's later than you usually call. I thought you. I thought something might be wrong.'

'Oh, right. No, no. I'm grand. *Absolutely* grand. I was just ringing to tell you how proud I am of you. I am *so* proud of you.'

'Why?'

'Just… Can't a father be proud of his daughter, Lou? My Lulu?'

'He can I suppose.'

'This car competition. Going out on the road for people in need. I think it's so brave. You're so *brave.*'

'Thanks, Dad. Not my idea but I'll take the credit! How are you anyway?'

'Oh, me? Fine. Grand. Living away here in my own little bubble. Minding my own fukken business.'

'What do you mean?'

'Oh, nothing. What do you mean what do I mean? Isn't that what ye want? Dad to keep his fukken distance like? God forbid I'd trouble ye…'

'Who have you upset, Dad?'

'What? Why have I upset someone?'

'Well it sounds to me like you've upset someone and you're ringing me to vent.'

'Not in the *slightest.* I love both my children. Despite their feelings about me. I might not be required anymore now that neither of ye need feeding, or loans, and there are no spins needed, but I'm still out here *in the void*, loving ye all with all my… with all my fukken heart.'

Lou shifted slightly, away from Marta.

'How's Deborah, Dad?'

'You tell me, Louise.'

'Ah. So it's Deborah.'

'I wouldn't want to butt in on her life now that she's doing so well for herself, now that she's happy in her relationship. Sure why would I want to know how she's doing now that she's not coming running to me with her problems, begging me to get her out of holes. God no. She doesn't want to hear a peep now out of her own fucking father.'

'Were you talking to her just now? Did ye have a row?'

'A row? You'd have to be granted an audience with her to have a row with her. I didn't even make it past that fucking waster she calls a husband. That fucking… He's flavour of the month again now of course so he answers the phone and tells me she's busy. The fucking cheek of him. Oh she's busy alright. Shopping on Amazon probably, running up bills that I'll end up paying after she comes bawling to me saying they've *quarrelled*. No, your sister doesn't even bother coming to the phone to me nowadays. I'm yesterday's fukken… newspaper. Your Marta would never be so uppity… She's got a heart in her chest. You—'

'Ah Dad, she's probably just busy.'

'At nine p.m. on a Tuesday night?'

'Who knows. There's no need to get yourself worked up.'

'Worked up? Who's worked up? Sure who'd want to talk to *their own father*?'

'Well, Dad, you're not exactly easy to talk to in this— at these times.'

'What's that? *In this* what? In this condition? Lou, I had two glasses of wine with my dinner. Am I not even entitled to a glass of wine now, is it? Am I supposed to be ready and sober and willing to drive ye anywhere, is it? In case I'm needed, is it? To run up to South Doc? To drop someone to work? To loan *you* money?'

'Two glasses of wine, Dad?'

'You've some cheek, Louise. *Some fucking cheek.* I've supported you. Every decision you've ever made, I supported you. And they weren't all popular decisions as you well know. I've been there for you through thick and thin. No questions asked.'

'If you're referring to my coming out, Dad, then thank you. Though it was quite a while back no—'

'And when other people criticised you, I backed you to the hilt. *To the hilt.* And what do I get now? My daughters don't want to talk to me because I'd a glass of wine with dinner. You know what, I better get back in my fukken box—'

'Dad, you know I love you.'

'No, I know when I'm not wanted. I'll just sit here on the couch and wait til I'm needed again. I'll just rot here on the couch.'

'Dad, I love you, and I'm grateful for everything you've done for me and for all of us.'

'Yea. Oh you do alright. Feeling guilty now, is it? Well don't fukken bother—'

'Dad?'

But the line was dead.

'Two *big* glasses of wine,' Marta said, giving Lou a squeeze of the kneecap and picking up the remote again to unpause the show.

'Could you hear him?'

'Is he okay?'

'Yea. Just busting for a fight. The usual. He won't remember tomorrow. Play it on there; I want to get to bed early and have some fun with our little box of tricks.'

'Oh,' Marta said. 'Uh. Maybe not tonight. Maybe I'm going to go look for Tabby again. I'm worried.'

'Oh yea. Of course.' Lou shifted again. 'Sorry. I'll come with you of course.'

'No, no. It's fine. You have to work early. I can go. Late shift tomorrow.'

'She will come back, Marta.'

'I know. Well, I hope.'

'She will. Cats do this all the time. They breeze in the door after months away.'

'I know. I know. You said.'

'I've got my appointment with the white witch next week. I'll ask her where she is.'

Marta laughed humourlessly. 'White witch. Hah.'

'Just don't be worrying.'

'I can't not be worrying. I have Tabby my whole life in Ireland. Nearly ten years.'

'I know, I know. Sorry. You're right. It's just it's been a while. Since…'

'Yes. A week.'

'Wow. Feels like a year.' Lou tried to make it funny by pinching Marta's tummy playfully.

'Not a year. A week.'

'Yea, well. I'm horny.'

'Yea, well, I worry about our cat.'

'Sorry.' Lou took her hand back. Sorry sorry sorry sorry.

'Hit play, will you?' Marta said.

BROADCASTING SIMULTANEOUSLY on 5264 kHz + 1420 MHz…

playback: the pale moon was rising above the green mountain / the sun was declining beneath the blue sea…

first voice: *[static] five… one… nine… three… five… three… four… seven… i hear these things.*

second voice: *yawn.*

first voice: *i form my own image, like i said. all this i assume, i note down as the possible backstory. as how it might be out there. or might have been. it strikes me that people are like cyclones made of words. the power… the frenzy… [static] five… one… nine… three… five… three… four… seven… but in the middle of those cyclones, what is there? what sustains them? around what are they propelled — what's at the core? trauma? love? hunger? nothing? perfect calm? the truth? eternity? some inner eye? i hear these things. i listen to the voices. i form my own image. i note them down… [static]*

second voice: *yea, you note them down alright. i'll tell you what's at the core — you, a babbling brook. like, what is it you're actually doing here?*

first voice: *listening [static] hearing.*

second voice: *i got that. you like this particular radio show. you have it recorded or something. [static] you like to imagine the lives of the people who broadcast it.*

first voice: *[static] it broadcasts.*

second voice: *yes. but. you listen to it over and over. you re-broadcast it. you make these things up about people's lives.*

first voice: *i build the world from it. it tells me of the world!*

second voice: *why do you keep talking about the world like it's gone?*

first voice: *hmmm… [static]… would happen to the radio waves — to these voices — if there were an apocalyptic event? would those voices on the radio waves scramble? or disappear? or distort? or would all these voices we listen to end up floating across the world's breezes for eternity, roaming the air of a rejuvenating world? or an empty world, depending [static] .*

second voice: *[static]… several ways it could go. the end i mean. nuclear. viral. chemical. overheating. something we don't even know about yet.*

first voice: *but you'd wonder whether TONY and LOU, or any of these people, ever considered the fact of their recorded voices, that those voices might be broadcast long after they were gone. that once digitised, every word they* *ever uttered ON AIR would or could last forever. every word that came out of their skulls might wander the earth's airwaves and data storage facilities forever…*

second voice: *god, imagine being the very last human on Earth, sucking in the very last of the [static]… you're after depressing me now!*

first voice: *well, you know, depression, apocalypse… they're not so far apart. have you ever been depressed? like, really depressed? [static]*

second voice: *no? well, i don't think so…*

first voice: *[static] oh, look, don't mind me. i'm glum by nature. a cyclone of glumness. that's all i am, revolving around my own sad fuck of a self. anyway, that's all for today's show, folks! stay tuned for some other voice! safe home now! [static]*

sea
of
typhoons

OFF-AIR, as they rolled eternally backwards, the giant head asked him from the back seat: 'Have you a wife, Tony?'

'I do,' Tony replied. 'Nuala. Married twenty years.'

'Good man. She's well?'

'Ah, she's great.'

'And how would you know that now?' the gaunt woman asked him, beside him there in the passenger seat. 'Sure you'd have to spend time with her to know.'

'We have our ups and downs I suppose. Anyone would over twenty years. I suppose you never really know if someone's right for you. No matter how long it goes on, you—'

'We went to the Land of Women once, Tony!' the head bawled.

'Oh, yah?'

'The one time. It was a year. What a year, Tony! But when we came back? I didn't know a soul.'

'Listen to the two of ye,' the gaunt woman said. 'And the thoughts ye do be thinking.'

'Go on, you!' the head said to her. 'Did you ever think about this though, Tony? Where does a fly live?'

Tony thought about it. They rolled backwards in the car, down the hard shoulder.

'You've got me there, my friend.'

The gaunt woman huffed impatiently, her hands covering her face in mock anguish. 'Put him out of his misery.'

'A fly lives nowhere, Tony! And yet everywhere. On the wind, on the wall, under a leaf, nowhere at all… The fly lives *in the world*, Tony.'

OFF-AIR, a message via the internet:

03:24

Hi Tony,

Its been a long time! How are you? Believe it or not Im living in Ireland now and somehow we heard you on the radio here yesterday. I came back to Galway to run a pub for Daddy last year and then today I hear your voice on the radio and of course the London memories came flooding back. how are you? Im good, happy to be in Ireland and away from the Trouble. Galway is lovely. I thought about you a lot Tony over the years. I missed you. It would be so nice to see you again. I dont even know how much you remember about those London days those times. They are still dear to me. Well youve done really well for yourself since you came home! I'm very proud of you I have to say. You're running a radio show Im running a pub, we're doing okay! Do you still remember me Tony? Your car competition sounds great. Come to Galway? The pub here is called the Silver Branch. Its near Connemara, a place called Furbo. Lovely place. Very peaceful. Near the sea like Brighton. Happy memories Tony. Hope you are well.

Take care of yourself.

Lorraine (Lolly)

OFF-AIR, a bright grey morning, windy on the road. Lou held the jacket close around her as they called for the cat.

'Taaabbbyyyy,' Marta called gently from the opposite pavement.

Wind like that would cut right through you, was how Lou's mother had described it on the ferry over to England that time. She'd been making fun of the way Lou's father spoke. Wind like that would shave you, Lou.

'Taaabbbyyyy.'

Aboard with Mam and the truckers and the Travellers and

50

people with dogs and bikes and motor homes and all of them rocking and swaying and sliding with the brutal tilting of the vessel. Wind like that would cut the face of you, girl.

'Here, Tabby.'

And later, a calmer boat up the Thames, to Embankment. Mam getting mixed up about what 'dawn chorus' meant. Wind like that would rake your garden, Lou! Wind like that would clean your windows wind like that would rear your children wind like that would wash your car. They got on so well, her parents, except when they didn't.

Marta crossed. 'We will never find her like this.'

'We'll keep trying,' Lou said. 'It's fucking windy though, isn't it?'

Marta looked at her. Shrugged helplessly.

'We'll find her,' Lou said.

'I talk of loss,' Marta said. 'You talk of wind.'

'I am looking,' Lou said. 'Amn't I? I'm fucking agog for Tabby, Marta. I'm looking.'

Marta crossed the road again and crouched to look under a gate and call.

That wind'd strip your skin, Lulu! Her eyes wet with laughter as Mam ran on with the joke. She had bright grey eyes, her mother, and they'd be wet while she was still grinning. That wind is worth six points! Wind that'd drive the roads clean, child! Wind that'd stand you a pint! Wind that'd raise the *Titanic*!

The odd car passed along the road, the engine sound emerging from and returning to the gale sounds, where Marta's calls to the cat travelled too. A pigeon up in an evergreen beyond a wall clung on for dear life. Dad might be getting up about now, stirring at least, on his own all these years, grabbing his forehead and feeling the hangover. Or not. Maybe he didn't get hangovers anymore. And Mam, well she was long in the ground. She wasn't getting up! But it didn't hurt anymore, not really. Just a twinge maybe. The awareness of a vacuum. But it was hard to know all the same what lingered in terms of pain. What was held and what was repressed. In many ways, Mam dying was the only awful thing that had happened Lou. And she had a job she loved now and a partner she loved. Or presumed she did. So then why the constant butterflies of worry? The sadness? Was it still something to do with Mam? Or her parents in general – the fighting, the shittiness, the drink? Or just something in her DNA? Some anxiousness? Lou gave up trying to hold her head so that her hair stayed flat and let it fly. She let the wind happen to her.

'Some day!' she roared as a man pushing a bicycle approached and passed her. She forgot to show him the picture of the cat.

'Great day to be a flag!' the man roared back.

ON-AIR

TONY
… Lou is watching me here from the producer's booth and she's giving me that stern look because I'm going off script entirely. Sorry, Lou, but d'you know the way that music can bring you back in time, the way it can transport you? Well, I'm cycling home last night – *yes* I try and keep the weight off by cycling home the odd night, and *yes* I'm as surprised as ye about it! – well I'm cycling home down the line and this particular song came on my shuffle-all and I wasn't cycling the line anymore. No. I was walking down Deptford High Street, in south-east London, of a Saturday in the late eighties, most of a week's pay in my back pocket, and I was smelling the smells of a food market and hearing the calls of the vendors and feeling that grumble in my belly that said *Saturday Morning Hangover.* I was there, guys. The Specials

brought me there. That song I just played for you transported me, just like in one of those teleportation devices they had in *Star Trek*. Amazing how that happens... I remembered cold Christmas nights on the streets of London, warm ales, old, old buildings. I remembered the smell of... let's call them *funny* cigarettes... on our road in Brockley. I couldn't make head nor tail of it all. There used be a Turkish restaurant there – Mezze Something? I don't quite recall – and it was only massive that place. I always went there on payday. Filled me boots. I was working in London like so many Irish before and after me. So many in a town now under siege from guerrilla terrorists. I remember the graffiti, I remember the endless urban sprawl, and the gorgeous little parks then. Little oases in that concrete jungle. The amazing thing about London, coming from a small place like Passage, was the noise – it was never quiet, *ever*. And the multiculturalism! Like, lads, every single type of person you could imagine. And I'm not just talking about race and that; I mean fashion too. I could never have imagined humans could be so various, and I think that's stood to me my whole life since. And so of course it breaks my heart, *breaks my heart*, to see what's going on there now. And to hear the kind of report you're about to hear. Lou's giving me a tentative thumbs up now, but a very clear signal also to wrap it up—

OFF-AIR, her mam had the radio on – something about another attack in London – and of course the radio being on reminded her of the house, the kitchen, frantic mornings getting ready for school, toast burning under the grill, the kettle boiling endlessly, the shouting up the stairs and through the bathroom door.

'Jada.'

She was nudged again in the bed, her mam's voice low in that cramped room.

'Jada.'

'Uhhhh – what?' She didn't turn yet. Pretended to be still in the throes of sleep.

'Would you go to the shop for us before we have to leave for the day? Be good to have milk for a cuppa, before.'

A room could be just sounds if you kept your eyes closed. The radio; soft knocking from inside the walls; the dryshifting of shoes on carpet; the whispered play of a child; long drawn breaths; things being constantly moved out of the way.

'Can't you go, Mam?'

'Grand, I will so. And you'll pack us all up then?'

She sighed and rose from the duvet. 'Grand. I'll go.'

'And take your sister with you, please?'

In school, they'd learned about the famine. Back then most families all lived in the one room. With animals and all. It was normal. She sat up in the pillows and looked about her. The bags were lined up at the end of her camper bed, and Mam and Dad's duvet was all trussed up at the end of the double bed where Sally was using it as a mountain her dinkies were driving up. *Vrroooommmmm.* And stuff – bags, toys, cups, a plastic water bottle – lay all over the floor between the places they'd slept. How in fuck's name did people live in one room on a normal basis? Jesus Christ. Well, no animals here at least.

'Can't we just rob a bit of milk off someone else, like before?'

'Jada, please just go.'

54

Then the door opened and Dad came in wrapped in a towel and still soaking wet.

'Morning all!' Too loudly. Too fucking loud.

She looked at his pale flabby skin, freckles all up his arms, and she collapsed again onto her pillow and pulled the duvet over her head.

'The night owl in a bad mood!' he called out. He knew better now than to grab her foot or pull the duvet off.

'Darren, you're fucking soaking the place,' came Mam's voice, no longer low.

'There was a queue! Didn't want to keep people waiting.'

'So you've flaunted your nipples to the whole guesthouse and now you're making soaking wet footprints all over the carpet.'

'Right!' Jada jumped up out of the bed, fully dressed. 'Come on, Sally! Off for an adventure!'

'YAY!' Sally jumped up from the dinkies, ready for road, and Jada pulled on a hoodie and her FILA coat, which was much too big but handy for stashing spray cans.

'Where ye off to?' Dad asked.

'Shop.'

'Will you get hair gel for me?'

Mam looked up from helping Sally into her coat. 'No hair gel, Darren.'

'How am I supposed ta— Aah, forget it.'

'Come on, Sally!' she said, dying to get out that door now while Sally tried to jam all her dinkies into her coat pockets at once.

Mam pulled a tenner from her rattling mess of a bag. 'A milk,' she said. 'Toothpaste. Cereal bars. And one treat each for yereselves.'

'Fags?' She liked trying to buy fags.

'No, love. Not today. One nice thing each. I'm expecting change.'

She zipped the tenner into the coat pocket with her phone and grabbed Sally's hand by the door.

ON-AIR

HARRY

I had a ground-floor office, Tony, in a fourteen-
storey building, and I felt the weight of the
whole place down on top of me.

TONY

Sure you were doing the work of three people,
Harry.

HARRY

That's what the HR Generalist said to me after.

TONY

God, that's awful... Look, stay with us for
a minute, Harry, we have to take a few
messages—

[jingle redacted]

[static] … the jingles are louder; they have to be,
because they cover the dead air. there can't really
be dead air, because dead air's seen as the void,
the gap between noise. that's a horror not to be
contemplated, because it makes space for thinking,
a fertile field for… because if it crept out from
beneath the jingle (or the ad, or the song, or
whatever) that void might just prove to you once
and for all that the noise is all gone, a memory, a
conjuring, and the earth itself is an empty plenum,
and we're all just— [static]

[static] —ah here… seriously? [static]

TONY
We'll take you back to Harry and his story shortly, but before we do, it gives me no pleasure in bringing to you more news of chaos in London. News of another attack, in the London Bridge area we believe – and I remember it well – and while we're hearing about crashed trucks and machetes, nothing is confirmed yet. It's all still going on I think, so bear with us as we try to—

OFF-AIR, the pink sky rippled and all along the waterfront where they walked the shops and offices and apartments were mostly crumbling and paint-flaked. She didn't understand dereliction, or those ghost estates in the suburbs and on the country roads. Horrible looking places, with plastic flapping from walls and mounds of earth and dark smeared windows. Like, a place just started to crumble because people weren't in it? What was that? And why in fuck's name did they have to be left empty? Could they not just be given to the people who needed them? In what kind of world could homeless people be surrounded by empty properties?

'Isn't this sky beautiful?' she said to Sally as they approached a line of gulls on the riverside wall and the gulls took off one by one. That was the kind of thing Mam said to avoid reality.

'Pink sky in the morning, shepherd's warning,' Sally said, quite seriously.

'Very good.' She squeezed her sister's small, cold hand. 'Pink sky at night?'

'SHEPHERD'S DEEEEEE-LIGHT.'

'You *genius*!'

She burst into a run, dragging Sally by the hand as she squealed and scrambled to keep up.

'Jaaadaaa!'

'Jada?' Sally asked when they were catching their breath, waiting to cross by the Bridewell garda station. 'Jada?'

'Yea?'

'Where do you go at night?'

She looked down at Sally's white little face in the dark, fluffy hood. 'Just walking.'

The green man lit up and they crossed. From the city came strange metallic clangs, and clunking sounds and drilling sounds.

'But it's scary to walk at night. On your own.'

'Well, you know the fox and the owl?'

'Yea.'

'Well, they're night-time animals, right? They're *nocturnal*. They sleep in the day and go out at night.'

'Yea.'

'Well, I'm like them. *Nocturnal*... And look, can you keep a secret?'

'Yeeeaaaaa!'

'You won't tell anyone?'

'Nooooo!'

'Not a soul?'

'No one! Not one!'

'Look, the truth is... I'm a superhero. I *have* to go out at night.'

'A superhero?! No you're not! What's your superhero name?'

'I'll tell you next week.'

'Tell me now!'

'No. Next week.'

And she sprinted on a ways again, down the island pavement, through the exhaust smoke of the queuing traffic. All those people in their cars still just lived in normal homes. They got up in the morning and went for a piss and had breakfast and the bathrooms and the kitchens were the same as ever. And those people would walk from room to room, turning on and off lights and looking for slippers and calling out about cups of tea, and not ever notice the rooms they were walking in... Here and there – on a doorway, or on the alley wall down by the Asian market – she saw her name, the name Sally didn't know, her *true* name, her mark. She was *all*-fuckin-city. Would it have been nice to show Sally and tell her the truth? To give her a tour of AERO's city? To show her not just the little scrawled ones, but the majestic block ones. The one on top of the Rock Steps, that looked all the way to St Fin Barre's Cathedral. Or the one over the river down by the Lee Fields. Or the one at Meadowlands that watched over the road to Dublin. Her true name stretched like a DNA strand across the entire city, claiming it in white and neon green and black and red, calling out from every door, wall and rooftop.

AERO

'Jada, what's your treat gonna be?'

'Hmmmm… Chocolate Hobnobs I think. What about you?'

'Hmmmm… I dunno.'

'Come on, we better hurry or we'll be late back and THERMATICO WILL EAT US!'

And she took off sprinting yet again.

ON-AIR

TONY
Now, it's not often I would go and visit someone's house, but I happened to get this letter and I was compelled to do something. To see for myself. It's not often you get a handwritten letter these days, and this one was written in the most beautiful and disciplined handwriting. *Old school* this was. But there was something about the paper. It seemed to be dripping with sadness. It was, in fact, damp

to the touch. I read it, and I won't repeat it to you... But I'll tell you that this was from a woman in her seventies, a very private woman, living in the same council flat for fifty years. *Fifty years.* And this woman is at the end of her tether, and wrote to us out of pure despair, so having read the letter I went to see her, and this is what I found—

[static] a recording follows, made using a dictaphone, and full of cave-like echoes and drippings and scratchings. it is a desolate recording, an echo itself, a memory [static]

I'm standing in a hallway... and it's very dark, very dim. The smell of dampness pervades... My nostrils are full of this wet, musty, dank smell. You'd swear something was rotting somewhere... The hallway walls are soft, almost crumbly to touch. The dank smell hit me the second I walked in the front door... If you'd even call it a front door, banjaxed auld thing...

[static] moments of prolonged scratching and dripping mark the passing of time, the passing from one room to another, breathed upon by resonant footsteps and grunts. i imagine that TONY felt he could sense the reel of the tape turning. i rebuild TONY from these echoes and drippings — the type of person he might be [static]

I'm in the toilet now and it's falling apart. You barely have room to turn around in it... The bath is full of dirt and debris. The kitchen is two feet away and it's in no better condition.

Cupboards wet through. Doors missing off
them. Black mould in every corner, spreading
out like a cancer... Here in the bedroom it's
the same story. Everything is running off one
socket. The bed is broken, falling apart. She's
using a cardboard headboard to keep the mould
off her head when she sleeps, and even that is
soaked through. There isn't even paint or paper
on the walls. Everything has flaked away. I've
been in every room and I've seen a total of two
chairs, one of them bockety as a pair of auld
knees. This woman is living in squalor. A wet
rag of a place. She needs a new bed. She needs
a washing machine. I wouldn't take a present
of this place... You'd swear it was 1970, or 1870,
not the twenty-first century. I'll tell you what:
I'm lost for words...

[static] mechanical silence clicks off into fresh
studio silence, and TONY gives it that extra second
of dead air to let the squalor settle into the
minds of listeners [static]

> [static] oh i'd say he does alright! he's a real
> pro that way! [static]

Now, this can't be allowed to happen, lads. Not
in this proud county. This is a lady paying rent
her whole life. She's not a sop or an addict,
though she's had the ups and downs any person
might have in life. This is not some woebegone
era – it's the twenty-first century. I'm appealing
for help for this lady. You heard the recording:
she needs a bed, a washing machine, a few
chairs. The place needs treatment for damp

– damp I haven't seen since the great floods –
and a dehumidifier to keep it off, and a fresh
coat of paint throughout, and curtains, and a
new kitchen if possible, and a new bathroom
while we're at it. She needs fresh, clean – not
necessarily new now – *clean* bedclothes and
linen... What can you listeners and local
businesses out there spare? Look, I'm not going
to name names here, because this is a very
private, humble lady we're talking about, but
I'm going to say let's get together this morning
and solve this lady's woes in these few hours we
have. Phone in to us. Or text in. Or call in to
the station. Pledge something. Pledge a chair. A
table. A few cans of paint. If you're a business,
donate one of your products to us. A bed, a new
cooker. We'll give you all the plugging on the
show that you could want in return – *I don't care.*
Are you a tradesman with an apprentice who
can spare half a morning to do something here?
Please. I'm asking on behalf of Cork. We're a
proud county, and this shouldn't be happening
to one of our own. The damp there stays with
me even now. I feel it in my lungs... I shudder
to think of it. So what can you spare?

[jingle redacted]

OFF-AIR, back in the guesthouse, she tried to give her
mam the change from the shop.

'Take it for school,' Mam said, pushing it back. 'You might
need a few quid.'

'But what does that leave ye with? Have ye enough for the day?'

'Don't you worry about us, Jada,' Mam said, already turning

for her bag, their belongings in backpacks for another day. Dad was already gone with his. Dad always went back to the car, and sat and smoked in it – she knew this. 'You worry about getting to school on time now,' Mam was saying. 'It's already half past eight. Have you everything you need?'

She crouched and pulled the schoolbag from under the camper bed, untouched since yesterday. 'Yea, I'm grand. I've everything.'

'And what classes have you this morning?'

'Double Geography. Then Religion, then English and Irish, then double PE. You don't need to check up on me you know.'

'Right, well. Don't be late.'

'... Are you sure you don't need that money though?'

Mam gave her the eyebrow. 'Jada, I'm *sure*.'

And so she took it. Even knowing that her mam had fuck all money. Took the money and the schoolbag, and hugged Mam and hugged Sally, who was giddy as shit for school every day, and away she went back into the city, back through her labyrinth of signs and memories and dereliction. And was she going to school? Was she fuck. School was a waste of fucking space.

OFF-AIR, Tony was thinking of that late-night message from Lolly, the mad coincidence of the timing, when he'd only been thinking of her the other day, as if he'd summoned her back into his life somehow, and anyway he was in his early twenties again, loving London, in love with Lolly, who was perfect. He couldn't want for anything else with her, in the early days at least, and yet it somehow ran its course and in the end she stayed on to run the family pub when he came back. Oh the half-Irish, half-English lilt in her voice, daughter of a London–Galway dance. Lolly was a big girl – five eleven, maybe six foot in good form – and broad of thigh, with a stoutness and a firmness and a paleness. Love that he could scale again and again, feet to face, and feel alive, feel... Pale and loving – cold feet and hands in the bed. Kisses of the neck and the forehead. Father PJ had said to him maybe a year after his return from London – in a particularly low period – that there were some injuries in sport that stopped you from ever playing seriously again.

'Sure,' Father PJ had counselled from the blindside of the confessional, 'you can tog off for a game of five-a-side the odd evening, or stand in corner-forward to make sure a fixture is filled for the parish – I've done that myself – but you'll never again throw yourself into the fray with real intent, into the pure white heat of championship. You'll never again give your whole self like that... My knee, at twenty-three...'

Father PJ had made the sound of an explosion.

'Hence the limp, Father?'

'Hence the limp. But do you know what I mean? About being broken?'

Tony had understood different things about that little confessional sermon at different stages of his life since.

And you'd wonder sometimes why you make the decisions you do. Had it been so important to come back to Cork? If he hadn't come back, he wouldn't have got in with the station when he did. It was only junior researcher, he'd told Lolly then, but it was a start in the place. And he'd been right. Here he was, however many years later: his own show; two great kids; Nuala his Dancing Queen up in the palace at Rochestown Heights.

And Lolly, living in Galway now. How would her head have withered and changed? Would she have carried the charm of her eyes and the great splendour of her limbs all these years? Or would she have thinned out? In London, when it was hot on the weekend and there was no hurling game, they often went to the park to lie back and just relax. It got far hotter in London than home, he told her, and hotter more often too. Around where they lived in Brockley the parks were all on hills, so from where you lay in the grass you could see the city through the heat haze, far away and below, all the stacks of buildings and the necks of cranes. The vast endless shimmering of it made Cork look like a medieval village. It was nice to be in a park on those days, looking down on that city but being surrounded by old trees, with your back on the grass. When you looked up you could see all the seed pods of the plants lifted away on the breeze. Bright little specks filled with sunlight. It was Lolly who brought him to the parks first. They were her favourite places in London. They felt real, she said. You'd take trees and grass and nature for granted in Ireland, she said, but not here, no.

Jesus and the litter and the life and the smells of Lewisham on a stifling morning too! POUND A BOWL! POUND A BOWL! All that concrete and tarmac, the heat bouncing all over. And walking to her flat or to her pub from Brockley – the weaker sunlight and rustling leaves of the Wickham Road, the pavements buckled by trees... They were good to each other a long time, him and Lolly, and then the ending of it was all him really. Five years in and he was lost to her, taking himself away in distant moods and vague statements of everything being fine. Stupid things had annoyed, festered; the putting away of his clothes; the squeezing of the top of the toothpaste tube, rather than the bottom. More went unsaid than said. The arguments then were like icebergs, with volumes of rehearsed words beneath the surface of one comment, which itself had nothing to do with the vague hurt bursting from it. It all became so useless and frustrating that they stopped even trying to open up to each other. Him and Lolly. Lolly and him. He certainly sealed himself off. By the end he made it impossible for her. A cold valley between them in the bed each night; different bedtimes, separate lives again. He left her there in London, the promise of the radio job more a way out than an opportunity. A start in the place, he'd said. That was five years of their lives. And then gone. And now a message from the blue.

But memory was a wilderness, wasn't it? And when you went back you got caught up, entangled in it, and everything seemed to catch you. It was wrong to even consider this kind of thing. Poor Nuala, if she only knew what he was thinking.

And yet still he hadn't deleted Lolly's message. And there she was now, in Galway, sending him a note after all these years.

OFF-AIR, what she did when school just wasn't a bearable notion, was she walked most of the way to school, the new school, where they barely knew her to know she was missing, and then instead of going up the hill she veered off towards Wellington Road. Went past the radio station and on a bit, and then up around Military Hill and the barracks and all that area and then doubled back to the old house. Their *home*, as it had once been known. She doubled back around and she minded to make sure the hood was up and that nobody would recognise her, and, well, yes, she did; she snuck up on the old house and she fucking staked it out. She watched it. She watched how the new people nearly always had the living-room blinds drawn. She watched how they kept the front garden, small as it was, trim as fuck. Pride of the fucking terrace. All those tiny lawns and this one with perfect grass and with flowers who gave a fuck what the name of them was. They made her want to do some real damage. And on this particular day, feeling that, seeing the blinds of her old gaff drawn, having doubled back on the gaff, the old homestead, the house in which she'd grown up, where Santy had called to them every Christmas, in which she'd got her first period, in which Darragh fucking Gooch had fingered her in her bedroom while they were watching *Scream* on his phone. In which Sally had been brought home that first time, a little wailing pink terror... Yes, on this particular day, on the hop from school, she doubled back on her doubling back. She went back out of the estate, as if she was going to go to school after all, to double Geography with some teacher whose name she didn't know, and who wouldn't even register her as missing, but once she was past the back of the houses she went back along the dodgy lane behind the gardens. Because you could walk down that lane – it went around to the main road on the other side, towards the barracks and towards the prison – and once you were about halfway down it you could cut into some undergrowth on the left, and down into an old

66

dried-up stream, and you could climb up from that through brambles and bindweed and you'd be at the back of the houses, and some of the houses had block walls but theirs just had a shitty wooden fence, half rotten. And the new people hadn't fixed that yet. And there she was then, leaving her schoolbag down in the weeds behind that rotten fence, and going through the age-old gap in it – Dad with a football, way *way* back, drunk with his friends and fucking around – and through the gap in the fence to the side of the garden, watching the house for signs of life, of which there were none. And she was going up the side of the garden, very low and very slowly, using all of her graffiti stealth, her shoulders slack, her fists clenched, and she was up to the back door, which, if you looked closely, had all these scuff marks low down on the frame of it, from when she'd thought she could rub a rock off it to start a fire. To set the house on fire basically. That was after a particularly bad row, when she thought it'd be easier just her and the baby on her own – no Mam, no Dad. But of course she couldn't start the fire. Probably didn't want to. But the scuff marks were there. Even now, when they weren't. That was what a house was.

And at the back door she stopped and listened. What would she do, once she was inside? Maybe she could actually set the place on fire now? Send it up in flames. Because that was the thing, wasn't it? However shitty life was in the gaff, it was fucking *way* worse without it. Mam and Dad actually got on better now, but she'd take this house back and put up with the stupid fights again in a second. Hands down. She'd never write again, never smoke again, never do fucking *any single thing* wrong again to be back in this house. Back with her friends. Back in her room, herself and Ró up there with their backs on the bed and their feet on the wall chatting shit. Climbing up on the back roof to smoke, all that clichéd shit. Ah, fuck. She had her hand on the back door. It was unlocked.

How had she felt when her mam told her about the house? It was like having her whole self torn apart. It was not okay. It was fucking soul-destroying. She felt like a black hole had opened up inside of her, right there in the middle of the shopping centre. And that lasted for days. Mam tried to make it sound like they were only staying at Auntie Claire's until some supposed new place was ready, but she knew there wasn't a new place. She wasn't a fucking idiot. How long did Auntie Claire's last? A month? Then fucking Wayne came back from college and needed his room back, and then it was a hostel for a week – the last of the money, she of course overheard – and then it was the car for three nights. By the time it was the car she was numb from the hurt of it, almost like it had happened long ago. It turns out there is only so much wishing you can do. And all of that crying and wishing takes its toll – it sucks something out of you, leaves you numb, or hollow, or detached, or something else.

And yet here she was, her hand on the back door of the house; the door unlocked.

She opened it.

To someone else's kitchen.

The counter was in the same place, but it was wooden now – not the black stuff they'd had before. And new lino. And the cabinets were either new or painted. A new fridge. Someone else's kitchen. Cunts.

And out of nowhere, voices. She pegged it.

Left the door open behind her and fucking pegged it.

Down the garden, through the fence, smashing her elbow on something, taking another rotten stake with her, grabbing her bag from the weeds and fucking lashing through the undergrowth and the dead stream and back down the lane and fucking gone gone gone.

ON-AIR

TONY
... Now, we don't normally do this kind of
thing, but it's our own dear producer Lou, and
we're on the lookout for her missing cat, little
Tabitha. Lou, when's she missing since?

LOU
Since Tuesday last, Tony, so eight days now.

TONY
And where from? What happened?

LOU
We don't know exactly what's after happening
to be honest with you, Tony. She doesn't go
out much – she's timid enough – but she went
out about six in the evening, we reckon, last
Tuesday, and we haven't seen her since. That's
really unusual for her so we're pretty worried.

TONY
And whereabouts should people be keeping an
eye out?

LOU
Well anywhere in town, really, but particularly
the Shandon area where we live. She stays very
close to home normally. She'd wouldn't even go
as far as the river. But we think something must
have spooked her...

TONY
What does she look like?

LOU
She's small, Tony, white with patches of tabby.
She's easily identifiable by a little tabby patch
around her eye. Hence the name. Tabitha. Tabby.

We've put up posters all around town, so details and a couple of photos are on those. And on the station's social media pages too.

TONY
Well, guys, keep your eyes peeled for little Tabby. And check the social media. And for god's sake check under your car before you take off if you've parked it up around Shandon or the quays there. I won't tell ye that horror story. Fingers crossed, Lou. And look, we'll be right back after these—

KFLDMANDHTNEMALDJFHTNENFBT
HGOLEPELAMNDNDNRTBTYBTBYBY
MMWEFFFMRGNTHAMWLEKJENTNTY
NDMDDJSNENDHSPOALDMFNTHEME
KALWQQQAMDNRB INTHES TATIC
it's a habit they always had, leaving the radio on when there was no one home. To deter burglars who might put an ear to the door. So that the dog wouldn't feel lonely when everyone was gone. And so the voices — Tony's voice, the voices of callers, the jingles, Lou talking about her cat — spoke to the empty kitchen, to the breadcrumbs strewn beautifully across the creamswirly formica countertop, to the stapler on the kitchen table, to the rinsed but unwashed crockery in the sink, to the Lidl receipt — folded not crumpled — for €86.17, which perhaps had come to rest near the kettle, to the kettle, to the bottle of raspberry cordial left out, only a drop left, to a pair of fluffy Penney's slippers pointing different ways on the tiles, to the 'Dance Tango' fridge magnet, to a couple of happy birthday cards still pinned

to the noticeboard. The kitchen door would be open, and from the hallway beyond would come the shuttershift push and papersplat of post coming through the letterbox, to which the radio voices responded:

… now he wasn't the captain of the ship, but became captain of the ship when the captain died of… what was it again?

Where did they come from, those radio voices? They often came from homes, like this one, speaking aloud into phone receivers that magicked them through the walls and up into telephone masts. They were transported via radio waves hundreds of metres long, via electricity, carried from pole to pole still yapping away in the electromagnetic signal, as it crossed roads, fields, ditches, rivers, crossed air, passed birds flying, over farms, beaches, housing and industrial estates all along to the radio station's transmitter. The beacon. This was all electricity! Radio waves! They surged through the air of the world! Received, they came down into the station through tubes and wires into one room, where they were decoded to voices again, where Lou, Bernie and Mark heard them, ordered them, tested them, briefed them and queued them for *his* room. Tony's room. The studio. Just another small room in a small city, in an insurmountably vast world.

And to the voices in his room he listened, and with his own voice he responded. And he encouraged them to respond to each other, and

the voices were both voices and electromagnetic
signals, travelling through time and space at the
speed of light, and the ways he transitioned were
beautiful too, and included:

            john, good to have you on: talk to me —
ann, what did you see on the glanmire road? —
to line three now; karen, how are you? —
            julius from kinsale disagrees —
where am i going, line one is it? —
ray, you were there yourself, is that right? —
    now, who's on two? bríd, is it? —
    but where are they getting the phone
                numbers, áine? —
why haven't we heard this before, michael? —
what i want to know, teo —
            who should be on line three, lou? —
is why do people keep going back? —
how's a person end up with a name like julius? —
                            father dan —
                            line one —
        what's your read on all of this? —
should we be afraid, akinbaye? —
gillian from togher called in a couple of
                months ago —
who's on line two? wad? jud? waajud, is it? —
                waajoode? —
marie, what in god's name is going on down there? —
    frances is on line four to tell us —
but we could talk about that until the cows
come home —
and i want to bring in teresa —
        i'm gonna bring in jason here —
        go on, josh —
        you're on, joan —

you're up, jane —
you're through, jim —
are you there, jan? —
what exactly *did* you see, james? —
you disagree with the last caller, mike? —
welcome aboard... marek —
you're just in time, ed —
carol, was it dettol the young fella drank —
you've just got time, gráinne —
... first-time caller. it's about time, graham! —
your response, tony two? —
amanda's got a real problem —
what is it, amanda? —
we're getting call after call on this. tom? —
how's it going, frank? —
where exactly are you, flo? —
how's she cutting, francis? —
how does it look from passage, pavel? —
how did ye get up there, kathleen? —
how are they getting on in mallow, joe? —
ber, i believe you were watching this on the
tele last night? —
how now, bernardo? —
hello all! hello dean on line one! first
caller of the day! i hear you've a very
specific problem, dean? —
where will it end, rory? —
rory? —
what's the reality of the situation, claire? —
sorry, conchita, is it? —
who are we going to next —
jamesie, is it? —
yache? yanchev? ah, i'm not even gonna try —
... go on, pj?... —
get up out of that! —

                        go on out of that! —
                        go on away from me! —
                        get out of it you! —
                          go'waaay! —
                        good lord above —
                        good night, irene —
                        god willing —
        i don't know. i don't know at all. noel is
        on line one. noel, help me for the love of
                                              god —

And, of course, at the very same time the voices
were transmitted back out of the studio, via the
same wires and tubes, up through the transmitter
and out, to all the rooms and yards and cars
of that city, and beyond. You could listen —
anyone could — simply by tuning to a particular
frequency on a box. Electricity. Radio waves. The
voices could reach you. Abroad on sine-waves, the
voices are always there, always speaking through
that frequency, which surge through the air of
these places, into these places, speaking into
this kitchen, speaking to the dog that comes
in to crunch on the bowl of dry food, speaking
to the office, to the garage forecourt, to the
girl fleeing down the back garden, through a
woman's headphones as she walks to work, to the
baby's crying, to the lad with his hands in the
waistband of his tracksuit pants waiting to get
his hair cut, to the dog as, alone again now, she
settles into her basket to go back to sleepppddm
enfahdnweldmenanbddntgtmmmfnfnfreefreeellllddmmmm
sfkfhsbnnandmflllldkapfpfofnrnnsdsmdnfhgntherewwa
lkfjtrpoiytutmncbxzasdhfnrehwwwsjakdmmffffffffffn
nrhebaddebenenebdmdlllldpppdd

74

ON-AIR

TONY
Now, something that annoys us all. It especially grinds my gears. I'm talking about graffiti. I'm not talking about street art – the skilful images you might see along by the Kino there – I'm talking about these ugly marks you see along the walls, everywhere in our city. Just names, slogans, *rants*, stupid things like that... Lou is telling me from the producer's booth here that they're called *tags*. Spray-painted on walls throughout the city. Scrawled on walls. Dragging the place down, making it look dishevelled, dirty and downright derelict. As if some parts weren't bad enough already... And they do it *everywhere*, Lou! They're besmirching the good walls of our city! They drive me nuts, Lou, and I'm not the only one. Barry is on line one there, and there's a particular... *tagger*... who drives Barry round the bend. Barry, back me up here!

BARRY
Tony, listen, call 'em what you want. I call 'em scum. I'm living up here off Barrack Street, and there's this sort of a name I see everywhere I go. AERO.

TONY
AERO?

BARRY
AERO. Like, for a start, what kind of a name is that, Tony? It's a chocolate bar, like, d'you know what I mean?

75

TONY
It's a bit *weird* alright, Barry. And where are you
seeing this tag?

BARRY
Oh, everywhere, Tony. Literally everywhere. On
the walls up the lane where I live. On the gate,
on doorways, on shop shutters, on the gable
end of the house at the end of our terrace.
This gurrier, as you call him – I'd call him
worse myself to be honest with you, Tony – has
literally pissed up every wall and door from The
Lough to St Fin Barre's Cathedral.

TONY
And you know, I saw it myself, cycling home
the other night along the line. And for people
who haven't seen it, or noticed it *yet*, what kind
of mark is it? Is there any craft to it?

BARRY
Craft? You must be joking me, Tony. Sometimes
the lettering is sort of… cartoonish. There's one
– the biggest one I've seen – is up on the Rock
Steps there, by the North Mall. It must be about
four feet high and about six feet long. It's like
something out of a New York ghetto, Tony!

TONY
It's just a bit much, isn't it?

BARRY
The whole place is riddled with it. I was only
unlocking the gate out the back of my mother's
place yesterday and turning the key I looked
down, and there scrawled in what looked like a
Tipp-Ex pen? AERO.

TONY
Ridiculous.

BARRY

The whole place is riddled, Tony. This mindless, stupid stuff...

TONY

And Nicole joins us now. When are these guys at it, Nicole? When are they actually doing the graffiti? The brazen so and sos...

NICOLE

Well, Tony, god knows. Hardly during the day I suppose. And that's another thing. If these scuts are out at night defiling our city's walls then there's a bunch of parents behind them letting them out. It all goes back – and I've said this before, Tony! – one way or the other it all goes back to irresponsible parenting—

OFF-AIR, a small crowd gathered outside the station on the Wellington Road to see Tony and Lou off. There was the radio station gang and Jerry Collins with a couple of others from the Mazda publicity team and they all chatted over folded arms and kicked at the pavement and waited for the leaving to happen. Like their hoodies and their jackets, the Mazda was decked out in the various logos of the station and the *Talk To Tony* programme. Carol Lehane – the Mazda publicity guru – would have had a few final remarks about visibility to send them off with. Walsh might have been passing with the dog and stopped in to say hello and good luck. And at that point Lou – fidgeting, grimacing, grinning, rubbing at her face, feeling the need to take big deep breaths – might have said that they'd better get going, and they were off then, on the first Friday of the car competition, out past the train station and the terraces built into the sheer rockface above the Lower Glanmire Road, and down past the trees of Lotamore House and onto the Glanmire roundabout and over the Dunkettle Interchange and out along the N25 dual carriageway, then eastbound unto the vague fields on each sides, the hills rising and falling away, the acreage and hectares and boundaries that spread out in the map, the county beyond the city.

BROADCASTING SIMULTANEOUSLY on **5264 kHz + 1420 MHz...**

playback: the pale moon was rising above the green mountain / the sun was declining beneath the blue sea...

first voice: *[static] ... five... five... seven... two... they did this road trip. it happened. i've heard all the recordings, seen the photos. i know the name of the one who wins the car...*

second voice: *[static]*

first voice: *hello? ... are you there? ... what is it like where you are?*

second voice: *[static] yawn.*

first voice: *[static]*

second voice: *hit play there til we listen to some more [static]*

ON-AIR

JONATHAN
Go on anyway, Jimmy. You've called about the
news that a string of known and registered sex
offenders have been found to be living within
one square mile of each other on the outskirts
of the city. We don't know who they are, or if
they know each other, but we know that they're
all there in the one community.

JIMMY
Yes. Exactly. What I want to know, Tony, is, like,
do these animals know each other? And if so, do
they hunt in packs like? Do they get together
and make plans for catching the kids?

JONATHAN
A harrowing thought, Jimmy...

JIMMY
Like, whatever the chance a child would have in
outrunning one fella, they'd have no chance at
all against three. Or five. I mean they could be
waiting around corners with nets, and one fella
chases the child in the direction of the trap... I
mean, Tony, Jesus Christ like?

JONATHAN
God, yea. Thanks, Jimmy. And it's Jonathan here.
Standing in for Tony, who's on the road today,
though we can't say where.

JIMMY
Go on away from me, Tony!

JONATHAN
There you have it. Jimmy wants to know if
they hunt in packs. We'd love to know what
you think, so do get in touch. But listen, as I

79

just mentioned, our very own Tony and Lou
are on the road as we speak. We cannot reveal
where they're going yet, but I *can* reveal that
they are on the N25, heading in a particular
direction. A bad day for driving but driving
they are. They'll be on the phone to give us a
clue about their destination within the hour...
And just to remind you that all the returned
exile that you know has to do – be it yourself
or a friend or relative – all they have to do to
win a brand new Mazda 2, is find the car. The
chance to win a Mazda 2 and a year's petrol is
all I'm saying—

OFF-AIR, the market town rooftops of Midleton falling
away to the side of them, Lou complained as she drove: 'Ah
fucking hell, Jimmy... Fucking hell, Jonathan. Fucking hell
tonight – what is he playing at, entertaining that stuff? A giant
net for fuck's sake.'

'What?' Tony asked defensively.

'Scaremongering about paedos?'

'It's a legitimate worry! I wouldn't want these guys a few
doors down the road.'

'Eh, Tony, there's providing a measured, balanced view and
there's giving airtime to lunatics. Giant nets?'

They both faced the road as they argued the point, Lou
hunched over the wheel and far too tall for the car; Tony lounging
back, with his arm hanging from the handle over the window.

'But, Lou, Jimmy is a common man and the common man
has worries. So that's a legitimate voice.'

'The common *man*, is it? The common *man* is a sexist, racist
bigot, Tony.'

'And?'

'And what?'

'He might not be right but you believe in freedom of speech, don't you?'

'I do believe in free speech, Tony, but it's not designed so that some poor guy gets beaten up because someone thinks he's a sex offender.'

'See, this is the problem with your generation. Everybody your age performs these sort of perfectly PC personas. Climbing over each other to be seen to be tolerant. Whereas my generation just voice their paranoias and get on with it. It's healthier *our* way.'

'Tony, are you saying it's healthy to be racist? Or sexist? Or to scaremonger people about paedophiles in their area?'

'All I'm saying is be wary of the liberal PC attitude, Lou. This performative witch-hunting thing; people getting *cancelled* left, right and centre because of some remark they made off the cuff, or some costume they wore back in nineteen-dickety, or because they don't fully understand paedophilia. It leaves no room for nuance, or context. It alienates the common *person.*'

'And all *I'm* saying, Tony, is that people should be challenged if they express drastic views that might get other people hurt, or stir up fear in the community. That's not crazy, is it?'

'It's not.'

She sighed and shook her head and they were quiet for a bit. She was lost to the conversation now, and this was the thing with Lou: there was a burst in her of passion, enthusiasm, fierce care, profound seriousness, the greatest of craic too; she'd be literally trembling sometimes, as if she couldn't contain herself; and yet it could evaporate just like that, and then she was barely there, as if she'd vacated the place. But by God when her dander was up she was a passionate woman alright!

The road stretched into the drizzlemist. The corners of his eyes clocked ghostly clusters of hillside bungalows, and pylons and vague monstrous turbines looming over ditches and smaller roads that ran away from the hillsides like rivulets. Kilometres were counted down through roundabouts and traffic lights. Rinn grew closer. Nothing approached in Ireland; all encroached.

Tony asked in consolation, 'Do you ever wonder about the callers though?'

'In what way?' Lou replied.

'Like, whether they're just lying. Or how often they're lying.'

'Oh yea?'

'Like, they might tell you they're working as a teacher for thirty years and have three kids and *blah blah blah*, but it could all just be lies. They might have done their teacher training and one measly term substituting for someone on mat leave. Nothing more. They might have babysat their nieces and nephews a few times, and never had kids of their own. Or they might tell you they were in such and such a place when such and such a thing happened, but maybe they weren't there at all. Maybe they're just making it up to get some point across or back up their opinion.'

'Mad,' Lou said. 'I never thought that, no... I'm thinking it now though!'

'...'

'The thing I sometimes think about,' she said, looking out at a gull flapping its way back towards the city, 'is that they're real people, in houses, with lives, jobs, kids, all that stuff. That each caller is a human being, with memories of all the things that have happened them in their lives.'

Tony put his coffee cup back in the holder. 'Well, yea. I don't generally forget that, to be honest with you, Lou!'

'I suppose. I just sometimes forget that they're anything but opinions. Voices. Bits we have to use to get from one point to another.'

The odd car coming the other way beeped at them, and drivers opened up their mouths and shook their fists in encouragement.

'Fucking liars the lot of them!' Lou suddenly roared, slamming on the horn to beep back at a Corolla with all that enthusiasm again.

'Fucking blaggers!' he laughed.

And they relaxed into their seats then.

ON-AIR

JONATHAN
... So headed east and crossing a border. Make
of that what you will. And now, staying with
cars, we've been having a good laugh with
listeners' car names here this morning. We've
had Petunia, The Beast, Kitty, The Banger, The
Tank, Penny, Slugger, The Langer, Two Slaps of
A Hammer, Mick, Brenda... Tell me, Maureen,
you actually have a process?

MAUREEN
I do, Jonathan! Every time I buy a car, I name it
after the fella I bought it from. The current one
is called Alan!

JONATHAN
Brilliant! Shirley, good morning to you.

SHIRLEY
I've a Polo, Tony, so I called her Minty!

JONATHAN
Gas! I get it!

SHIRLEY
By the way, Tony, I met you before!

JONATHAN
Shirley, I'm actually Jonathan. I'm sitting in for
Tony as himself and our producer Lou are on
the road to a secret location to try and give
away a brand new Mazda 2.

SHIRLEY
I met you in 1967. In Mallow!

JONATHAN
Shirley, in 1967 Tony was hardly born I'd say!

83

SHIRLEY

You were one, I think. It was the Cobh Fair.
You'd more hair then, Tony, even at one! And
they still called you Anthony then!

JONATHAN

Janey Mac! You know, Shirley – and I think I'm
probably talking for Tony here too – I don't
remember that at all.

SHIRLEY

You were a lovely baby, Tony. Bye now. Bye!

JONATHAN

A Polo called Minty, belonging to a woman
who met Tony when he was one. You couldn't
make it up! And sure look, cases of mistaken
identity happen all the time...

PDFMRNTHANDNFIFIIGLSMMFNGT
BRHEWDERNDBFNRTHROHGUHFNAM
NAEEMHHDNDBFGRHEJKSNFBDDDH
EDEDEDENFNOOOOOUGHKKDHFNTB
EGAHDIN TH E STATIC in the early
afternoon, here she was now, the mother with the
child in a sudden drizzle, the child having come
out of school with a temperature, and they were
heading across the car park towards the automatic
doors of the Dunnes in Blackpool, Calpol on their
minds, when the child saw something and broke off
the held hand and started trundling towards one of
those euro coin rides they have outside shopping-
centre doors everywhere on Earth it seems.

'Sally, no!' she said in her low, first-warning
voice. She knew that she hadn't the euro to spare,
but knew immediately that she'd say instead that

she hadn't change. *We'll get change*, Sally would say. *Mammy, Jada gave you change when we came back from the shop?* But she'd say, *I gave Jada that change back for her lunch. And I don't have time now to be stopping and getting change so you can waste the money on a one-minute ride.* But of course time was the one thing she did have, wandering the city from one hour to the next, waiting til they were allowed back into the hostel in the evening, browsing all the things she couldn't afford for hours on end, giving herself jobs to do and trying not to look at the time on her phone...

Following a child, there was a thing that happened, a process that kicked in, whereby the child was a particular distance ahead, say three or four feet, and while she, the mother, wanted the child to turn of her own accord and come back to *Mammy*, she, the mother, also had to close the distance between them in case anything happened. For discipline's sake, for development's sake, the child had to turn of her own accord, based specifically on her mother's command, and yet she, the mother, couldn't but maintain a sort of pursuit, which while she called out closed the distance between them.

'Sally, I'm warning you!' she said again, low, yes, but a little louder.

She watched the way the soles of Sally's runners flicked up brown watery specks, spitting them in her direction. The drizzle came down lazily, and cars moved slowly in low gears, in various directions along the gridlines of the car park. Sally was reaching out a tiny hand as she trundled, sort of waving to the euro ride — was it Thomas the Tank Engine?

85

'Sally, come the fuck back here!' was when she had to start running after the child, was when she was feeling violent, though of course she'd never hurt her little angel.

'Sally, there could be cars!' was when she'd given up on Sally's voluntary return yet still hoped the child would swivel back to her, an act that would of course lessen the rebuke (though there would still be a reminder of rules and responsibilities no matter what — i.e. Sally was in for a fucking scolding). And this was when the notion occurred to her, the mother, and not for the first time, that when you're not a parent, you remain convinced that there's a way to parent that doesn't involve nagging, and giving out constantly. That you'd never swear at your child. But when you become a parent, well...

Sally trundled along the car park's dark tarmac in her navy school tracksuit — the only new clothes she'd had in a year — one hand held out, one pendulum-swinging by her side, as if she was in an awful hurry, impatient for this magical train ride, and the mother was less than five feet behind the child, calling her name more and more insistently. Exhaust fumes that had been suspended on the air began to rise; and the light, even at lunchtime, struggled.

'Sally!' she shouted. She was jonesing for a smoke. She just wanted to get the Calpol, which if it was still around six euro would leave her with about thirteen euro in her account until Thursday, which was already not enough, and even as she almost had Sally in her grasp she was already having conversations in her head, and while she should have been looking each way for cars — especially

on this slick drizzly road, where they wouldn't
be able to stop so quickly (something she'd
been trying to teach Sally on the interminable
moneyless days of drifting around town) — she
was already realising that the question of money
could now form itself around Sally's potential
illness, her need for Calpol, the price of Calpol,
the trip to the doctor (which she'd decide later
whether was actually required or not), but that
that was seventy euro she could legitimately and
non-guiltily ask her sister for (though there
would of course be the requisite guilt that must
be mentioned and felt, or performed if not felt,
as part of the asking conversation, and of course
there was the low-level, deep-seated guilt that
was always, *always* there, and which could only be
buried, forever temporarily, forever shallowly,
through a matrix of self-explanations and backstory
and promises and abstract reasoning, and smoking,
which...) 'Sally, one more fucking step!'
   But she was laughing as she grabbed the child,
laughing at this beautiful child, this beautiful
friend in her life, just messing about in a car
park, just wanting something simple, just *dying*
to go on the train thing when they were supposed
to be getting Calpol for her temperature, when she
was supposed to be sick. Yes, call it laughing,
laughing, as that Vauxhall hit the brakes a little
too hard, for effect, to make a point, and beeped
at them performatively, and she, the mother, gave
the car the finger with one hand at the same time
that she hit Sally a hard slap to the back of the
fucking head with the other, and said, 'Sally,
don't you ever fucking do that again!' It was all
hard lessons, this fucking life.

OFF-AIR, Lou explained that there was movement essential, which was the movement of your soul, and movement local, which was the movement of your body. 'Like we're doing now, Tone. Crossing the land physically... And this tribe had covered such a distance in terms of movement local – hundreds and hundreds of miles on foot with this explorer – that they had to sit down and wait for their souls to catch up. They just refused to budge until their movement essential caught up with their movement local.'

'And this is the kind of thing you were studying in the college?'

'Exactly this kind of thing.'

'Madness!'

By the time they came down off the N25, with Dungarvan Bay opening up like a soggy landscape painting, the silences and the chat – the snippets of story and speculation they shared – must have made things comfortable between them. They must have realised by that point they'd be okay in each other's company on these road trips. It would all be fine.

ON-AIR

TOMMY
I'm after coming back from fishing in Kerry, Jonathan, only this morning, and I'm after seeing a huge crash on the N22.

JONATHAN
What happened, Tommy?

TOMMY
Hard to tell but it was a family in a car going one way – one of these soft jeep-looking things – and a white lorry coming the other way. I saw a child coming out the back window of the car, Jonathan.

JONATHAN
Jesus, Tommy.

                    TOMMY
    The body is a frail thing, Jon. A frail thing!

JONATHAN
What did you do, Tommy? I'm presuming the
worst here?

                              TOMMY
        I called 999 and tore away on down the road.
        The car was needed at home. Sure what else
        could I do? I didn't even see where the child
                                landed, Jon.
JONATHAN
My god. The roads in this country have a lot
to answer for. We can only pray they're all okay
– the child in particular – by whatever slim
chance. Tommy, you do need to sit down with
someone – be it a professional or a friend or
a relative – and you need to process what you
saw.

                              TOMMY
    The body is a frail thing, Jonathan! Impossible
                to tell who was to blame—

OFF-AIR, the place they chose – the first 'hiding spot' on
that first Friday – was a small pier in Rinn that looked across the
seaweed and humped shorerocks of the bay to Dungarvan town.
There was a pub on the pier – Molloy's – which was, of course,
closed at ten in the morning. Tony had last been here one night,
decades ago, when they'd drunkenly rowed from Rinn across
to Dungarvan town to find a nightclub. Returning to the pier
afterwards, they'd found the punt gone again, and it being too
late for taxis or spins they had to walk the black road all the way

back to Rinn. Dungarvan was a scattered necklace of lights then, and yet now a grey urban haze.

'What'll we do now?' he asked Lou in the car.

Lou returned from her own thoughts, pulling her phone from its holder and hitting the power button on the radio. 'We'll phone it in, I suppose.'

ON-AIR

JONATHAN
Tony, are you there?

                                             TONY
                    **I am, Jon! Strange to be on the other end of
                                              the line!**

JONATHAN
I'd say so! Well, look, I'm keeping your seat
warm for you. Give us a clue as to where you
are, Tony? The phones and the social media
pages are going wild here – people squeezing
the shoes on left, right and centre – and you
were definitely spotted passing through Youghal
and over the bridge into Waterford!

                                             TONY
                    An bhfuil cúpla focail agaitse, Jonathan?

JONATHAN
Tá cúpla focail agam, Tony, cén fáth?

                                             TONY
        **Well, we're down in a particular heritage area,
         in which a particular language is spoken, just
              over the border into the splendid county of
         Waterford here. Many's the night I did the disco
             in Dungarvan back in nineteen-dickety, Jon,
             and I'll give ye a clue: when I was DJing in**

Dungarvan, I used to be looking across at this
particular town. Well, let the hunt begin! Get
motoring, folks!

JONATHAN
Good man, Tony. Listeners, callers, ye've got
two hours—

BROADCASTING SIMULTANEOUSLY on 5264 kHz + 1420 MHz...

playback: the pale moon was rising above the
               green mountain / the sun was declining
               beneath the blue sea...

first voice: [static] i haven't gone as far as rinn
               of course, but sometimes i imagine
               cycling around to these different
               places. the roads are cracked, run
               ragged with loose grit and potholes.
               they say the land remains barren until
               the right question is asked, and i
               imagine these potholes and dents in
               the road filling up with puddles,
               over and over again, for eternity...

second voice: [static] the wind would fill your ears
               in a sad, lonely way too, wouldn't it?

first voice: the wind!

second voice: mad thinking of a place as big as the
               world as a place that might be empty...

first voice: ... now i wouldn't be much of a cyclist; i
               wouldn't have the heart for exercise.
               and the sight of the open sky can
               be a bit of a shock at first... but
               i do imagine trying, struggling on
               past the various houses and shops...
               [static]

second voice: ... you'd pass a lot of rooms over the
               course of a day alright. you'd see
               them through windows. you might see

91

a person inside, watching TV, or a whole bunch of people, sitting around a table eating, drinking, chatting. or the rooms might be empty and dark either; they might just seem to be waiting for the people to return to them...

first voice: *now, i don't know exactly how to be in rooms, but you do. or you did once. you were good in a room alright i'd say.*

second voice: *i did! i was! i love people, and i mean that. but what i might do now is i might tour the floors of one of the various shopping centres, at some random hour... [static]*

first voice: *[static]... there i'd be, just cycling around the place. i'd stop at the traffic lights and even though it changes nothing—*

second voice: *all pointless i suppose—*

first voice: *i'd count the seconds out. at the lights. three, two, one, go! counting feels like a layer of consciousness beneath thought, you see. beneath experience.*

second voice: *and of course there's thought. always.*

first voice: *and i think of you, of course.*

second voice: *oh, you old romantic! my old comrade! go on. give's some more of TONY and LOU and all those other poor souls. i'm in the mood for it today! [static]*

OFF-AIR, a short man with grey hair and a goatee came along the pavement, accompanied by a bearded, short-haired spaniel. Hands in pockets, collar pulled up against the drizzle, this man leaned in the window as Lou lowered it, and the spaniel cocked a leg to the front wheel.

'Is this the car off the radio?'

'It is. Are you back from London?'

'I'm not, no. I only came down to have a look. I thought I saw ye alright.'

The man whistled and stood straight to take in the whole of the Mazda. 'She's small enough. What would you get to the gallon on her?'

> **JONATHAN**
> **Did God not say to Adam and Eve, go forth**
> **and multiply?**

'I'm not sure,' Lou said. 'I can't think in gallons anymore. They say it's economical though.'

He was looking at her wryly, like she'd failed the test, when in the wing mirror she spied Tony coming back with the coffees.

> **A VOICE**
> **... Blackwater motors: Fermoy, Skibbereen and**
> **Turner's Cross! The new Renault range. Deposit**
> **required. Now giving more for scrappage than**
> **ever before—**

By and by, the potential contestants came. Most had misunderstood.

'Have you come back from London?' Lou or Tony would ask, depending on whose window the person came to.

'No. Why?'

'The car is for someone who's come back from London,' one of them would explain.

'Because of the Troubles,' the other would add.

'It's for an English person? It's for the English?'

'No. A person who's had to move home, back to Ireland, because of the attacks on London.'

'Why?'

'To help them out.'

'And what do the people who didn't abandon their country get?'

'... Do you know anyone home from London by any chance?'

'Sure who would I know from London?'

It went like this, repeatedly, and having prepared for such, they gave these people goodie bags for their trouble, containing air fresheners, stickers, connector kits, handsfree units, chargers, garage vouchers and catalogues, which the people took as they sighed and looked at their watches or phones. Counted the time they'd wasted. They came in Toyotas, Seats, Fords, Skodas. They approached the Mazda unsurely, like teenagers asking adults to buy drink for them.

'Do you know what time the pub opens?' one woman with a Northern accent asked.

'I don't,' Tony said.

[static] the rose of tralee? [static]

'Only I thought it might be open,' she said.

'I'll give it a google for you,' Lou said.

'A what?' she said.

Eventually, a man came who said his son had returned from London a couple of months back, and he was calling the son to get him down. He was working twenty miles away in Killeagh; could they wait til half eleven?

ON-AIR

JONATHAN
Now, apologies for the delay, but I've really wanted to keep going with the prostitution–motherhood story. Fascinating stuff, and

dividing opinions to say the very least. But
we're ready to go back now to Tony, because
we have a brand new Mazda 2 to give away this
month. And ye guessed it! Tony and Lou are
in Rinn today and they've found, I believe, a
returned exile to stake the first claim on the car.
Hello, Tony?

TONY

Hello again, Jonathan!

JONATHAN
Tell me, much interest in a free car down there?

TONY

Oh, plenty. Plenty of visitors to the pier down
here.

JONATHAN
And the first was?

TONY

I've a young gentleman, also named Jonathan
funnily enough, alongside me in the car here.
I'll put him on.

JONATHAN
Tis all name games here this morning. Hello,
Jonathan?

JONATHAN
Hello?

JONATHAN
A fine name!

JONATHAN
Thanks.

JONATHAN
...

JONATHAN

...

JONATHAN
You're recently back from London, Jonathan?

                    JONATHAN
                    I am. About two months.
JONATHAN
And how was it?

                    JONATHAN
                    Ah, grand... Well, not great I suppose...

JONATHAN
... And what were you doing there, in London?

                    JONATHAN
                    Carpentry.
JONATHAN
And how long were you there for?

                    JONATHAN
                    Nine months.
JONATHAN
And tell me, what was it like? Was there an
atmosphere of fear there? An anxiety?

                    JONATHAN
                    It was okay. Once I got work. But then, I
                    suppose... It was... Ah, not great really.

JONATHAN
Were you afraid for your safety?

                    JONATHAN
                    Not really, no.
JONATHAN
You didn't fear for your life?

                    JONATHAN
                    It was a bit... It was difficult to get around. Lots
                    of delays, lots of checks...

JONATHAN

And did you experience any terrorism?

JONATHAN

There was a shooting in Ealing. I lived there.

JONATHAN

Crikey. How many died?

JONATHAN

One, I think... I'm not sure if he died actually.

JONATHAN

And did you know him?

JONATHAN

Oh I didn't, no. It was drugs-related I think. I
wouldn't touch the drugs myself.

JONATHAN

... And you left because you were scared? You
came back home?

JONATHAN

I wasn't scared. I... yea. I suppose it wasn't a
great place to be.

JONATHAN

And are you glad to be back?

JONATHAN

I am. I missed home. The beer there is awful...

JONATHAN

... Tell me, did you hear us on the radio or did
someone else alert you?

JONATHAN

My father told me about it.

JONATHAN

And where is he from?

JONATHAN
Killeagh. But we live in Dungarvan.

JONATHAN
He's an exile himself so!

JONATHAN
The what? Is that it? Have I won a car?

JONATHAN
Not yet, son! It's not that easy!

JONATHAN
Oh.

JONATHAN
But you are the first name in the hat for the
draw for a Mazda 2, all courtesy of Jerry Collins
Motors on the South Douglas Road. And you
have won a year's free petrol courtesy of Circle
K! Are you absolutely delighted, Jonathan?

JONATHAN
Oh, yea... That's great, yea. Thanks. I don't
actually dr—

JONATHAN
Thrilled! Well, welcome home, Jonathan, and
congratulations, and hopefully you'll all tune in
again next Friday to see where Tony and Lou
park up next—

_____

OFF-AIR, on their way home from the first Friday of the
competition, they would have stopped for a break, for a cuppa, at
an expansive, neatly landscaped garage and service complex, an
off-road outpost. Trucks, vans, cars: all would be parked at rough
angles throughout the forecourt and adjacent car park. Like a

small shopping centre, the complex had everything the person in transit might need: a shop, a couple of fast-food counters, toilets, a shower room, and some chairs and tables to sit at, by a glass wall that looked out on road and pylon and field. People moved through the forecourt and the interior facilities in a stilted way, as if their bodies made little sense to them, stretching legs and hips as they limped back into a rhythm, extending arms and bracing, yawning, scratching, rubbing their eyes, stretching their necks, squeezing their eyes shut as if trying to awaken a reality.

Tony might have hurried to the toilet, the radio echoing throughout the various zones of the complex, motor sounds infiltrating the space with each swish of the automatic doors, distant hand dryers blasting the same sudden note of fast air. They'd have bought tea and sandwiches and, pocketing their receipts carefully, sat in the window of the café zone. Looked out on the road, and a fringetattered billboard, while cars wound down off the overpass and were drawn by. And maybe Lou's eye fell then upon a distant house on the hill opposite. Grey finish, perhaps unpainted. It seemed empty, its windows dark, no car in the shale driveway. The notion of an empty house was a sad one, and yet what kind of life would await her if she drove up to that house now and gave it purpose? Herself and Marta, and a bump in her belly growing, her hands resting often on the bump, her father coming up to visit and they all sitting together on some decking, watching the road and the fields. Well, her life would be emanating something then, and it would be beauty, rather than the completely unearned sadness. What was it that made the privileged people of her generation so sad, so anxious? Mainly: why in the fuck, for the two minutes Tony went to the toilet and she was undistracted, did she feel so fucking weirdly, manically helpless? It shouldn't have been the case. Everyone had grief in their past. Everyone had fucked-up parents, lives… The world went on and people were okay. Not everyone had a great job and a loving partner. Was it the lack of a cause? Was it something to do with technology, with the internet? Device dependency? Changing images of self? The ease of access to everything, all of the time? Did the speed with which they moved through the world leave their souls behind – did she need to stop and wait for the soul to catch up? Did they all?

'Well,' Tony laughed as he returned to the table and squeezed into it, 'Rinn was a bit of a disaster anyway!'

She shook her head, began to chuckle. 'Young Jonathan wasn't very talkative!'

They looked at each other, grinning with a sort of disbelief.

'I wonder whether the bollocks was home from London at all.' Tony pushed the crusts of his sandwich to the side with finality. 'Well, I wouldn't have bet that the son could be even less interesting than the father.'

'I know, yea!'

'Not the best start to our venture.'

'No.'

'...'

'Maybe we need to prep them a bit better next time. Draw out the stories a bit more before we actually get them on the phone. And if there aren't stories, we need to find them.'

Tony sipped at hot tea through the lid; Lou removed her lid to drink, suddenly exhausted; and then Tony's phone rang, the Dancing Queen popping up on its screen.

'Well, my love,' he answered, getting up, and Lou would have smiled up at him as he stepped out, then looked back to that hillside house...

[static] who's our next caller? [static]
     [static] hi there this is tony cooney calling and
  as a husband to a dear wife — aka the dancing queen
     — and the father to two teens, i just want to say
   that i think lou is dead right to want a family of
  her own. bad genes be damned! sure in this day and
              age what even is a normal family? [static]
[static] ain't that the truth, tony! [static]

OFF-AIR, the city said:

fuk u

RKD

FREE MUMKEY JONES

CHASE

JC ★ PAZ
RUN DIS SHIT

AERO

PRIKAZE kiss

AERO

SMASH THE CHUPS

PHOOH   10000 HOMELESS

HISTORY IS A NITEMARE FROM WHICH IM TRYING TO AWAKE ←

u need to
talk bro

VIVA VENEZUELA

NICE

```
[ain't that the truth, tony!
   ain't that the truth, tony!
      ain't that the truth, tony!
         ain't that the truth, tony!
            ain't that the truth, tony!
               ain't that the truth, tony!
                  ain't that the truth, tony!]
```

BROADCASTING SIMULTANEOUSLY on 5264 kHz + 1420 MHz...

playback: the pale moon was rising above the green mountain / the sun was declining beneath the blue sea...

first voice: *[static] four... four... seven... three...*

second voice: *so here we are. the hydrogen protons still spinning.*

first voice: *here we are.*

second voice: *... which is where exactly?*

first voice: *hah. i dunno. beyond terror? up on the weather hill? out in the universe, on the other side of the delta orionis, the red shift dragging us away back through time? in [static] and LOU's heads? in our bedrooms or sheds playing with our transmitters?*

second voice: *eh... okay... let's simplify this. what do you see?*

first voice: *i dunno. em, oceans of darkness. a sort of filmy substance, perhaps, that might be code?*

second voice: *really?*

first voice: *or maybe i just broadcast with my eyes closed, to better savour the sine-waves... but i see words floating. i see them in my mind's eye... maybe? [static] can't tell the difference between the mind's eye and the darkness...*

second voice: *[static]*

first voice: *no. look, i'm only being dramatic i suppose. if i'm honest, i see TONY. i see him at the front door of his house. am i in TONY's head or is he in mine? now there's a question...*

second voice: *fuck's sake! you always bloody see TONY!*

OFF-AIR, the way the argument started was that a man came to the door selling knives and Tony, who had answered the door but felt that specific exhaustion that came after travelling long distances, said to the man: 'Let me stop you right there, my man. See, each of us' – here he indicated with a sweep of the ruby-carpeted hallway behind him, his wife somewhere inside the house – 'each of us has the things we're in charge of, and knives – well, cutlery and the kitchen in general – that is her thing. All interior design, in fact, is her arena. My arena is the washing-up. The bins. The lawn. The bathrooms. So before you say another word, let me get her for you if you'll just wait one second...'

And the poor knife salesman didn't even have that second to take the first sample out of the Morphy Richards box, because Tony was already shuffling back down the hallway in his slippers calling, '*IT'S FOR YOU, NU!*' leaving the man in the driveway of the four-bed detached 'HQ' up in Rochestown Heights.

And of course a mere minute later, Tony heard the closing of the front door again from his chair by the record player in the front room. He was just pulling out some Sven Libaek to ease his tightened brain, and was in fact thinking about those tribesmen who all sat down for weeks in order to let their souls catch up with them, when Nuala put her head in the door and said, 'What the fuck was all that about?'

'What about?' he said.

'Sending for me like I'm the fuckin help?'

'That's not my thing though, love. The kitchen's your arena?'

'Tony, you're not on the radio now, so cut the bullshit. A guy comes to the door selling shitty knives at six in the evening; have the balls to just send him away. Don't fob him off on me.'

The vinyl hung from his limp hand. 'Nu, it's been a long day. I'm up since five. I've been to Waterford and back. I'm exhausted. I'm sorry I came to see if you wanted new knives. I'm sorry. I'm sorry that I'm tired after getting up in the dark to do the job that pays for this house, your art, the fucking knives we already have and all. I'm sorry I'm tired after doing the job, and I'm sorry I want to relax when I come home. Is that enough apologies for you? Is there anything else I can apologise for?'

She said, 'Fucking hell,' as she closed the front-room door behind her, but she quickly came back, right into the room, and stood over him in the chair with her hands on her hips. 'Actually, yea, there's plenty more you could apologise for.'

He leaned back in the seat, as hours before he had reclined in the passenger seat of the Mazda with Lou. 'Go on. Enlighten me.'

'You could apologise for essentially being a ghost in this house lately. Barely acknowledging your wife, your children. You harp on and on about the fucking Dancing Queen on the radio, and being a family man, and fucking losing Aaron, and yet you come home and go through the motions and listen to your beloved records and you seem to forget all that stuff you say about being a husband and being a dad. I mean, do I need to remind you that you've two kids here? You treat us like colleagues for fuck's sake, not family.'

'Nuala, what can I do? You tell me and I'll do it. I thought we'd agreed that they related better to you on the... hormonal stuff. They're teenagers; they want nothing to do with their lame dad anymore.'

> [static] but actually, was it more that they'd
> outgrown him already; that from ten upwards they
> weren't his anymore, they were their own people, no
> longer his arena? [static]

'Hormonal stuff?'

The physical choreography of the argument was typical. She paced about the room and tidied or moved objects while he sat up straight in the seat and made motions with his hands. Their movements seemed to punctuate the argument – its warp and weft – and of course eventually he was standing, and they both paced the room, and then ended up in the kitchen, by the knives ironically, cycling through the same points and counterpoints, accusations and counter-accusations, again and again, while the kids in their rooms upstairs sighed and listened to the muffled back and forth of their parents' lowered-but-somehow-raised voices with a grim acceptance, and no little annoyance at the prospect of the bad vibes that would reverberate through the rest of the weekend.

'Hormonal stuff? Tony, what is hormonal about self-harm? Sadie is self-fucking-harming and you're saying you don't deal with the hormonal stuff? Get a fucking grip, boy. You go out of your way to avoid these things but they're real. And they're not going away…'

'No,' he said. 'They're not going away. They'll never go away. You wouldn't let things like that go away, that's for sure.'

'What's that supposed to mean? You think I'm perpetuating it? You think I'm making it worse by caring about it while you swan about the country in a car? And tell the *proud people of Cork* what a family man you are? Need I remind you of some of the things that have gone on in the past? In *my* past? Do I have to spell things out for you, Tony, in order to persuade you to care about our daughter's mental health?'

'Woh,' he said. 'Okay. Wasn't this about knives?'

'Ah, Jesus Christ, Tony.'

'Right, right, okay. I'm here. I'm here to help.'

'Tony, it's not about *helping*—'

'Okay! I'm here to talk to Sadie. I'm here. Whatever you want. I don't want to fight. I don't think you perpetuate anything. You hold this family together. You're the glue. You're the—'

'Oh, Tony, fuck—'

'No! I mean it. I'm in the wrong. You just keep going on about my role as a father and I sometimes wonder is that all I am to you anymore. The father of your children. And is there any more than that? Any love? Any fun?'

As he said this, he might have caught sight of himself in the gold-painted mirror in the hallway, or the glass in the conservatory, and he might have seen the balding and the sagging of his jowls. Pure old-looking. And he might have been asking himself even as he said it, where had he gone as a father? The love was there always, but did it feel dormant now? Or routine? Not the fire that burned with—

'Tony,' she would have been saying while he regarded himself. 'I am telling you that your daughter is self-harming because of something going on at school that we don't know about, and you are making it about yourself. About your fun? She's been pulling sickies for weeks on end now, to the point that I don't even challenge her – I leave her home and I write the note – and you're looking for love? Seriously, Tony?'

His eyes no doubt would have found the ceiling. He would have rubbed them vigorously. Sighed the sigh of an exasperated man. 'Ah, god, no. Sorry. I'm sorry. I'm wrong. You're right. I'm selfish. I'm sorry. Let's go talk to her right now.'

'Tony—'

'I'm not being sarcastic; I mean it. I'm sorry. Is she upstairs? Let's just go and get it over with. I'm sorry. Mea culpa. I am a shitty man sometimes; I am a shitty husband. I'm a shitty father. Let's go. SADIE?!'

And he started trudging up the stairs, calling, leaving Nuala in his wake.

OFF-AIR, Mahony asked: 'Does your uncle still have that place up on Patrick's Hill, Lou? The grand place?'

'He does, P, I think.'

It was Friday night. They were sat at the counter in the Friary, their mobile phones hanging out of them – Lou, Marta, Mahony, Val and Joe – facing the mirrors beyond the counter, the reflections of themselves occupying the mirrored pub, with its handful of tables and the posters for the various 'nights' they had, and the tall windows that looked out onto the North Gate Bridge and the dark river of rippling streetlight.

'Is he going to do anything with it?'

Lou shrugged; a gesture meant to convey that she hadn't a clue, or had no interest.

'I heard he has a fella working there? Or staying there?'

Long delicious pintgulp. 'He does, yea.'

Marta was smiling. They had agreed to take the night off from looking for Tabby, or worrying about her, and it was the first time Lou had seen that smile in almost two weeks.

'And is this fella paying rent?'

'The contrary,' Lou said. 'Dan's paying him.'

'It's *crazy*,' Marta grinned.

'For what? Is he renovating the place?'

'Nope.'

'He's being paid to stay in a derelict property?'

Lou drew thoughtfully from the pint. 'He has a job alright.'

'Is this another radio station thing? Has Dan given the place to a returned exile, with pocket money thrown in?'

Val intervened. 'Lou, put this poor creature out of his misery, will ya?'

Lou lifted her face to the light and then turned to Mahony. 'He's no refugee, or exile. His remit is simple, P. Just keep the place as it is.'

'As it is?' Mahony guffawed. 'In ruin?'

'No,' Lou corrected. 'In a state of disrepair. Larry – poor creature with all the trouble he's had in his life – has the sole duty of keeping that house in a state of disrepair.'

'A state of disrepair! To maintain a state of disrepair?! That beats all! That beats all!'

They all laughed, took pleasure in the strangeness of Lou's uncle, and Mahony the burgeoning estate agent's frustration at prime real estate let to lie fallow.

'Does he not realise the money he could make on that place, without even touching it? Does he realise the profit to be had?'

Lou shrugged again.

''Tis drowning in madness he is! Christ almighty!'

'How'd ye get on in Rinn today?' Val asked.

'Ah, it was a bit shite to be honest with you, Val, but it'll only get better I'd say. We've three more places to go.'

'Where else are ye stopping?'

'Dublin, Galway and Cork…'

'Lovely. How's Tony to travel with?'

'Ah, he's grand.'

'He keeping his hands off you?' Mahony grinned, and Marta grimaced.

'Eh, he understands the meaning of the word *lesbian*, P. Plus he's far too mad about his *Dancing Queen*.'

'I like him,' Marta said. 'But a man that can't drive in this day nage? It's crazy.'

'Speaking of crazy,' Mahony said. 'Lou, gimme your uncle's number there. I'm going ringing him first thing in the morning.'

Lou only shook her head at him. 'P, one day he'll fall down dead with a stroke, or a heart attack or cancer, so I'd say let him do what he likes while he's here.'

'…'

They were all suddenly checking their phones, or checking the weather out the window, in embarrassment she imagined. Jesus Christ. She hadn't meant to make it sombre. To have them all suddenly thinking of her mother. Of death. Jesus Christ!

Then Val said: 'There was that woman on the show, the other day. Stage four cancer. Jesus she was a brave woman her. Said she was in pain but that it was all an adventure. She was half fucking mad on morphine I'd say.'

'I heard her,' Mahony said.

'She was going on and on about *the mystery*,' Marta said.

'That's the one.'

'Ann,' Lou confirmed.

'Yea.'

'…'

'And what d'you think, Val?'

'I want to be cremated when I go. Don't fucking dare drop me in the ground, Paul!'

'I'm here,' Marta said, 'to enjoy the world as much as possible. And then... goodbye.'

Lou turned and gave her a funny look. 'Eh, okay.'

'What?'

'Don't worry about those of us left behind, like?'

After a time, Mahony asked: 'Are ye afraid of it?'

'...'

'Not really,' Lou said. 'I mean, I'm not relishing the idea of it. I hope it's fast when it comes... But I don't really think about it, to be honest.'

'...'

'I am,' Val said. 'I'm afraid of all the things around it. Who'll find me. Where I'll die. In what condition. Whether I'll blabber on like a baby. Whether I'll keep breathing for days or weeks and everybody will be relieved when my chest stops moving.'

'...'

Marta said: 'I don't want to be one of those yellow bodies hooked to the machine, like a milk cow or something. I just want to go.'

'...'

'...'

'Lou,' Val said. 'When you go to the white witch next week, she'll read your lifeline. She'll tell you exactly how long you have...'

'Great.'

'It's a freaky thing to hear, whether you believe in it or not.'

'I'm looking forward to it actually.'

'Ah, she's brilliant. I always come out full of beans when I see her.'

'...'

'...'

'Would ye prefer to die alone or in company?' Mahony asked.

'...'

'... Alone, probably. To die in front of people would be awful embarrassing.'

'Aye. It would actually.'

'Probably better to say nathing to no one, take to the bed and stick on the tele or the radio and just ease out like that.'

'Why the tele or the radio? Why not peace and quiet, you know... at the end?'

'Well... to let yourself know that life goes on. That you weren't the be-all and end-all.'

'Lou, you're too obsessed with your work.'

'She is! Never stops!'

'Sure who needs peace at that point anyway I suppose. You're going into an eternity of peace one way or the other. The prime real estate is worth nothing then, P.'

'It is, actually! It's an asset to leave for your family.'

'Hear him?! 'Tis far from *assets* you were reared, Paul O'Mahony!'

'My main problem is I'm sitting here with three bloody feminists – two of them rampant lezzers – not one of whom understands how the real world works!'

'Listen to him!' Val shoved a thumb at Mahony's face before turning to him. 'Didn't I have to show you how to boil an egg when we first started going out?'

'It's not like we'll have kids to give estate to anyway,' Marta pointed out.

'Hold up, love,' Lou said. 'You never know.'

Marta took a sup of her pint. 'Oh, I know.'

'...'

'...'

'I heard a story though,' Joe said, thoughtfully, at last, 'about a woman who died alone, in front of the tele, and no one found her for something like three years.'

'Where'd you hear that?' Lou asked.

'Don't remember. On the tele probably. They said there was

a mountain of letters inside the door – bills, pizza flyers, eviction notices. It was in London. They'd come to kick her out, and in the end it took her teeth to identify her. She'd just crumbled there on the couch, tins of food still good in the cupboard, tele still on.'

'Christ. Think of that. The tele still on at that point. Years after you'd passed.'

'Years of history playing out on the screen. The new becoming old in front of your…'

'Corpse…'

'And you with no eyes to see it…'

'And the world moving on, babbling away to itself, not a clue about you.'

'…'

'Did nobody miss her?'

'I guess not. I think she'd no family. Or she was estranged from them or something.'

'An awful curse, that.'

'I'm sure the programme explained it all but I don't remember now.'

'…'

'Still, probably better than murder. I wouldn't want to be in London now in a cinema or at a play and all these gung-ho lunatics come in guns blazing.'

'Or on the tube on the way to work when some maniac opens his backpack and kablammo. Look at this—'

The Friday night Friary crowd arrived intermittently, flotsam delivered by the tide, each arrival announced by the banging of the door. Still too easy on the hinges that door. People reacted differently to its clattering behind them: some got a fright, their shoulders leaping; others threw it the stink eye; some apologised to the gummy air, checking if the door was okay by exercising its hinges; others tried to see a way to fix it; some shot a nervous look to Mike, as if they had done something wrong; others didn't even notice, were already bounding across the floor.

Out of the buses they came, and out of the taxis and the lifts, and after brisk walks, with smiles, tucking away the masks or just not bothered with them anymore, with keys and coins jingled in pockets, bags unhooked from shoulders. So careful with those early pints, gathered up in twos and threes. Come midnight, only the nearer faces were clear. Jolly heads and shoulders bobbing. The loveliest kind of yellow light. Hands held. Arms draped. Wonder of the pint. Wonder of the deranged posters on the walls. Voices unravelling many spools of tales all at once, the palaver chewing and consuming and digesting and regurgitating itself. The selves unfolding. It didn't matter what you said. Hours sinking in the watch. Deep hearty laughter. Jolly place. Waiting for Mike's attention for ages. Random conversations, strange people: students; gamblers; the Apple crowd; that musician, that rapper dude; the swing crowd; the Icelandics with their Mohicans; the rugby-mad postman; the gamer; Toe Head; the taxi man; that African busker; yer wan with the art studio above in the Firkin Crane; Sheffield Chris who did the quiz of a Wednesday; that Traveller lady who was always about the place; four heart attacks right there; a campaigner there; lonely, they said; couldn't even kill himself right, they said; hiya, John! hey, June!; transformed groceries was all they all were; pasta and muesli converted; plans and problems; outrages; no shocks here though; all was punditry; punditry was all; stories of the guards; voices in the void, repeating what they heard on the radio and on the television and on the web; no phrase so terrible as the beef industry; the match; the world put to rights; yes; yes; ho–hum; hey-ho; ahwell; herenow; gowan; gluck; goway; buck up; your hole; me hole; upoutofit; when I get you home, girl, I'm gonna do filthy things to you; ah come'on, cheer up; that could be us, Marta, that could be us, with photos of our own baby on our phones; don't be so dramatic, Lou; please, let the bombs start falling now!; tell no one, even now; even now; say nathin'; not a word of boasting; not one to gloat; share the luck, I say; share the news; not one to boast; not one to gossip; not one to walk away; not one to give in; we'll find her, I promise; not one to take shit; not one to stick my nose where it doesn't belong; not one to talk out of place; not one for the dogs; not one for bold statements; not one for doing; I love you; I know you do; would a run help, you know, if you feel like that all the time?; maybe fresh air is all you need, Lou?; exercise?; do you not think about the future? what it might be like?; I think the world is going to hell; we'll find her, I swear; you said; but we will; we will; we will; I love you; g'luck, lads!; I think I'll go for a run tomorrow; exit all, eventually, all ghosts, to leave Mike alone, counting the cash, busting for that second-last fag.

the
noise
floor

OFF-AIR, the giant head asked, 'Who are you anyway, Tony?'

The cardboard box of records on the back seat slid forwards and backwards and side to side as Tony tried to negotiate the steering of the car he couldn't drive as it rolled infinitely backwards, his revving in vain.

'I'm a DJ. On the radio.'

'What's that when it's at home?'

'Like, I host conversations. I play music the odd time. We talk about what's going on in Cork. Cork issues, like.'

'Right, yea. But who are you?'

'I'm… I'm… a man. In my fifties. I love music. I'm a family man; I have three kids and a wife. My family are number one to me. I come from a small fishing town, just down the river there, though it's more of a suburb now. I'm a Passage West man. I loved hurling as a boy, played it until I was an adult. Played it in London actually.'

The gaunt woman reached to the back seat and lifted the box of records into her lap, holding it steady.

'Yes, Tony, but I repeat: *WHO… ARE… YOU?*'

'Jesus Christ! I don't know what you mean! WHAT ARE YOU FUCKING TALKING ABOUT?'

And the ground erupted as the car slipped off-road, from the hard shoulder into the grassy verge, and in a pub then he was interviewing some lads at the bar counter about who would win the Rose of Tralee. The floor was soaking wet. They gathered; they postured; they gestured; they more or less agreed on the Galway Rose.

DDMMGNTISISKAKAJRHTHEVEVSI
APSOPYITIJDBDBDNDJDIDODODO
DOEKKSJEJEJEJEHEJDJRIFIFOG
OGOYOGORODOEOSJWBWBRHDHDHD

IDIDODODOOWJWNJEEEJKKIOFOO
OOSHWHHGGTDHEVWQVSSJDJWWWJ
KKKHEUEHEUNBBBRBNOOOOOOODDD
INTH ES TATIC the engineer found the
light switch, and illuminated the small room,
and there still was the broom in the corner, the
empty cardboard box, the pile of odd nuts and
bolts on the shell of the old transmitter, the
transmitter now used as a sort of storage space.
And with the light on, he went to his work,
which was to check the alternate RFs, to steady
the drift, to fine tune the dissipator again.
In the shelf stack the new transmitter blinked
away, the smallness of it still so curious to
him — the size of a VHS player now where the old
one had taken up the whole wall — and on a tiny
school desk he watched, as he felt out his tool
belt for the spectrum tuner, the CCTV footage of
the transmitter station's exterior. Steel grey
fence, block walls, corrugated roofs, weeds.
He felt the signal around him, in him, there
in the no-space, the block hut surrounded by
weeds, the weeds rising up towards the concrete
plinth from which the antenna itself rose, the
antenna carrying the hum upwards and pushing it
out across the county, the skywave, the unified
fields, to the radio on in the Nissan Micra,
reporting terror in London yet again — a shopping
centre east of the city this time — and, beyond
the windscreen of the Micra, the blast of horns
to accompany every change of the traffic lights,
as if it were the apocalypse and they were all
trying desperately to get out of the city. As
opposed to just getting to work of a Wednesday
morning, amongst the channels of Cork city's

plastered buildings and the drift of exhaust fumes, with their car radios on, with their teas and coffees in their holders by the gearstick, receipts spilling out of side-door compartments, all these drivers' eyes on the road but their minds ruminating on things, or their hands rooting through bags on passenger seats, looking for glasses, for phones, for ibuprofens, lozenges, letters, a pen, the diary, edging forward in first gear, gambling up to second, daring to dream, only for the Opel people-carrier in front to come to a full juddering stop again. Edging forward, in first again, the radio going, the chat, the jingle, the news, the song, and coming to a complete stop again two or three seconds later, not even the chance to let someone else into the lane, the traffic lights still unseen way up around the corner, and yet dictating this flow of objects, this stream of cars, of engines, of drivers with places to get to, and worries on their mind and bank accounts and phones and cups of tea or coffee and their left foot on the clutch and their right foot hovering over the accelerator, then the brake, and some cursing, some muttering, some answering to the radio as though it could hear them, as if they weren't just static, some accusing, some praying, some clenching their teeth, or grimacing, projecting some argument with a colleague, or a father — and again the stuttering of inbound traffic, of a Wednesday morning, and if everyone just FUCKING CHILLED OUT they would all get to where they were hoping to get to in one piece, so just FUCKING CHILL OUT… AND FUCK YOU TOO BUDDYYYYYY YYYYYYYYYYYYDDDDDDYYYYYYYYYYYYYYYYYYYDDDDDDDDYYY

YYYDOODNNGBIOITTNNGPPOIBRBBNITNUNUIINNNNNMMMAJS
SJDJRBAAMAINASSHHHDNNNTNEANAINANINRBEBAINABEIJA
SSSPACFEENNNDMKDJJJJUUUUJUUHDGTBTBTOPPPSMRBTHWO
WLSLDNRNTJFUDJSNENENENKEOOAPRNRNRBDDEYDUUSUISSS
INNRPPPDDSADKKKKKFDNNSNAAAAJJJKKDDNDNNRPPLAAWER
NNNNDDYDUODD

ON-AIR

TONY
… absolutely awful that we continue to hear
these types of reports out of London, and, like,
you have to ask yourself, when are they going
to act decisively – get their act together and
come up with solutions? At times, I wonder
are they their own worst enemy over there…
Now, closer to home, I'm going to bring in Neil
Cahill, a guard from the Bridewell barracks,
who – the only way I think you can put it
is – went *above and beyond* the call of duty last
week. Neil, can you tell us about what you
encountered up on an estate on the Northside
– which we're not going to name – when you
were on a routine patrol last Tuesday afternoon?

GARDA NEIL CAHILL
Morning, Tony. Well myself and Gearóid here
were up on the estate having made a routine
call to one house, and we were heading back to
the car when a young lad came running up to
us – clearly distraught, Tony – saying, *My mam,
my mam!* So we followed him to a house, where
we found the door open and in the kitchen – a
small enough kitchen, Tony, if you know what I

mean – and in the space between the table and the counter there were four kids around this woman's body. The only way I can describe it, Tony, is that the older ones were taking turns trying to give her CPR.

TONY
Jaypers... And how old were these children, Neil?

GARDA NEIL CAHILL
From four to thirteen years old. Four of them, Tony.

TONY
And no other adults on the scene?

GARDA NEIL CAHILL
No...

TONY
And tell me, what happened next?

GARDA NEIL CAHILL
Well, we ascertained that she'd collapsed putting away the shopping and that they'd just called an ambulance when they saw us from the window. The woman was not breathing, so I began to administer CPR while Gearóid gave the ambulance more information over the phone. Then Gearóid brought the kids into the living room. Like, Tony, nobody wants to see their mother in that position.

TONY
Very true. You *have* to take them away from the situation... So was she breathing at that point?

GARDA NEIL CAHILL

No, she wasn't. See, Tony, CPR is mainly a way
of keeping the brain alive with oxygen until the
more powerful machinery arrives... But anyway,
the paramedics arrived quickly and did an
incredible job. Very professional. Very fast. And
they took her to the CUH.

TONY

And it's what happened next that really interests
me. Tell us!

GARDA NEIL CAHILL

Well, we were left in the house with the four
kids, waiting on a social worker to come, and
I asked the oldest one what had happened and
he said she'd just been about to cook the dinner
and she'd collapsed. So I asked had they had
dinner and he said no. So we stayed on and
cooked them dinner...

TONY

Wait now, Neil. So you're telling me that two
guards on the beat stayed on and cooked dinner
for the kids?

GARDA NEIL CAHILL

We did, Tony, yea.

TONY

God! Ye're great men. Two *legends*... And what'd
ye make?

GARDA NEIL CAHILL

Eh, we made spag bol, Tony...

TONY

Brilliant! Great gas! And did they like it?

GARDA NEIL CAHILL

They weren't complaining anyway, Tony!

TONY
Great men! And tell me that's not all, is it?
What'd ye do after that?

> **GARDA NEIL CAHILL**
> The washing-up, Tony!

TONY
God above! There should be more like ye. I'll
tell you, if every man and woman in the world
was like ye it'd be a perfect world.

> **GARDA NEIL CAHILL**
> I don't know about that, Tony...

TONY
... And any news since
on the mother?

> **GARDA NEIL CAHILL**
> It isn't good news, Tony.

TONY
Jaysus. It's a cruel world.

> **GARDA NEIL CAHILL**
> It is.

TONY
Anyway, look, we've a great picture of the two
guards doing the washing-up in that house,
aprons and all. Taken by one of the kids I
understand; get online there and have a look
for yourself. And I won't ask who washed and
dried, because that's a personal choice, and it
causes enough trouble in our house, and *each to
their own—*

[static]... and throughout the morning tones of
incredulity flowed, words of disbelief uttered
again and again, and TONY's voice was the conduit
through which it all flowed, swelling up from the

123

*barber's shelves and surgery waiting rooms and
kitchens and garages as people divulged their
selves. He was a man with the ability to be
all citizens across any one morning: the stoic
father figure; the proud mother, the exasperated
mother, the Irish mammy; the defensive parent;
the activist, the rebel; the conservative; the
conversationalist; the conservationist; the next-
door neighbour; the politician; the outraged
customer; the wise publican, common sense
personified; the man who'd seen it all before; the
man who was perpetually amazed; the fool; the man
not to be taken for a fool; the spiritual; the
atheist; the amateur historian; the forewarned
victim; the uncle; the how-many-times-have-we-
heard-this-before…; the auld spud; the failure; the
blow-in; the mischievous kid; the giddy goat; the
slacker; the reformed slacker; the aggrieved; the
local; the furious; the guy who worked his way up;
the old lady who knew exactly the place you were
talking about, there by the courthouse, where years
ago they used to have the used book shop, where
everyone would spend half of August queuing up for
their school books, years ago, before the virus and
social distancing and all that jazz, when summers
were still hot and winters cold… [static]*

WEENNFIOAOOOFJDDJDJFJFJE2
BDBBAAOOFFDHJJDYSUAIIOOFN
SJSHFHFHDHSUASUSIDISOSOSO
SPPPWENRNRNTTTJJJSSSUUII
DIDSNENENENEEKLEEOOOGHHHTB
RBSBBGYIJSBHIFOKNDVHDUSIIF
DWHJRVVSKAOOODHBDBBHDHSYSD
UDUSSSUZOOOONDBDHDHSAJJDSO
SPPGPGGNEHAHDBTNEOOEEEOJI
NTHESTA TIC a passing greyhound sniffed
the air on Nash's boreen above behind Holyhill,
and by the time he'd smelled the mark of a missing
tabby cat the signal had already reached the
apartment down on the quays, where the baby no
longer cried, but was watching these fluffy,
bloated characters on the screen of his phone.
The baby had no idea yet what a phone actually
was, or what the characters signified, but some
visio-chemical formula bathed her eyes and balmed
her mood with moving images. He'd sworn they
wouldn't use phones with her — he'd been the
adamant one — but that was before reflux, before
croup, before sleep therapy, before not knowing
what else to do, before being too strung out to
think. She was gone out for her break now — two
hours, and god knew she deserved it — but god he
wished that she was still there. It wasn't that
he didn't know what to do — actually he could
change a nappy faster than she could, and he was
a better burper too — it was that... what? What was
it? Here he was, on their couch, with the child
just about able to sit up alongside his hip, the
two of them, father and daughter, sharing their
warmth, sharing a couch in a small living room in

a one-bed apartment, her looking at his phone, he absently listening to the usual radio talk show — guards cooking, London fucked blah blah blah — the gentle hush of the odd car passing on the street below, the buzz of the fridge clicking on and off to some timetable he didn't know, the click and thrum of the heating coming and going again while the oven clock counted up towards her return, while a flapping beyond the living-room window indicated the movement of a pigeon, while whatever grey light there was filtered in through the blind, moved from the DVD shelf to the mantelpiece to the dusty African drum he dreamed the child would one day pound on, which now only served as the plinth for a cooling coffee cup, his watch still ticking onwards to next bottle, to her return… was it that with her not here it made less sense somehow? Or that, alone, even briefly, he couldn't do it? Didn't have the courage or the emotional language for it? The child suddenly sneezed loudly — *AAAACHOO!* — and he put his handkerchief to her little nose, by which point the signal had long since reached and expired upon the horizonnnnhiiiiifdntnnykk epsspprnnrbrrhaahsshahahqhqqqhejrjdjddjsziiotntv evrgsyyeswwnbnrkkooffdhshrbrbsgsydususooorbnnrbb bsashjjffoooooojnfffbbbdssffvvvcuiifrrhhhaakkppp gggfddjjjgbbbdssjkkksspdddebrbsuuonrouooubnddsbb eeeeaaanbtkoknnddsskooorttbbbnnddddrhuyaaaaasyu uiooognehrhruioeewppoebbeeaaaasjfkiggreeewwhuuif ggggi

ON-AIR

DONIE

C'mere, Tony? I'm just after seeing the most
spectacular thing!

TONY

What'd you see, Donie?

DONIE

I was walking along by the South Terrace there,
by the apartments there, d'you know? And out
of the corner of my eye, I seen a whole host of
brown leaves falling from the trees. Hundreds of
them. But what did the leaves do, Tony?

TONY

What'd they do, Donie?

DONIE

They turned in mid-air, Tony. They turned in
mid-air, just above my head almost, and they
changed direction, and they flew off into the
sky in a beautiful shape, changing all the time,
and weaving these gorgeous formulations. They
were *birds*, Tony. Not leaves, but birds.

OFF-AIR, the lights changed and Lou was off again, the traffic heavy eastbound on the South Ring, cars rolling with ease from slip road to slip road, switching in and out of the lanes. She navigated it all with a sort of muscle or machine memory, driving without thinking about driving *[a consciousness beneath thought]*. All the cars and their drivers seemed to. But maybe more than that too. These indications she made as she drove – that they all did – the physical spaces between vehicles and road markings created and closed and let out again... Sometimes it felt as if all that movement was pre-ordained somehow. As if, driving, she were on a conveyor belt, being pulled along gently,

127

through some between-space. As if the road and its roundabouts and slip roads were another existence, at a remove from the idea of Cork as a *place* that she grew up, where countless were born and grew old and died, as history, as a marsh once, as a frozen land before that, as homes and offices now where *citizens* – the *population* – all had their various roles to play and jobs to do. It felt like ebbing, out here in infrastructure, the architecture of the landscape diminishing into something new and separate. She thought again about movement essential versus movement local. Words like 'route' and 'commute' came to mind. Billboards off the dual carriageway offered 'office space' and 'scrappage'. Banks of scrubland slipped by her, and industrial buildings and office blocks amidst car parks. All this minutes from their home in an ancient city. The more she tried to think about it, to cover it in her mind, the less sure she was of what she was even trying to understand. Was it the world she was trying to figure out, or herself? Was the soul out there somewhere, lost in the sprawl?

She remembered now when she'd worked in the East Village bar in Douglas, collecting glasses – how old had she been then? seventeen? – and she used drop Mark home after work. Her first and only boyfriend. He lived in Blarney, or near it, and when she'd be driving back the pitch black road from Blarney into the city, she'd try to look into that great dark sky – an entire, ever-expanding universe – and she'd try to make out the meaning of things. The pub uniform stinking of beer and binjuice and smoke. Her eyes pricked open but unable to see what she needed to see. Sometimes, at night now, she still felt it, in bed, next to Marta, awake, unmoving. She hadn't scratched the surface of that massive blackness. There was surely more to life. An immensity to be fathomed. Losing her virginity to Mark, she remembered saying in the back of the car, *Just don't get me fucking pregnant*, and him laughing in the gloom. Then Marta's voice came back to her: *My alcoholic, cancerous parents? Your cancerous, alcoholic parents? Are you crazy?* And yes, what kind of a dying world was it to be a parent in; she heard the stories every morning. She produced the stories, for fuck's sake. But yet why was she now constantly thinking about having babies? Was it just another modicum of safety, of protection from the desolation, from the inexplicable… Why spend thirty-odd years getting over a lack of emotional control only to introduce some wild element and relinquish that control again? Why let your life be blown asunder? Why prolong the suffering of the human race?! But then what had Mam said in London? *You came along then, Lou, and kicking away inside me you kicked even more room into my heart for loving.* She saw, in the distance, the tops of cars moving along another flyover, pulled by a parallel conveyor belt, another circuit repeating, and then, without it seeming like another moment had passed, she was out in Cobh, parking neatly along the kerb by a long grey wall, and the music on the radio died with the engine, and the sun was coming out along the pavement.

BROADCASTING SIMULTANEOUSLY on **5264 kHz + 1420 MHz**…

playback: the pale moon was rising above the green mountain / the sun was declining beneath the blue sea…

second voice: *[static] … and you've your passports, you see, your birth cert, your COVID cert, your PPS number, your email address, your driving licence, your—*

first voice: *[static]… and all those itineraries mashing into each other — converging — in that wasteland, looking for some sign, some confirmation of [static] trying to talk about what they were by talking about what they were not. does that make any sense to you?*

second voice: *it does and it doesn't.*

first voice: *it's like a feeling of a place being completed by particular words, spoken in particular ways. like slang being*

                        a sort of password to identity or
                        [static] making it more or less
                        impossible to separate collective
                        constructed identity from some private
                        other, unperformed sense of self…

second voice: [singing] IN CORK HE'D BE KNOWN AS A
                        LANGER! A LAAAANGER! A LAAAAANNNGGEERR
                        [more softly] in cork, he'd be known
                        as a langer…

first voice: i read somewhere once that an old
                        person dying is like a library on
                        fire. [static] six… four… eight… one…

OFF-AIR, the heavy painted steel gate was a bastard to open, jammed into its own latch, but the bang of her fist jolted it free. As she crouched under the arch, she saw her shadow along the wall, a looming, arachnid echo of herself. She couldn't seem to catch her breath.

Behind the wall and down a few steps, it was a big old house with an overgrown garden going around the back onto a low wall and then the river, wide and flat and murky today, and on the other side of it the hills appeared dark and wooded. Distant screeches of gulls came to her over the creaks of unseen riverboats and the groaning, scraping machinations of nearby dockyards. Hydrangeas, briars and ivy sprawled across the wonky paving down the steps, and she battled them out of the way as she beat a path to the front door, next to which a bulging black bag and a warped cereal box stuck out from the half-open lid of a wheelie bin.

She lifted the iron knocker and rapped with it three times, then folded her arms across her chest, then put them in the pockets of her cardigan again, then let them at her sides, then held them behind her back, then shoved them into her pockets again, like guns. Her breath still heaved gently when this woman answered the door, herself panting.

'Hello!'

The white witch held the door wide with complete openness. She didn't lean against it, or sidle into it, or withdraw herself with the arc of the door; no, she held it open at her bare right arm's full length and stood opposite Lou with her posture square and open and upright. She smiled. 'Louise, is it?'

Neither did Lou expect the strong East Cork accent.

'That's me,' she grinned.

'Come in, Louise!'

The house was dirty, was the only way Lou could describe it, if she ever would describe it to anyone in the end. Small tied bags of rubbish around the place; dust and hair strand grown brazen throughout the floor. So much of it was normal – the terracotta flagstones, the white skirting, the brown carpeted stairs, the HOME SWEET HOME mat – but yet it was a house she could not explain to herself. The first living room – which she only caught a glimpse of – had two deep couches, one with worn indents where the white witch must have rested each night in front of the flatscreen television... But then there were the salt crystal lamps and the strange Eastern paintings and this second living room with the low coffee table that looked like a ouija board and the two low futons either side of it, both bulging with cushions of orangey and purply colours and silky materials and sequined patterns. Candles and large hardback books had been parked in or on every cupboard and bookshelf in the room, of which there seemed to be at least eight of various shapes and sizes. The place smelled like the Chinese shop in town where she'd bought her family Christmas presents as a teenager, and she thought too of the samurai sword they'd seen over the office door in the Mazda dealership, Tony whispering, 'Don't say anything that'll get us in trouble here, Lou!'

[static] lower glanmire road [static]

'Sit,' the white witch said in that second living room, righting a few things around the table. She was just a normal person really, in normal clothes – black vest and loose black skirt – with a normal face and a normal accent.

'What a lovely location,' Lou said, pointing through the narrow gap between dark curtains to the window's vista of water as she settled cautiously, knuckles first, on the nearest futon, ending up too far back on the futon and trying to re-balance, like an ironing board unfolding itself amongst the few silky bejewelled cushions. 'Right on the river!'

'Yes,' the other said. 'It is.'

The white witch insisted on making her tea; Lou didn't admit that she took sugar.

'Before I forget,' Lou said, when the witch came back into the room with the cups, as Lou rolled among cushions looking for the notebook in her back pocket and the brown envelope within its pages. 'Your money.'

The witch said thank you and slipped the envelope under her futon. 'Now,' she said. 'Why are you here?'

Lou, who had finally found a comfortable position leaning forward off the futon, said, 'Emmm…'

'Don't give me too much detail. Just a sentence. A purpose.'

She couldn't say it was just to see whether something like this would work on the show, and she couldn't come up with another answer, so now Lou could only think about the fact that it was her turn to say something and for some reason nothing was coming. She had been making the *emmmm* sound for a while when the witch said: 'Try a sentence that begins with a *to*. Like, *To buy cigarettes.*'

Lou laughed; the white witch did not. She had a well-defined bone structure, deep eyes, and her dark hair was greasy and her black top had pastry flakes on it. Her futon was about three feet from Lou's futon, and she sat cross-legged, her legs and hips giving a tent-like structure to a loose skirt that covered her down to the ankles, on one of which Lou could just see a worn brown bracelet. Her feet were bare and tanned. She waited patiently, but without smiling, and seemed to be massaging her own legs as she

132

sat open to Lou. Jesus, this was hard to do! To be supposed to be thinking of one thing but to be thinking of a hundred other things!

To find a cat.

To see what's going to happen to me.

To find out whether I'd be a good mother. Whether we could have children? Should have?

To learn the truth about myself.

To ask where my mother is right now. Right this very minute.

To find out what's wrong with me. To ask why it is that I feel fucking sad all the time.

'Some people,' the witch said, 'say, *To seek guidance*, or, *Because I want to feel inspired*, or, *To help find my way*, or, *To help me make a decision.*'

'Yes, yes,' Lou said. 'That middle one. The *Because* one. Because I want to be inspired.'

'Okay,' the witch said. 'Good. We can certainly try to help with that one.'

Then she slid forward from her futon and leaned over the low table and she asked for Lou's writing hand, and as she did, a lamp that Lou had not noticed on the table came on. She had not even realised it was gloomy until there was lamplight.

'Your hand,' the witch repeated, and Lou gave the witch her hand.

As the other took her hand, she began to re-write the moment in her mind, as it might be framed for a radio segment. *She takes your hand then and…* As she might imagine Tony describing it. *And listen, what happens next is…* His voice, in fact, began to overwrite the moment. Everything, she realised, whether it was for work or not, had this weird overwriting to it now, where she would frame it as she imagined it might go down on radio.

'Concentrate,' the other said. 'Concentrate on something simple, like your name.'

Louise. Louise. Louise. Lou. Lou. Lou. *Producer Lou is giving me that look from the booth again! Ain't that the truth though, Lou?* Stop. Find it in Marta's voice. Lou. *My Lou.*

It was like a massage – the witch's fingers and thumbs coursing the pathways of her palm. It was so sensual all of a sudden; the witch didn't seem interested in anything now but her hand in the light.

'Mmmm,' she said, full of thought.

Lou felt something begin to stir in her, as if it understood some mystic call, as if this woman were some kind of snake-charmer.

'Relax, Louise,' she said. 'You're very fidgety.'

'You have a strange aura, Louise,' she said. 'Strong. Very strong. But restless. You were meant for something – I can't see what – but you are festering… But there is serious power…'

'Hah,' Lou said. 'Great!'

The white witch sat back a moment, as if she had come up for air, and rearranged herself on her futon. 'I'm sorry,' she said, looking about her. 'I never get a moment to tidy the place… to wash my hair even.'

'Oh,' Lou replied. 'I didn't even notice…' She trailed off and chuckled. Said nothing more. Was that part of the woman's power, to read minds?

And the white witch came back for the hand then, which had hung aloft in her absence. 'You offered your left hand,' the witch said, 'and so I'm reading from the left…'

Strange to Lou, she started in the past. Not married, she said. Few lovers. The witch looked at her: 'If you had married that first lover you would have been together the rest of your days. But you wouldn't necessarily have made each other happy.'

Lou asked if she could take out her notebook and make some notes, but the witch said she'd do it for her, producing a pencil and a scrap of paper from the folds of her skirt. She massaged her thigh for a moment with her free hand, as though for relief from an injury. 'Louise, your mother and father were in a deep love, a kind that is rare in Ireland. Something happened, I don't know what.'

'Oh, she died,' Lou said. 'She was very young.'

'Yes,' the other said.

Lou's incredibly strong aura, the witch said, was probably a product of that love. It was a hell of an aura, she said, and a strange one at that. She'd never experienced anything like it. 'It's as if you're bursting with life but you don't have any use for it,' she said, squeezing Lou's hand, bent forward from her futon. 'It's as if you're a place on fire.'

Confused, and lacking an appropriate response, Lou grinned and nodded. She liked the pressure as the witch thumbed her hand. Then the sexual thoughts started. She really hoped the witch couldn't read her mind.

The witch said many things about family, and work, and health. 'You will think clearly til the end, Louise. Your lifeline is one of the longest I've ever seen. But it wavers gently, to suggest some trouble. The way it curves back a little – it's as if you are haunting yourself...'

Later: 'There has been a parting of ways with a close friend, or perhaps a sibling. It's not dramatic but neither is it redeemable...'

She did not ask Lou to corroborate anything she said.

'Have you been thinking about a journey?'

'Well, sort of. We've a lot of travel coming up for work the next month. And I was thinking a lot about roads when I was driving over here.'

'Remember, Louise,' the white witch said, 'that places live under all the tarmac and concrete. Real places. Look beyond the hard shoulder, Louise.'

'I will.'

'And take that journey.'

'I might so.'

'You will see a solicitor in the next year. I recommend a local Cobh man named Harry Bailey. He represented me once and was very good. Honest and reasonable.'

She wrote down the solicitor's phone number on the scrap of paper.

She never let go of Lou's hand. She gave context to every comment, though most had nothing to do with anything true in

Lou's life, and she said that such a line was crooked, and explained what that signified; that such a line had three intersections with smaller lines and that these signalled important opportunities in the future and past. At no point did she give Lou a chance to ask any of the questions she'd now come up with, about love, or kids, or sadness. It just increasingly felt like something was... *happening*. All Lou was doing now was squirming in the seat, having the hand felt off her by this witch. Had the witch looked into her writing hand and seen her wanking hand? Lou's heart pulsed gently.

'You hold things in,' she told Lou. 'You seal the internal stuff off from the external. You'll burst that way. Do you mind if I come and sit on your side of the sofa? I can't get enough of that aura – I want to bask in it!'

'It's your house!' Lou gibbered.

The more the witch spoke, the more she was squeezing Lou's hand, and repeating herself and then trailing off, and soon enough she was practically in Lou's lap.

'I never do this,' she said, as they started to sort of kiss and she tried to undo Lou's belt buckle, rooting for a way inside, as Lou half moaned and half protested with sounds because words wouldn't come, because she certainly wanted it, sprawling back in the futon like a daddy-fucking-longlegs. But between the awkwardness and the wanting it and the discomfort and the fear and the darkness and the realisation that she was very likely going to sleep with this witch, and that this would be a disgusting thing to do to Marta, the actual love of her life, and a terrible thing in general, resistance returned and desire fell away.

'No thanks!' she finally blurted out, raising her arms above her head in a weird sort of defence position.

'Oh god,' the witch said, scrambling away. 'I'm so sorry. I never do this. I couldn't help it. You've the aura of a fucking minotaur. Christ, that was so inappropriate. I'm so sorry!'

Lou's heart pounded. 'It's fine, it's fine. I was... eh... feeling it too. I'm in a relationship though. I love Marta to bits.'

'Yes,' the witch said. 'Yes, sorry. I gathered that. I'm sorry. I don't know what came over me. Oh god, I'm so embarrassed. You could have me arrested!'

'It's fine,' Lou said, finally figuring out how to stand up and do her belt buckle properly. 'Honestly, it's fine. There was two of us in it.'

The witch was already on the other side of the table again, sitting down, fixing her skirt. 'Do you not want me to finish?'

Lou was considering the question, when the witch said, 'The reading! The reading I meant. Do you want me to finish the reading? Jesus Christ almighty, what am I like!'

'Ahnoyouregrand,' Lou said, turning, and then the witch stood again, and a polite argument ensued in which Lou tried to leave and the witch tried to return the money or insisted that Lou stay for the rest of the reading and get what she paid for. She promised she wouldn't touch Lou again, and in the end the witch's will was stronger and Lou sat down to listen rather than take back the envelope, and so the witch continued, looking at Lou's hand now rather than holding it.

'The numbers five and seven are good for you. Pay heed to that...'

'Your journey, the one you're taking for work, will be long not in days but in spiritual searching...'

Twice more, she recommended local businesses – a travel agent and a creative writing class – and she finished by reminding Lou that the lines could change. Yes, some things were fixed, but you could change most things. The right hand, she said, considering it only briefly, looking at it without touching it, pretty much reflected what the left hand said, so there was no need to read it too deeply.

'You and your partner,' she said earnestly, 'you will find what you're looking for. That is certain to me.'

Finally, came a warning.

'You came here wanting to feel inspired,' the witch said, 'and I hope you have something to go on now, because if you don't discover your purpose in life in the next ten years you will wander restlessly for the rest of your days. Louise, I am so, so, so sorry again about what happened there. I swear to god that's never happened before. And won't again. You were well within your rights to call the guards for god's sake!'

At the front door the white witch said sorry one more time, and gingerly, careful not to touch Lou, handed over the scrap of paper with notes on it. Said, 'Come back again in six months for a free consultation and I swear I won't touch you.' And she laughed nervously with her hand on the door and Lou laughed nervously and said one more time that it was fine, there was two of them in it, and that nothing really actually happened, and then the white witch closed out the door and Lou stumbled back to the car and fumbled for her key on the bright grey road.

OFF-AIR, the hospital was so quiet now, after visiting hours, that you could hear the electric hum of the strip lighting on the corridor. Shadows were cast at angles from the doorways and corridor beds and machines and offshoot corridors. Neither of their shoes squeaked as they thought nervously about their mother.

'Did she say *left* at the end of Corridor B?' the daughter asked.

The son lifted his head. 'I thought she just said to follow the yellow footprints.'

'Oh yea.'

Both siblings held their shoulders the same way, sort of proudly, and both had their hands planted in the depths of their pockets; hands that would remain buried a while, until exclamations, explanations and complaints would draw them out and make shapes on the air in front of them. Following the yellow footprints down an unlit corridor, the lights not clicking to life about them as they expected, they came to a set of glass doors that wouldn't open. There was a gloomy ward on the other side, and a thin shard of light glinted across the few empty beds they could see through the glass.

'This is definitely it,' the daughter said, peering up at the sign that said WARD 52.

'Here's a buzzer,' he said, and pressed it.

There were distant sounds: tappings, mechanical shiftings, a buzzing, the odd wail or moan seeming to come from inside the walls.

'It's not exactly brimming with life down here,' the son said. Then, 'Don't!' before the daughter could make the joke.

The corridor where they waited was glass-panelled, and, outside, on both sides of it, there were tiny square courtyards landscaped with uneven paving slabs and grass plants that quivered. They didn't seem like places for rest or fresh air; he couldn't even see a doorway out to them, only other glass corridors on the other sides of the courtyards.

'Are you nervous?' the daughter finally asked him.

'I don't know,' he replied. 'I don't think so. I guess we've been through this a few times now. I guess we know what to expect.'

Eventually, an unfamiliar nurse sauntered out to let them in, opening the door to them curiously, like a distant relative might greet an unannounced visit.

'We're here to collect our mother,' the daughter said. 'Ann?'

'Oh yea.' The nurse stood aside for them, smiling. 'She's just had a cup of tea and got dressed. Some woman for one woman. She's doing great.'

They went towards the source of that shard of light, passing the quiet heaps of bodies under duvets in beds, and then, in the half-light, came to their mother, sitting up on the bed, hands planted each side of her, looking pale and waxy and stiff and yet horribly soft.

'You're under arrest, Ann,' the nurse said, busying herself with the curtain about the bed. 'There's two guards here to take you away and there's nothing I can do about it.'

Their mother looked up and her eyes swam a bit before she smiled. 'That's my daughter and my son.'

'Hi, Mam,' they said.

Movements then – the nurse handing the son things to carry, and repeating the medicinal instructions to Ann, but for the children to hear too, Ann repeating that she was feeling a bit weird, a bit *out of it*, that her head felt swollen, and looking up at her kids like they were familiar strangers when they asked her questions or tried to make jokes. They assured her that Jerry was waiting with the car at the A&E entrance, but Ann looked shaky, and confused, and it seemed no surprise to the nurse when she eased herself back onto the pillow heap on the bed and said, 'Can I just have one more cup of tea before we go?'

'No problem, girl,' the nurse said.

'No problem, Mam,' her kids said.

The daughter took out her phone to text Jerry, and the son began to look about for two chairs.

'I just need to get my bearings,' Ann said to the ceiling, and then, sitting up a little, repeated to her children. 'I just need to get my bearings.'

OFF-AIR, it was like being a ninja, getting out of that room unheard. But, like, easy-level ninja, because even if she knocked one of the empty cans by the door, or toppled the bottle of wine, her parents probably wouldn't wake. And Sally slept like the dead. At what age, AERO wondered as she placed each foot like a ninja, and turned handles like a ninja, until she was back out there in the dark, crisp city street, at what point in a person's life did sleep become hard to do? Sally let her head on the pillow and it was as if she shut down til morning. When did that stop? Thirteen or fourteen? How long had she herself been sleeping badly, worrying into the night?

Just the one throw-up that night, on that hoarding near the Lidl, just around the corner from the Bridewell garda station: a hell of a space. There were fewer and fewer good spaces these days, so you had to act quickly. And it was an impressive spot this, because it was on the main thoroughfare along the river and there would often enough be people still coming home from the pub, or a friend's house, or their night job. College students didn't care what night of the week it was, so there was nearly always someone stumbling drunkenly along, glaring about them or half asleep, or singing. And being so close to the garda station you could have a squad car coming past at any point. The risk was what made it though. In terms of method, you kind of needed to become a master of time to do this stuff: to be quick but never to rush anything; to be attentive to your surroundings but focused on the work. Rushing was how you ended up with the scrawly stuff, which of course she'd done plenty of, but if you were zen enough, in half an hour you could write a decent sign, a piece even, if you had enough paint. Then you could embellish and improve and so on, dashing off strokes casually, looking up, taking a short walk and so on, returning, dashing again. That was Ró's method too. That was where she learned it.

It was getting misty. Bad for writing. With the E done, AERO turned and saw this small guy in a big Puffa jacket, trundling along by the riverside wall, and he didn't seem to be in any hurry, peering over the wall now and then. The night was all diffused streetlight, diffused traffic light, concrete and tarmac and low limestone wall. The river was quiet – was he watching her? She decided to take a break, and pocketing the spray can she walked casually towards Paul Street. Pulling her hood tight, she listened, again like a ninja, for other footsteps. There were none.

She turned at the opera house, saw no one, cut back to Paul Street and back onto the river. No one. Just the sound of a distant house alarm. The slow rush of a car somewhere between all the buildings. And, by the river wall, where Puffa Jacket had been, only a tabby cat limping along. AERO stopped to watch the cat, which moved slowly, deliberately, pausing every few steps to look about and smell the air. Was it badly hurt? Ró had said about setbacks what the counsellor had said to him: life was full of them. You had to soldier on, to make sure that each setback

141

made you stronger, or better somehow. *So you have to move out of your house? It'll be grand. There'll be other houses, and you'll appreciate them all the more. Your parents making those mistakes now means you won't make them when you're an adult.*

But what if there was never another house, Ró? What if there was never another fucking house? Or another friend like you?

She started to walk again and the cat watched her closely, head dipped, from the other side of the road.

'Don't worry, cat,' she said. 'You'll come back stronger.'

Wary nonetheless, the cat limped back along the pavement and went down the steps from the pavement to the river – one of those old mooring spots for small boats in the olden days – and AERO went on to get the last two letters done, wondering if the guy in the coat could possibly have turned into the cat.

OFF-AIR, he wrote:

23:36

Lolly!
My god, it's been years. I was glad to hear from you, though I must say it was a shock. We are on the road every Friday for this car competition, we might try and get up to you alright. It would be great to meet again after all these years. Send me on your phone number and I'll be in touch?
Lots of love / your old friend Tony

OFF-AIR, as he began to fall asleep next to his Dancing Queen, Tony said to himself, to his imagination, to the listeners of Cork, on-air: I don't often stop and think about what things mean. Have meant to me. But I wonder now – now that London is falling to pieces – what Lolly meant to me. Or what losing her meant to me... I came back to Cork. I got on with life. I was upset, sure, but I tried my best to move on. I'm sure I buried myself in work, or in music or hurling or something. I met my Dancing Queen eventually. I'm happy now. But when your heart is broken like that – like with our first little boy after – when your heart is broken like that, it's an atom bomb to your spirit. Right? No matter your age. When Lolly and me... I was torn asunder by the end of that, lads. I wandered streets where no one I knew would see me, crying. Weeping openly. And of course it was all my own doing, my own fault, but a hole was blown open in me, and how did I fill it? How did I heal it? I didn't drink so much, as you might think. I worried I might become an alcoholic if I did that, or that I might do something stupid... So I stayed away from the drink, but I had conversation after conversation with her in my head. With her, with others. I never sent that letter in the end. I suppose time passed. I healed somehow. Something else grew around the hole. Or filled it I suppose. Like a tree hit by lightning, I was changed forever, but I found a way to grow around the wound. How many of us are out there now today, grown around such wounds, carrying these sealed-off holes in our guts, our spirits, our psyches. Call them what you want. I think of my own daughter, going through things now – things changing her, not that we can get it out of her, whatever's going on – and, you know, I just think there's trauma somehow, occurring or reoccurring in everyone. When myself and the Dancing Queen lost Aaron so soon, only days old, was that another hole in myself that I grew around? Was that another lightning strike? How warped and twisted am I by all these traumas? Carrying them around every day... Is my whole personality really just the story of a heart I broke myself, and a child we lost without ever really having? Are the lot of us, all the listeners and callers out there, shaping and re-shaping ourselves around these wounds? Trauma, I suppose I mean. Something, I bet, has happened to each of us, has put a new shape on us at some point in our lives, even if we're not aware it happened. Are our two teens formed by the loss of our first boy, even though they weren't on the planet when he was born and died? Probably.

They must be, in ways. Jaypers, the way I'm thinking now, it's a wonder any of us out there can make it through a single day! I'll shut up. All I'll say is, I *think* I'm well within my rights to see Lolly now, after all these years. But tell us what *you* think.

And as sleep turned into him, as his inner voice passed through to the sleep side, he began to imagine, and then dream, the calls and texts coming back into him. The giant head, for example, texted in to say that we were all going to our own funerals, every day of the weather-damned year.

OFF-AIR, they took the cat's two bowls – the dry food and the wet – through the city, in the night, clinking them together in that special way – the way that meant that Tabitha would come bounding from wherever she was to come curling stiffly around Marta's legs – clinking the bowls and calling her name as they lapped the city in a loose figure of eight. Lou felt sick the whole time. The guilt was a squirming pit in her stomach; she played and replayed things in her mind. Nothing had actually happened. Nothing had actually happened. They'd stopped. They'd not actually done anything.

The trajectory was based on places Tabby had supposedly been seen: Pope's Quay; UCC; Paul Street Car Park; the apartments behind The Bierhaus; Blackpool Shopping Centre; Glanmire… They remarked on how noisy the city was, even at night; too loud to hear the soft miaow. Lou tried to conceal that trembling in her voice that started in her gut. They saw the odd cat watching them from a broken weedy wall or the underside of a car or a fence before slipping away. None of those cats were Tabby. They both did the special whistle again, they clinked the bowls together again, called her name, came face to face with poster after poster of her, and fruitlessly they returned home and to bed, where Lou festered on and on, replaying the thing, lying awake next to Marta, who lay awake next to her, both of them with eyes closed. Neither said anything, or opened their eyes, or turned.

BROADCASTING SIMULTANEOUSLY on 5264 kHz + 1420 MHz…

playback: the pale moon was rising above the green mountain / the sun was declining beneath the blue sea…

first voice: *[static] five… one… six… two… [static] and maybe LOU dreamt that she was on a dark road, a road that unfurled across a dark landscape [static] ditches rustled and loomed; the shape of giant turbines rose above the black silhouettes of trees on the dim hillside horizon. a distant figure might have been jumping from tree to tree [static] the road she was on undulated in the dark, was still unfurling, all the time. she was a car on that road. or, her body had decayed in the car and she had become the car, and she moved along the road now feeling the gear changes within her, making no sound but engine. going backwards and forwards at the same time [static] she was seeking, she knew, a bridge of moonlight somewhere, though she couldn't yet see it. the road undulated [static] the road was a dogfish. a stupendously long dogfish. and all the journeys of days and nights — summers, springs, autumns and winters — were held in its colossal scales. she journeyed across the tundra of dogfish, the motorway of dogfish — it felt an almost sexual thing between the car and the dogfish road — and she realised that it would be a journey of writhing, and she might have to do it many, many times before she would find the bridge of*

	moonlight, if ever she'd find it. her mother was looking at her over a box of cereal at the kitchen table: a look of concern. all the dreams of death and aliveness, she might have felt them there, alone on the dogfish road [static] the undreamed and the dreamed, the unmanifest and the manifest, an immense tangle of living things.
second voice:	*or maybe that was your dream? it's very specific.*
first voice:	*it all gets so confusing, this business of living and imagining and dreaming in the one skull.*
second voice:	*[static] whatever about the living, i'd be wary of the dreaming. sure dreaming is only the static of the day. don't be reading too much into it now!*
first voice:	*[static] … and all this in the same week that there was a rise in bus fares… [static]*

ON-AIR

TONY
Do you think it's fair, Máire?

MÁIRE
Fair, Tony? How could it be fair? It's not even fair on the bus drivers, the ones who have to put up with the abuse. 'Tis worse the buses are getting. They keep upping the prices and yet it's worse the service is actually getting!

TONY
Five per cent is no small amount.

146

MÁIRE

It all adds up, Tony. I get the bus twice a day,
every day of the week—

___

TONY

Producer Lou has a story about a memorable
book. Go on, Lou, mic up there and tell us!

LOU

... I remember, Tony, reading a book as a child
– I must've been eight or nine and this was an
awful book that I read. I was an avid reader, Tony.
I used empty the library shelves. Margaret was
the librarian's name and she couldn't replenish
the stock fast enough for me. She had grey
hair as long as I could remember, big, curly,
glamorous grey hair. Anyway, I must've been
eight or nine, and I got a book out that was
definitely too old for me, because I was reading
the first few pages of this thing and I was *bawling*,
Tony. *Bawling*. It was about the aftermath of a
nuclear bomb being dropped, on England I think,
and this young lad wakes up to find his dog dead,
his brother dead, his mam and dad dead.

TONY

Crikey, Lou.

LOU

Well that was enough for me, Tony. Slammed it
shut, went up the hallway bawling for Mammy.

TONY

And what did Mammy say?

LOU

Well she was up on the couch watching some
TV show or other, and I'd say she got an awful

land at the state of me. I blabbered out the
story and the next thing I know she grabs the
book out of my hand, jumps up off the couch
and throws it straight into the fire, Tony!

TONY
Jaypers!

LOU
Blazing in seconds, Tony.

TONY
I'd say Margaret had a word or two to say about
that down the library?

LOU
Jesus, I can't remember what I told her. I
must've said I lost it.

TONY
Well, not the kind of book burning we're used
to hearing about, Lou!

LOU
I know, Tony!

TONY
And what's the strangest book experience
you've ever had, listeners? Give us a shout on
the blower, or message us via all the usual social
media channels.

———

A VOICE
The accused, a native of Waterford with
an address at Ballinlough, admits stabbing
O'Halloran in the chest but has pleaded
not guilty to murder, claiming it was
manslaughter—

———

A VOICE
Is your heart beating right now, Tony?

TONY

It is, I think? Jaypers, I hope so!

A VOICE

And how is that happening, Tony? Would you believe me if I told you it was all electricity? We're essentially all frequencies.

TONY

Explain that to me now.

A VOICE

See, our bodies, Tony, are powered by electricity, which we generate ourselves, in our own cells. It's both biological and electrical. The electricity is generated in the cell itself, and travels from cell to cell via little ion gateways called sodium-potassium gateways. So when you feel pain that's your body broadcasting an electrical signal – at the speed of light now, Tony! – from the source of pain, your burnt finger say, to the brain. That's how the nervous system works too – leccy. And when your heart contracts and beats, that's also triggered by an electrical signal. And the movement of these currents at a particular rate, and the vibrations they cause, well that's called *frequency*. So, in a sense we're all frequencies. The body is essentially a transistor!

———

A VOICE

The minister has admitted that she does not know why it took so long to make a decision on the matter—

———

LOU

The process is called pre-implementation
genetic screening, Tony, and involves screening
embryos prior to implementation. A healthy
baby was born this morning at Cork University
Hospital and we've a very happy aunt for you
on line two—

———

SAM

I'll tell you where's a great place for a day out,
Tony: Mahon Point Shopping Centre. 'Tis like
a big spaceship landed in the middle of all the
roads and roundybouts there, and it has every
single shop and convenience you can imagine.
And, Tony, the beauty is that you don't even
have to buy anything. You can cruise around
shops and look away to your heart's content.
Doesn't cost you a blind penny. Now, of course
you can get a coffee or a milkshake if you want,
or even a glass of beer in one place I believe,
and you can head for a bit of grub if you want.
'Tis a wander – wait, is it wonder or wander,
Tony?

TONY

Isn't it the same thing, Sam?

SAM

But, isn't wan with your feet and wan with
your mind? … Anyway, 'tis a wander, with rain
the way it is in our country, that we don't turn
the whole place into wan big shopping centre
– sure what else do we need? Our clothes, our
food, the cinema… 'Tis big enough to walk the
liveliest dog, Tony! In fact, Tony, I'd go as far as
to say that Mahon Point is absolutely glorious.
It's the peak of our work on God's earth!

TONY

How long have you been working there, Sam?

SAM

Hahah, I wish, boy! Sure I haven't worked in
seventeen y—

A VOICE

These graduates think they can use big fancy
words like equitable and that that wins the
argument for them. Well, it doesn't—

A VOICE

—won't be beaten on price!

TONY

Ann, you're still alive, girl?

ANN

Still hanging in there, Tony—

TONY

We've had tip-offs about Lou's cat, lads – people
have claimed sightings in UCC car parks, on
Pope's Quay, up around Blackpool Shopping
Centre, on Blarney Street, up in Grán... but we
haven't found her yet. Keep your eyes peeled;
we'll bring her home yet.

A VOICE

Martyrs, Tony! These people think they're
martyrs? Well, they're not!

DEBORAH

I've been sleeping in my car with my family for
three months now, moving from car park to car
park...

———

TONY

Right, we're going to take you back to London
now – which I'll remind you is in a state of
martial law, with curfews in place – but some
are staying, even as these heinous attacks
continue. One of the people who is refusing to
leave is Seán, who's from Kinsale originally, and
we've got him on the line from London now.
Hello, Seán?

SEÁN

Hi, Tony.

TONY

Seán, you work in the *City* of London, right, as
opposed to London city centre? That's that sort
of financial district, right?

SEÁN

I do, yea, Tony. I work in the legal–commercial
department of a technology company that
provides virtual data room solutions for
mergers and acquisitions and IPOs and things...

TONY

Sorry now, Seán, but what's that when it's at
home?

SEÁN

Emmm... I read contracts for business deals
that involve a special technology. It helps keep
the deals private and secure online.

TONY

And your office is right by Cannon Street,
where those first bombs went off?
Which seems like years ago now...

SEÁN

Yea, that's it.

TONY

And what happened there two Mondays ago?

SEÁN

Well, at about eleven in the morning a security
guard came through to the reception on our
floor and said that shooters had entered the
building and that everybody should go out the
fire escape as quickly and as quietly as possible.
We were told to keep our hands visible in case
we met police or army on the way down or
outside. We were told to leave any belongings
behind—

TONY

Mother of... And had ye any idea how many
shooters there were, or why they were there, or
anything else?

SEÁN

Not really. We were just given that, and he went
out again. I suppose he had to tell as many
floors as possible—

TONY

I see... But you didn't go out the fire doors,
Seán?

SEÁN

No.

TONY

Why not? What did you do?

153

SEÁN

Well, there were just too many people trying to
get out the fire escape at once. Our company
has a hundred and twenty people and there's
only one fire escape. I just thought we'd be like
sitting ducks on that stairwell. And at that stage
someone said they'd heard a couple of shots, so
everything became very tense and panicky...

TONY

Janey, I'd say so... So where did you go?

SEÁN

Well, when all this started months ago, an email
was sent round the building saying what to do
if shooters came on site. It was like a three-
point plan: run, but if you can't run, hide; and if
you can't hide, fight. So I went to hide—

TONY

And what was the atmosphere like at this point?

SEÁN

Oh, chaos. Absolute chaos. But people weren't
screaming, not like you'd think. They were
just urging each other on, just like trotting
really quickly from their desks. As if a massive
game of hide and seek had started, except that
everyone looked very serious. Some people
were on phone calls and hadn't heard properly,
so they thought it was a fire drill and at first
they were taking their time. So I suppose it
was kind of quiet chaos. And then at a certain
point somebody said they thought they heard
shooting and suddenly it was everyone for
themselves. I remember some shouting from

outside. I think I remember hearing distant
shouting—

TONY

Janey. So what did you do?

SEÁN

Well, I hid. Luckily enough we'd a tall cupboard
in our department that we'd modified to be
able to hang our coats in, so there was room for
me to stand in there with the door closed, so
I got in and pulled the door closed behind me
and just... well... stood still behind the coats...

TONY

And could you see anything? Through a crack
in the door or anything?

SEÁN

Not a thing.

TONY

And what could you hear?

SEÁN

Nothing really, to be honest. Once everyone had
gotten to the stairwell, only muffled sounds.
I thought I heard footsteps once or twice. I
thought I heard voices in a foreign language.
But to be honest I was in there a long time and
I think I might have imagined things as well.
You know? Your mind starts playing tricks on
you...

TONY

And how long were you in there?

SEÁN

About four hours.

TONY

Four hours? Did no one come through before
that? Police or army or anything?

SEÁN

They did, but to be honest I was so afraid of
getting shot I just stayed in there.

TONY

Crikey. What did you think about for four
hours, Seán, if you don't mind me asking?

SEÁN

I don't know, Tony. I was just in a blind panic, I
suppose. I thought about my family. I tried to
guess what had happened around the building...
I don't know really. I listened... It probably
didn't feel like four hours.

TONY

And what had actually happened?

SEÁN

Four businessmen had come into the lobby
of the building carrying squash racket bags,
apparently laughing and carrying on like they'd
just played a game, and then they took out
AK-47s and shot the two receptionists and
the security guard on the barriers. They used
the security guard's pass to access the whole
building. They started working their way up the
floors. Our company were very lucky – we were
the first warned, so all bar two got out.

TONY

And where were those two? Hiding as well, or
caught running?

SEÁN

They were in the toilets. One in the men's, one
in the ladies'...

TONY

...

SEÁN

You'd never think, going for a number one or a
number two, that it'd be the end of you like...

TONY

I'm... tell me about your time in the cupboard.
What goes through a fella's mind at a time like
that?

SEÁN

I was terrified. Terrified. But I suppose I knew
that there were cupboards the same as mine all
along that wall, and the same cupboards were
all over the office, so it seemed unlikely they'd
check every one. But then my biggest fear was
that I'd give myself away. That they'd hear me
moving, or breathing. Your own breathing is
very loud when you're trying to be quiet and
you're in a box. It's all you can hear, y'know?

TONY

And you emerged then into what?

SEÁN

Darkness. An empty office. It was just like
they'd closed for the day. Like those dreams
you had when you were a kid where you were
locked into the school or the big shop for the
night.

TONY

And you just – what? Went home?

SEÁN

I did. Well, I started to. I walked out of the
building, which was cordoned off, but there
didn't seem to be anyone about, but then when
I was halfway to Cannon Street station I turned
back because I realised that they might be

157

looking for me. That my name might be on a
list or something.

TONY
Wow... And yet you're not coming home, Seán?

SEÁN
I'm not.

TONY
Why not?

SEÁN
Well, I don't want to give in to them. This is a
great city and has been for centuries, and if we
give in to them we lose it. I don't want to be
part of that.

TONY
And what do your parents down in Kinsale
make of that? You said you thought about your
family when you were in the cupboard?

SEÁN
I did, yea. I dunno. I think they understand.
Mam wants me home, of course. It's hard, you
know. It's a hard decision—

TONY
Would you not think of them and come home?
Let Londoners look after London? Come back
to your poor mother's side?

SEÁN
Eh. Jesus, I dunno. Maybe you're right. But
what are Londoners – only people who live in
London?

TONY
All I'm saying is, think of your family.

SEÁN
I will, Tony.

TONY
One texter here says, Tony, tell the man I'll pay
his flight. He needs to come home and put his
parents at ease.

SEÁN
Very kind of him. But I dunno. I have my
job. My girlfriend. I want to come back to
Ireland at some point, but my life is here at the
moment.

TONY
What kind of life is living in fear?

SEÁN
I dunno, Tony. Sure isn't everyone living in
some kind of fear?

TONY
Hmmmm... And tell me where in London
you're living, Seán, because I think we might
have an old local in common...

BROADCASTING SIMULTANEOUSLY on 5264 kHz + 1420 MHz...

playback: the pale moon was rising above the
                 green mountain / the sun was declining
                 beneath the blue sea...

first voice: nine... one... three... five... [static]

second voice: you hear these things, you see them,
                 but at this stage it occurs to me
                 to ask again: how many were actually
                 coming home? how real, how significant
                 was this influx of 'returned exiles'
                 from london?

first voice: ah, yes. hmmmm, yes. an excellent
                 question!

second voice: [static]

first voice: [static]

second voice: *and what's the answer?*

first voice: *hmmmm… does it matter? enough that there was talk of it [static] and a competition to help them out?*

second voice: *but not enough that they couldn't find homes and jobs? that they wouldn't be quarantined? [static] upwards of four hundred thousand irish would be living in london…*

first voice: *well, there were specific emergency funds made available to them, i presume.*

second voice: *were there enough coming home to warrant that?*

first voice: *well, one presumes… [static] listen, why let numbers get in the way of the noble cause of patriotism?*

second voice: *why do you even like this radio show so much?*

first voice: *… [static]… hmmmm… i dunno. it just makes me feel like i'm… somewhere?*

second voice: *and where would that be?*

first voice: *[static] cork? in the static myself? in a room, listening?*

second voice: *all real places i suppose…*

first voice: *[static] somewhere where time is a flat circle, looking at all things at once? seeing all things at once?*

second voice: *a legitimate place too, it could be argued! [static] i suppose it doesn't matter where you are [static] point made.*

first voice: *[static] suggested that we might be two simulations? programmes sent back through time, space, distortion, devastation… probes tasked with picking up these lost signals, these orphaned voices?*

second voice: *i would suggest perhaps that you'd re-watched THE MATRIX one time too many.*

first voice: *[static]*

second voice: *but i mean, the idea that everything is a simulation — [static] it sort of misses the point.*

first voice: *the point being?*

second voice: *even if none of this were real; even if TONY and LOU weren't real, even if we weren't real—*

first voice: *or even if there were multiple interpretations of us, and we couldn't possibly know which was the correct interpretation... [static] they do say your life flashes before your eyes...*

second voice: *[static] point being that even if we didn't exist, or know our true versions, or it was all made up, a simulation, or a figment of some gom's imagination, or what-fucking-ever, here we are, feeling it, feeling all of it, participating, communicating, so what difference does it make?*

first voice: *[static]*

second voice: *and sure how could we be programmes when we've a sense of humour, right?*

first voice: *what's a sense of humour?*

second voice: *[static]*

OFF-AIR, Tony woke early then that Friday morning. He wanted to turn and lie with his face into the window light, and to feel the quiet dawn behind his eyes. Before work, before the noise of parenthood. Warm light yet. He was turned away from Nuala; he turned back towards her.

161

ON-AIR

DIANE
*[sobbing, uncathartic, barely
controlled; a wheezing sort of a sob,
quiet for a while and then returned, as
if a sponge was being soaked in tears
and periodically squeezed out: a sad,
sad state of affairs]*

TONY
... Diane, listen to me. As their mother, you feel
that your job is to fix this. But it's not. You *can't*
fix this. No matter how much you try. What
happened to them was not your fault – it was
the fault of those... *gurriers*... and the idiots
who raised them. Because that's who I blame. I
blame the idiots who reared these children not
to know better.

DIANE
*[sobbing, release, a sigh full of
tears; a long, snotty sniff]*
But Tony I should have been there. I should
have warned them somehow. They're just
little boys. They didn't choose the colour of
their skin. They didn't choose to be beaten
up walking home from... *[sobbing as the
image is reproduced in her mind, as
potent as the first time, a thousand
times since; release; a sigh full of
tears]*... I mean, Tony...

TONY
I *know*, Diane *[his own voice very low
now, crumbling in sympathy, almost to
nothing, almost into tears itself]*.

162

I know, Diane. I know. I have two kids myself,
and we want to protect them from every bad
thing on Earth, but we can't. And you mustn't
blame yourself: you could do nothing about it!
[are you a father at all anymore
though, TONY, or only the shell of a
father that once was?]

DIANE

We told the teachers, the police... nobody
seems to want to do anything about it. I mean,
is this okay? Am I missing something? Is it okay
to beat up children because of the colour of
their skin? I mean, what kind of a world are we
living in, Tony?

TONY

Diane, it's absolutely *not okay*. Absolutely not.
Trust me – those boys who did this to your
two sons – they will suffer. Either sooner or
later. There's no future in their way of thinking.
And... look... your boys sound like great boys,
and you're clearly an *incredible* mum. So they'll
be okay too. Right, Diane?

DIANE

[silence, a long sniff, then a
collapse into sobbing again]

TONY

Look, Diane, if you don't mind my saying,
but you are taking this harder than anyone
else [voice crumbling again, almost
to nothing; broken grains of voice,
perfectly controlled, the very
frequency of sincerity]. I mean, you need
to mind yourself. Your self. Have you thought
about maybe getting some help? Someone
professional to listen to you maybe? That

163

could really help. Maybe we can fix you up with
someone...

DIANE

*[clearing of throat, presumed wiping
of eyes near a phone, with the heel of
the hand presumably, somewhere in the
city]* Do you know what it is, Tony? Do you
know... I was cycling recently. And whatever
way I turned, Tony, to get from the pavement
back onto the road, I came down off the bike
– I fell – and... I was fine, I wasn't really hurt...
But I hit my shoulder on the kerb, and do you
know that sudden shock of hurting yourself –
that shock you get when something frightening
suddenly happens? That shock of pain?... I
keep... I keep... *[breakdown into sobbing;
sobbing but continuing to blurt out
the words even through the tears]* Oh
god... I keep thinking of my two boys, nine and
eleven years of age, walking home from school,
minding their own business and suddenly
being approached on the pavement by those
other boys, and punched, and punched, and
pushed on the ground, and kicked, and not
even knowing what was happening to them, or
why – that pain out of nowhere, for no reason
– not even knowing what was happening to
them OH GOD... OH GOD... *[sobbing,
uncontrolled; sniffing]*

TONY

I know, Diane. I know. Diane, you need help.
I'm so sorry, Diane, I am. I'm *so* sorry. Take a
moment for yourself there. If you've just joined
us, Diane's two boys are mixed race. Nine and
eleven years old. They were walking home

164

from school on Thursday last week when they were approached, mocked and attacked by a group of idiots from their school. Scumbags. Now, we've stayed with this far longer than we should have, but that's because Diane needs us. She *needs* us now. So I'm going to go to some overdue ads and we're gonna come back to this. Send us a text so we can read out your support to Diane. More after these.

[static] advertisements and jingles redacted [static]

... Diane, the messages are piling in. You would not believe the amount of support out there in this county for you and your boys. 'Diane is an extraordinary person. Her compassion knows no bounds, and her lovely boys will make great men because of her.' 'Diane, you are incredible. Your boys will get over this and they will be stronger for it. Don't blame yourself. Life is full of...' I can't say that last word on air I'm afraid, but it's the right word, I can tell you. 'Diane, I had the same problem. No one did anything about it. This country still turns a blind eye to racism. Your boys will be fine with your support, but this country is gone to the dogs. Hang in there.' I could go on but they're coming in faster than I can read them out. 'Tony, congratulations on your handling of this. Your compassion is astounding.' Look, I'm just a parent. That's all I am. Just another parent, listening... We want the best for our kids, we want nothing but joy for them, but then the world just happens and we're powerless to protect them from everything that's out there.

Maybe, Diane, we can keep you on the line
after this, and find a way to compile all these
messages of support – scores of them, piling up
by the minute – and get them all to you, Diane.
How do you feel now, Diane?

———

GREG

Has anyone considered – I mean, look, since
ye were talking about the AERO signs on the
walls, I can't stop seeing them everywhere. I
work near Anglesea Street, but I live on the
Watercourse Road, so I've a lot of town to get
through on my commute, and I swear, they're
everywhere. *Everywhere*. And, Tony, has anyone
considered that it might be more than one
person? Like, a gang of AEROs, a collective?
Because it just seems too much for one person?

TONY

A good point, Greg, we'll put it out there. Sally,
you've been waiting patiently so I'm gonna let
you come straight in...

SALLY

Actually, Tony, I think that last caller is on to
something. Because I *have* noticed that there's
sometimes differences in the tag – like the 'A's
aren't all consistent. I'd presumed that was
down to whether he was spraying or using
a marker or whatever... Or sober or high or
drunk or whatever... But that it's a collective
and not an individual is actually a very plausible
possibility.

166

TONY
**Thanks, Sally. Joan has been waiting too; Joan,
you've got about thirty seconds before we go to
the news!**

OFF-AIR, the studio was a small boxy room filled in the
main by a large curved table, a streak of red neon running along
its curved edge. On the table were three bunched computer
screens and a couple of telephones. Two spongy red microphone
heads grew out of the table, and a couple more hung down
from above, all stamped with the station logo, while high on the
soundproofed wall was a large TV screen, silently playing one of
the twenty-four-hour news channels. And sealing the walls and
the desk and the computers and microphones and telephones
and TV, a huge double-glazed window that held the sky above
and the city of Cork below.

Yes, out the window, beneath the sky, lay Cork city, from
Merchants Quay to the Shandon Bells, from City Hall to St
Fin Barre's Cathedral to Sunday's Well, and beyond to turbines
in distant hilly fields. He could see it all, spread out from him
like a living model. And in his blue office shirt, deep in thought,
plucking a nostril, Tony looked over it all, as, not long after midday,
the usual drift of teenagers in uniforms came down the street
below the station, between the old Georgian houses, beneath
that massive clear sky. Somewhere out there – through the blue,
beyond the horizon – bombs were falling. People were shooting.
People were being exploded. Thousands were on hospital beds,
with festering wounds. Millions probably. Dying, being born,
being stitched up, in London and elsewhere…

And Lolly was out there, up in Galway, serving pints. And
Nuala, over in Rochestown, or maybe having a coffee with
Angie and Dora about now. And he caught half a reflection of
himself in the window then: pale face and sunken eyes, thinning
grey hair at the sides of his dull skull. Unburied skull, decades in

the wearing, tea-stained teeth inside of it. What kind of a fool was he, thinking of these things?

Lou stuck her head in the door: 'Ready for road, Tony?'

DEIIIEEDDNNNEEEEOOOWWWWAAA
AAAAABBBRTROOEOSJJJDNSVABR
IROPPENEBEHFHFHSHAHAHHHTJT
JDOOOOOAORBRBRFBSAOOOPFNNN
EWJAFIIKJNNRREEWAAAOOOCFFH
EBSHASJJJFFFCCUUIWBABRBTGG
GUXOAPPPJDHEERRHFFUDDFUFII
OODDDHWWERYDDYFFFIJJJJJJJJ
JEERRRBBBHHDFFSOOOORRJJJTOO
ODFFFHJJJTTTEESFVUUWQPPPPPO
RHHBRFYCUFUUUI NT HES TA TIC

Nuala, Angie and Dora watched the customers of the shopping centre go by and they sipped at their cappuccinos. Some of the shoppers took their time, with trolleys held before them like patient pets; others moved with purpose, on errands, or in an outright hurry, jangling keys or talking with clipped haste into mobile phones. It was a way of watching the world go by, of passing time, sitting in the Bewley's in Douglas Court with their coffees.

'And isn't it so mad,' Angie was saying to Dora, the newbie in the group, 'to be listening to your husband doing his job while you're doing the shopping, or in the gym or getting your hair done!'

'Crazy!' Dora agreed. 'How was it you met Tony, Nuala?'

'Ah,' she said dismissively. Was it that she was embarrassed to tell it or was it that she was tired of telling it? His voice had only minutes ago been echoing around the shops and tiled floors of the place.

'Ahh, go on,' Angie said. 'Go on. It was a wedding, wasn't it?'

Nuala tucked her long blonde hair behind her ears, her face hard to judge, her hair still damp after the shower at the gym. She rolled her eyes then, and submitted: 'Well, it was at the afters of a wedding. The disco. He was DJing…' The same eyes that told the story moved off over other tables and tracked other shoppers while her two friends watched her, smiling. 'I requested a song, and the fecker, he wouldn't play it!'

Angie and Dora cackled away.

'What was the song?'

'God, I don't remember anymore.' She could remember the dark, and the lights, and the tufts of chest hair coming out the top of Tony's shirt. And were there old framed photographs on the dim walls around the dancefloor in the back function room of the Commodore Hotel? 'Maybe it was The Kinks I was after, or something like that, but whatever it was he thought it was too old-fashioned.'

They cackled away, the lips peeled back gladly.

'He said I looked like yer wan from ABBA though, and of course I loved that!'

'And you still do, girl!' Angie cackled. 'Look like her, I mean!'

'Still got it, girl!' Dora bawled.

'Go on away out of it, ye!' Nuala giggled, and when the news was over then it was the pop music of the next show that came over the tannoy, which meant that Tony was away to Dublin, and she would never admit it but the

feeling about that was relieffdptnntirewnandsi
fiennndpppddjdjrbsbtbtbttbrthwsiiownnnrbrrgavgf
ydydioppppprbrbrffffhhdjjjrrtyyvbhewioopprrrdjjj
fffiopwntbrhjjwwsdfiiorpptnnwnwwiookttygggghfoo
ooowwweooojjtidhwbrifbygfuokrhehddjwoootbrbrffe
iiiiiofffyfgfyyyereeeeddofhwdfoihwerogiwhjwdlkg
nwelkwneflwqenfdwqlekfnwqelkfwjneflkwejfweriof
jwqepojwqepowejkfpowekfjqwokjworjkwrojmqnwerk
qwenmrewbtrekntrekjhbrkrtgbykrjehterkjtherklj
thwerotiwjherpijqepoqejkrpqwokerwpenqwlrkjqwn
elkwjepowkeporikqeikepddfowjhowiurghwruiogbwe
ifhvbqwefroqeqewpoqewqpoeiuhweqofbqehfjqbefoi
jqeboidbhqwoiudnbqsouxinszomzxmowinqowdihneoi
ufhrewiugheriotghrihiouhgierugnqrpouignrwepoi
ugfnwerpouginwergpoirengpoijewrngporeiugnperj
gunperiougn3pugpuigneqtnrreuhepruogheqrpoughr
pugpubgpuerbgpuioerbgpriouebgpqeruigeqpruogin
qrgioqthgrtgnetgnetjrtohjnrthoetoertyhoiptyi
pretjherjgnwkrejgfbfwqekfbqwkefbwqekjfbqewkj
fbnqwkjwoquiwhjqowuiweoqwuwqoeiuhaskjakljncz,
mznbvbxijhrewiogurwehoguirwehgourehgoergower
ghowrijwoigjworeighwrougbhaeiughouirehuibgbvd
fiobmgjiosngariugauigvbreaiugvaeruigvaewrgvy
euariogvaeruiogbrgberiogvberioqfgvirugvuiuh
brkrtgbykrjehterkjtherkljthwerotiwjherpijqepoqe
jkrpqwokerwpenqwlrkjqwnelkwjepowkeporikqeikep
ddfowjhowiurghwruiogbweifhvbqwefroqeqewpoqewq
poeiuhweqofbqehfjqbefoijqeboidbhqwoiudnbqsoux
inszomzxmowinqowdihneoiufhrewiugheriotghrihiou
hgierugnqrpouignrwepoiugfnwerpouginwergpoireng
poijewrngporeiugnperjgunpeffyfgfyyyereeeeddofh
wdfoihwerogiwhjwdlkgnwelkwneflwqenfdwqlekfn
wqelkfwjneflkwejfweriofjwqepojwqepowejkfpowek
fjqwokjworjkwrojmqnwerkqwenmrewbtreksdqwefdqw
eriewqruhweiugwehfiuwegfvbiweufgbweiufbgvwei

170

fubufogtreotuiyotuiqreyhreoiugheoifbwerhvew
jrkhgwvrmjehvfkwejhfbaewrfhbreowiuhewriopuher
ioutgherpoiugheqroiugthqeroiuthqeroiugtheroigu
heroiguqrhgoiuqerhgoiquerghoiqeurghoiqerughoqei
ruovhfsdkjfhdmnfbdhsfljkdfgjfdgeriopu4rutruriu
tuerwiouwpewpeprwefweprwwepoirwepoirhwekjrthwep
jtkhweptjherwptgyerugyrgipouhdfgopiudfhgwejkh
weljkhejklrgb

iguana
&
finch

BROADCASTING SIMULTANEOUSLY on 5264 kHz + 1420 MHz…

playback:	the pale moon was rising above the green mountain / the sun was declining beneath the blue sea…
first voice:	*[static]… three… two… five… two… i hear these things; i see them; i write them down… [static] this level of conjuring, there are of course times that you approach a sort of god complex yourself… like, maybe the whole lot of it is only happening in your head, but somewhere it is all real, all happening…*
second voice:	*[static]*
first voice:	*… but then would god or jesus or buddha or whoever have a ché guevara poster on their bedroom wall? a black argos coffee table [static] about 311 DVDs? the head & shoulders, the radox shower gel with the broken cap? a stack of half-filled writing pads? a cupful of half-wasted pens and blunt pencils? a plastic dishrack warped from the years? a few fridge magnets that were presents once, from those who were friends once? a corner medicine cabinet chock-a-block with half-finished blisters of lexapro?*
second voice:	*[static]*
first voice:	*… would god listen to the radio obsessively? and the radio playback too, the same shows over and over again? i lie if i say i listen only at certain times… [static] … would god broadcast her own musings? and was god's childhood dream [static] live in the home store + more on the kinsale roundabout for a year, sleeping on a*

175

	different bed each night, lounging on a different couch each day while the weather went on about its business outside?
second voice:	*[static]*
first voice:	*[static] the strangest thing when you died. because we were just talking to each other. just chatting, like normal, like this. but when it came to parting, you said, look, realistically, this could be it. if we're honest with each other. we might not see each other again… of course i was unreliable then. and you were very far gone yourself… i know, i said. and i knew. i knew i wouldn't see you alive again. and you said, you know i love you, right? i don't think we ever said that in all the years we knew each other, but it was always obvious to me. and i said, i know. i love you too. and we just hugged gently — because you were very weak then — and said goodbye. just like that. i have an image of turning away, not seeing your face a last time.*
second voice:	*the strangest thing, that.*
first voice:	*[static]*
second voice:	*you know, whatever we are, wherever we are, whoever we are, the mind is just not large enough to contain itself.*
first voice:	*[static]*
second voice:	*so here we are then.*
first voice:	*here we are.*
second voice:	*two souls on the same frequency at the same time. more or less.*
first voice:	*two souls out here in the void… in self-isolation i suppose.*

176

second voice: *ha ha [static]*

first voice: *[static] it's safer here, on the frequency, don't you think? you don't have to do all that living.*

second voice: *god knows.*

first voice: *[static]*

second voice: *[static] and sure what's living, only dying in slow motion. [static]*

first voice: *hush! hush! here comes another one!*

OFF-AIR, Lou didn't fancy the motorway for some reason, so she took the alternative route, demarcated by the brown signs for Watergrasshill, Fermoy, Mitchelstown and onwards.

'When we used first drive to Dublin before,' Tony said, 'it would take five hours, and you'd pass through about twelve towns. Amazing how quick you can do it now.'

It was a relief to be on the road, to be distracted, to be away from that feeling. Easing into the road's curve, Lou asked, 'So did Nuala used drive you to Dublin and you sat there in the passenger seat every single time?'

'Ah, she doesn't mind it.'

'You're an awful man, Tony. Wouldn't you just learn?'

★

Away from the motorway, he marvelled at the various species of ditch they encountered. Ireland and her landscapes slipped by in fleeting instances:

Distant smokestacks and pylons

Two empty petrol cans

A boulder that looked like a giant head

A round tower

Wooden fences

Green and white bollards on repeat

Wheelie bins

A GAA field spread out like a carpet
        Petrol garages in various states of disrepair
Bungalows, often magnolia
                Torn tyres
                        Cows in fields
                                Electricity wires strung with black birds
                        A road sign with a salmon on it
                Posters for Fossett's Circus
        Dirty traffic cones
Hills of green fields, hills of forest
Balloons, tied to posts
An agricultural dealership
A Corbett Court
        Patches of gravel around old gates
                Rocky outcrops
                                Pink silage bags
                        A giant ice-cream and a giant coffee cup
        A bath, with taps, in the middle of a field
                        Lines of trees, evergreen, deciduous
A team of men in overalls, strimming
                        Three rolling half-crumpled cans of Coors Light
                Signs obscured by overgrowth
                                Well-kept shrubs in gardens
                                Walls
                                        Windsocks
                Rain, then sun
                        Then rain
                Then sun
                        Bus stops
                Signs warning not to cut the Japanese knotweed
        A quarry, for sale

[static] everything (here) was built (here)!

178

But the towns he'd reminisced about all seemed dead now. Not a soul on the street, old jalopies parked crooked, towns stitched by FOR SALE signs and dark windows. As the Mazda crept through them, Lou said she felt like they were maybe being watched, by apocalypse survivors maybe, from the depths of those dark windows.

'It's almost as if there's cobwebs across the streets,' Tony observed.

'It's the motorway did this to them,' Lou said.

[static] four-thousand-euro scrappage bonus!

And of course the anxiety began to build again at the very mention of one thing doing something to another, and the notion then that actions had consequences, that you couldn't just *do* things to people like that, and so she suggested that they turn on the radio, and thus they were reminded that the same radio talk show as their own – the voices of that particular county informing and chiming and colliding – played out in all these other places too. They listened now to a DJ who was not Tony, who was Dee or Keith or Marian or Jason, but who still somehow seemed to be Tony. And the complaints and testimonies were the same, a multitude of disembodied voices telling their stories, finding at different times tragedy or warmth or comedy or fury in the play.

ON-AIR

SHANE

Well, what colour car you drive, Dee, says a
lot about you. It says everything about you, in
fact. It's funny in a way because people think
of colour as superficial – who cares about what
colour it is; *does the thing drive well*, right? Well,
I'm not so sure...

DEE

Go on, Shane. You have our ears!

SHANE

Well, let's start with the concept of beauty.
You agree that some things are beautiful and
some aren't, right? I mean, what is it about a
gorgeous crimson red rose, say, that just draws
our eye and warms our hearts? And the next
thing that's obvious – I mean, I don't have
to tell you this, Dee – but different colours
mean different things, don't they. Red can
mean danger or love. Green means nature,
or Go. These are called *connotations*. So now,
when you drive a red car, it doesn't signify
that you are dangerous, of course not. But
maybe it opens up that conversation, maybe
it hints at an openness to experience, to
danger, to living on the wilder side of life.
Maybe for you it signifies warmth, or love,
or your team. Blue cars are popular among
GAA fans in Dublin, for example, and I always
remember that story about Roy Keane saying
he never felt comfortable managing Ipswich
because they wore blue, and he'd been a red
all his life. He thought it was childish but I
say no, Dee, it wasn't. It was genetic. These are
connotations we're talking about. You have to
feel comfortable in your surroundings. Maybe
green is your colour – nature, Ireland, health.
Laois people or Dublin people might like blue:
the sea, eternity, freedom, the sky... Are you an
eternal soul, Dee? That's none of my business of
course... I drive a white car myself. You know
why?

DEE
I bet you're gonna mansplain it to me, Shane.

SHANE
I'm from Wexford, you see, Dee, the seaside –
you ever go to the seaside and see those white
breaking waves? Way out on their own, surfing
the ocean? Or the white gulls soaring, pure
and blinding in the sunlight? And those ocean
liners, far out on the horizon, like white specks.
Well, that's me. That's what I think of when
my machine is all washed and sparkling. When
I'm cruising along in my brilliantine white i30,
that's what I am: the breaking wave, the soaring
seagull, the ocean liner... Do you see what I
mean about colour now? And we have so many
colours to reflect so many souls. Celestial blue,
sterling silver, sangria pearl, burnished bronze...

DEE
S—

SHANE
And you buy a car from me, Dee, and it's
going to look back at you every day, that car,
every morning school run, every evening after
work, every trip you take. It'll tell you every
day what you think of yourself, whether you
value yourself in one way or another. And of
course it projects outwards into the impressions
other people have of you. Because we do
project ourselves. What will people think of you
when they see the colour of your car? Are you
someone who drags a dull grey banger around,
all covered in dry muck and scratches? Or do
you cruise about in a scorching red sports car,

181

blazing in the sun, all fire and potential? So,
you see, in a way, colour is—

OFF-AIR, in the passenger seat, listening to some weird
echo of his personality, Tony asked himself again and again, who
am I? Who am I? Who am I? As the image of that big boulder in
the field flickered. Who am I?

BROADCASTING SIMULTANEOUSLY on 5264 kHz + 1420 MHz...

playback: **the pale moon was rising above the green mountain / the sun was declining beneath the blue sea...**

second voice: *speaking of apocalypse...*

first voice: *uh-oh.*

second voice: *[static] the idea that humanity is coming up with new technologies and inventions all the time, and coming up with new technologies and inventions is basically like pulling lotto balls out of a big drum. and usually they're benign, the lottery balls, good things like vaccinations, or the wheel for example. but sometimes they might be dodgy things, like nuclear bombs [static] that drum is a black ball and that's the end. kablammo. but we don't know which one is the black ball and when its turn comes [static] imagine that for a second. how close we always are to the possible end of things. stick that in your shmipe and poke it, as my father used say.*

first voice: *hmmmm. [static] hmmm... but do you think that changes anything? would you be doing anything differently?*

182

second voice:	*[static] ah, i suppose not. i suppose it just puts things into perspective.*
first voice:	*now why in the name of christ would you want to put things in perspective?*
second voice:	*[static]… ha! eh, you have me there… [static] maybe you'd have more of a sense of what's at stake? what really matters?*
first voice:	*sure nothing matters! except of course the five per cent rise in bus fares, and the price of market trader licences on the coal quay of a saturday afternoon [static] the story of all humanity, the gospel in real time…*
second voice:	*we're talking here about whingers and soapboxers and pontificators and chancers. in all hindsight i think you had it at 'nothing'.*
first voice:	*[static] fair point i suppose.*
second voice:	*so why do we bother then? why are we listening?*
first voice:	*i dunno. i mean, what else is there to do?*
second voice:	*i dunno, live?*
first voice:	*ha ha. and how exactly would you go about that now?*

OFF-AIR, the Travelodge was somewhere in Carlow, sitting just off a roundabout, with a view from the uniform room of all that roundabout's exits, and the sounds of the cars coming onto it and off it again would filter into the room and into Lou's sleep the whole night, as though the room itself were the roundabout, or the roundabout there in the room, with the Travelodge's plastic canteen menu board perched on its grassy centre. Luckily they found a pub on the other side of the roundabout, The Traveller's

Rest, a cosy enough place where wood-panelled booths with green upholstery lined the walls either side of the horseshoe counter. And so there they were after dinner, happy out sitting at that horseshoe bar of a Thursday evening, halfway to Dublin, pints of Guinness in front of them, which were remarked upon as very good, and they were comparing notes on hotel rooms when a man came in and flung the rain from his cloth cap to the welcome mat.

'A bad night, Matty,' the middle-aged, bird-shouldered bartender said.

'Shocking weather, John,' Matty huffed, coming to the bar at the opposite corner and ignoring the two travellers. 'That scut of a Taoiseach has a lot to answer for!'

It was a quiet, transitory sort of a place. Groups of people came and went the evening long: worn-out tourists, travelling business people, the odd pair of locals. None of them lasted more than two rounds before moving on. Lou and Tony had a good chat. Lolly was often on the verge of his lips but he couldn't find a way to bring her up because Lou wasn't asking about London. Lou was more interested in why he wouldn't drive, how a relationship worked when only one of the people would drive. In what being a parent was like. He wanted to tell her that Lolly had been prone to whistling a strange tune, one he neither knew nor ever identified. The longer they'd known each other, the rarer he'd heard it. At the beginning it had annoyed him; when it was all over, he pined for the mystery of it. But instead they talked about Nuala, and her willingness to drive endlessly, and how she was a good one for the gym, and about work, and about his kids, and about Dublin, and Lou relentlessly asked questions that didn't lead to Lolly until by and by they got talking to an ESB man who'd come to sit at the bar, whose job it was to go to all the most remote parts of Ireland to read meters, where estimated bills had become a shambles. He was just that day in off Ireland's Eye, 'making peace with the locals,' he said, and was stopping in the Travelodge overnight before the next place.

'Even that old rock is metered,' he confirmed. 'On account of the Martello tower, and the tourism now.'

'That's fascinating,' Lou said. 'You must have seen some interesting things in your work?'

Tony could see the workings of her mind, thinking now of the show, of how this particular call might play out.

'A lot of islands,' the meter reader confirmed. 'Bucketloads of islands.'

He told stories of funerals, physical assaults, drunkenness, weddings, feuds, ghosts...

'People talk about ghost estates,' he said. 'Well I've seen houses, sat right there between two other properties, that shouldn't exist. Not on any ordnance map or town plan, no address, no name or papers, but a front door to bang on like any other. I've met people with no PPS numbers. I've seen hedge schools operating before my very eyes. Magic Ireland is out there alright, only it's not what you think...'

'I'm not being funny,' Lou said, 'but have you ever seen anything your own eyes couldn't explain?'

'Like what?'

Lou shrugged. 'I dunno. Like fairies or leprechauns, or actual ghosts, of actual people?'

The meter reader let down his pint and took off his coat and turned it inside out before putting it back on. Tony noticed Matty on the other corner of the bar, as old and ragged as the torn green blazer he wore, muttering away to himself.

'I met a man once,' the meter reader answered lowly, 'out beyond the Iveragh Peninsula, not far from Kenmare. He'd a fine big house on the side of a mountain – big stone place, fifteen rooms in it at least – but he hadn't set foot in it for twelve years.'

'Why not?'

'Said he'd come home one evening and before he'd even closed the front door behind him he'd heard two leprechauns plotting against him. He took one peek through the crack in the kitchen door and saw a big ugly leprechaun right there on the

185

kitchen table. This man walked out and never went back in his house. Someone sympathetic gave him a caravan and he lived down the road in that.'

'Fucking hell. Did you go in?'

'I'd to read the meter of course.'

'And what was it like?'

'It was like going back in time twelve years. I remember sheets of newspaper in the fireplace grate with back-page soccer stories from three World Cups ago.'

'Man. And did you see a leprechaun?'

'Did I fuck.'

Tony saw a pier leading out to the blue water, and green knuckles of headland beyond, falling into the sea. The Iveragh Peninsula. Lolly posing for a holiday photograph that was now, decades later, lost or thrown out. Where on the earth might that photograph be now? Rotted under a mountain of rubbish somewhere, or buried deep in the ground of another country, or incinerated... More squinting than smiling. But happy. She went swimming; he did not. She was mad for swimming. They'd bussed or thumbed it everywhere, and the adventure of it was only marvellous.

'An ex of mine's cousin saw a leprechaun too,' he told Lou and the meter reader. 'Walking home from the pub down a country road in Galway. Ugly as sin too, he said. Pure evil-looking.'

When the barman came back in from a cigarette, Tony ordered a round for the three of them.

'There's no moon in that sky tonight,' the barman replied, seemingly to Matty, and he set about pulling the pints.

The meter reader transferred the interrogation to their own purpose in transit.

'There's a dearth of new metal on the roads,' he said, when they told him about the car competition. But the car, the meter reader said, was everything. It was an extension of the self; it was a tool wielding great power. It could take you anywhere sure; in fact, it was not only an extension of the self but an extension

186

of desire, purpose, work. Tony wondered why everyone was so philosophical about cars all of a sudden.

'Imagine,' the meter reader said. 'You can traverse the twenty-six counties in only a few hours now.'

It was the great symbol of freedom, he said, humanity's last, and certainly Ireland's greatest. He raised a glass to Henry Ford, who'd brought cars and manufacturing to Cork before even the nation's birth.

'That's why it's such a great prize,' he finished gravely. 'It's freedom in its purest form. Freedom of the road.'

'We should get you working for us,' Tony said.

'Yes!' Lou agreed. 'We'll borrow those lines if you don't mind!'

Then from his corner of the bar, Matty piped up: 'Of course it is a weapon too. A lethal fucking weapon. No offence, pal.'

Tony laughed. 'None taken. We didn't invent the thing!'

And later again, the meter reader told them that he often stayed in that particular Travelodge. At the beginning he'd often gotten lost on the M50, and found himself at the Red Cow interchange – 'the outer circles of hell', he called it – and one time he stumbled upon this very roundabout, with a great pub and a cheap Travelodge, and he'd stopped here on Dublin trips ever since.

'I like to stay in the same places on my travels,' he said. 'To feel a sense of home away from home. But I like the anonymity too. I like the unknown faces.'

A smile grew over his face, more and more as he reminisced about different Travelodges he'd stayed in, and the warm feeling he got inside when he passed certain Shell garages. He recommended franchises for all potential destinations on the rest of their top secret journey, the trajectory for which they said they could not reveal.

'They're all on roadsides,' he boasted. 'Which is convenient. And with the chains now, you see, you know what you're getting.'

He sang a few lines from 'King of the Road'. He hadn't had such a good time in ages, he said. In the other corner, Matty watched him like he was a television show in another language.

BROADCASTING SIMULTANEOUSLY on 5264 kHz + 1420 MHz…

playback: the pale moon was rising above the green mountain / the sun was declining beneath the blue sea…

first voice: *[static] three… three… three… three… [static] you be LOU and i'll be TONY. go on, indulge me.*

second voice: *[static]… oh go on then.*

first voice: *i lived in lewisham actually, LOU. in london.*

second voice: *did you, TONY?*

first voice: *years ago. it was a busy place, lewisham. full of colour. full of noise. cheap fruit in big bowls for a pound. you wouldn't understand a word half the people were saying. not a thing! i loved it actually. there used be a house where all the plasterwork was formed into flowers. do you call them cornices? and the garden was all full of flowers too. and every different type of person you could imagine. blackheath was a big beautiful park then, and once or twice i helped the carnies take down the circus tent. you'd make a nice evening's drinking money doing [static] because the circus guys were so keen to get packed and onto the next place that they'd pay good money for the bit of help [static]*

second voice: *[static]*

first voice: *[static] i fell in love in lewisham, LOU [static]*

second voice: *did you, TONY? tell us.*

first voice: *LOLLY — a fine woman. she treated me like a child at times but i loved it*

188

really. they ran a good pub — the crane — on the lee high road. the lee high road also had an old record shop, and a graveyard. the smell of marijuana, LOU! rubbish stacked high on the pavements; the songs of hispanic children. i never loved anyone more than LOLLY, never opened myself more to anyone.

first voice: *so how did you get into cars, LOU? your father?*

second voice: *my mother actually! you know, i couldn't stand my mother sometimes... [static] well, i loved her. i was the one that mainly took care of her when she got sick.*

first voice: *my mother always embarrassed me.*

second voice: *people are embarrassing really. look at the state of us sure.*

OFF-AIR, Lou woke, gasping from a dry mouth, and reached for the bottle of water next to the bed, and she couldn't sleep then, and eventually put herself back to sleep by thinking about fucking the white witch.

*

And Tony awoke too, in the middle of the night, gulls going berserk somewhere, screaming to the unseen sky over and over. What outrage had occurred? What the fuck were gulls doing over a roundabout in Carlow? Was he still dreaming?

*

nd I could run away I could run away I could go
to Ró and say Ró I'm fuckin dying there with
them – help me out here. He could sort me out
with a small bit of money with food while I
needed it I could stay in any one of a thousand
empty gaffs in Cork I could get a job any job any
fucking job anywhere but here in this fucking
guesthouse. And the

lectricity would never fucking run out when I had
my own gaff every payday I'd give myself pocket
money and everything else would be rent and
bills everything else is living a fucking normal
life like the Walshes like the Obarzes like the
Smyths fucking electricity on food in the cupboards
always no matter what holiday once a year Spain or
Portugal or one of the other sunny green list
countries like that. How do you fuck up your
own life so much that you can't look after your
own fucking kids you can't pay the

ent how do you manage to still buy cans and the
house in the fucking dark and fags and scratch
cards it makes me sick. It makes me fuckin retch
you fucking irresponsible cunts you don't
deserve us fuck you I'll be gone tomorrow
I'll be fucking gone out of your lives tomorrow
and you'll never see me again except to come
back for Sally. Never mind me I'm broken already
but ye don't deserve Sally that perfect child
is too good for ye too good for all of us
ye don't deserve her so ye will lose her I
hope it I hope social services take us away
I'm fucking running anyway fuck the two
of ye and yeer shitty fucking lives. Sally
I love you I won't leave you I love you Sally
no matter what you will never feel alone
fucking hell fucking hell fucking hell when
will it end why can't we just go fucking

h   me

OFF-AIR, first, Dublin was the towering bland stack of a hotel, the windows of its rectangular face holding in them reflections of the infrastructure: a maze of flyovers and slip roads and various lanes and crossings. There at the Red Cow interchange thousands of itineraries converged each moment on twisting bands of tarmac, and that's all Dublin was to them. Gear changes, accelerations, the great lurch of a double-decker marked 124, the trill ring of a red line tram. Lou wondered was Tony seeing the very same thing, when Tony suddenly said that he hated Dublin: the size and sprawl of it. The busyness. 'The pace of life,' he decided in one of his radio voices. 'It's just... *wrong*.'

The misunderstanding was that they'd parked up at the Red Cow and were intending to stay there so that they didn't get stuck in loads of Dublin traffic, but then a phone call came in to say that the Dublin radio station had chosen a spot for them, and had already cordoned off an area of O'Connell Street. There was already a bit of interest, they said, so they told Lou in no uncertain terms to hurry up and get in there.

'We're on the move again so,' Lou said.

'O'Connell Street?' Tony moaned. 'How are we going to get there?'

'I'll get the maps up,' Lou said, hooking her phone back into the holder.

And away into it they went, buckling up again, crossing tram tracks, getting beeped at for not taking a chance on the lights, passing approximately seven petrol garages, and Lou was thinking then about Google Maps, about the fact that a while after Mam had died she'd been thinking about the virtual tourism, and she'd found herself on Google Maps, looking at her parents' house in the street view, and she'd noticed a timestamp in the corner, something like **Image capture: Aug 2011**, and she'd thought, Jesus, Mam is still alive in this image, she's probably still in the house right there on the screen, in the right now of that image, hoovering the hallway or watching tele on the couch… And enfolded in that memory somehow was a memory of her parents arguing in the car, Dad driving, Mam with the road atlas on her lap, they all utterly lost looking for some rented holiday home in Kerry, when Lou and Deb were still quite young, and the strange Kerry roads, like the argument, going on and on, the same fucking places repeating, the same accusations repeating, on and on, in circles, until Lou wanted to scream, until Deborah did scream, and the roads and the argument and the scream seemed to go on for the entire ill-fated holiday, and yet there was Mam stuck in that image of her home in August 2011, and there was Lou on roads again, years later, stuck in the endless map, driving.

ON-AIR

ALISON
I've never heard the likes of it, Paul!

PAUL
There's shite and paper everywhere, Alison. And worse. God forbid when a car comes down that road a little too fast and it gets sprayed everywhere…

ALISON
I mean, there's sewage leaks and there's *sewage* leaks.

PAUL
It's everywhere, Ally. Coming from under the wall. It's a health issue, d'you know? It looks like it's going to be some bleedin' job.

ALISON
Thanks, Paul. Ciara, you went down there for a look – what did you see?

CIARA

I said I'd go down there and take a look, Alison.
One little council van there. The smell is unreal,
Ally!

ALISON

Well, DO NOT go down there for your
morning walk, lads. I'm glad it's you down
there, Ciara, and not me. We've got to cut to
messages but more after this—

OFF-AIR, Lou had the car idling at a red light, and there
was this man in a red hoodie, sitting inside the window of a café,
and his eyebrows were furrowed and she couldn't see what he was
looking at but there was pain in his face. His frown, his arched
eyebrows, were the outer twist of some visceral anguish. She felt
it. Fucking hell she felt it. Was it work? Did he owe money? Was
the children's allowance late? Was it a fight? Was his girlfriend on
some maternity ward, pushing or bleeding? Or, like her, was it
something he couldn't say to anyone that was twisting his gut
and his face so, arching those eyebrows, stretching that face? Had
he too betrayed his love? *Say it, man!* she wanted to roll down the
windows and call. Whatever it is, just tell someone. Just say what's
on your mind. It'll help. As if sparked into action by her thoughts,
he remembered that his coffee was there and pulled it to him.
Remembered to take a drink out of it, and seemed to forget it
again then, with no sign that he'd tasted it, his mind still working
furiously on that anguish, his whole body expressing it, leaning
forward, the balls of his feet working the stool perch so that his
knees were bobbing up and down frantically. Like he was about
to confess, or cry, or explode. The eyes were wrung out. The
elbows were squared on the counter, either side of the coffee,
his shoulders rising and falling with a force of desperation, as if
with each breath a building was collapsing inside him. *What is it,
man?* Money? Is someone sick? Did you fuck the white witch?

193

Did you go to her house and give her your hand and let her into your fucking lap? Did you ruin everything? He twisted his head, wincing, looking about as if for help, and pressed a finger and a thumb to his temples, covering his forehead with a stretch of his hand. Then with that same hand he rubbed around and into his eyes as if he wanted to press them into his head. He lifted a spoon then, looked at it, put it down again. On a high stool at the window, there he was, on the verge of tears, or screaming, but holding on to it. *Say it, man!* Fucking say it. Out with it. Let it go. Fucking ask it. Fucking say it. Tell someone what's going on. FUCKING OUT WITH IT, MAN! Let it out! The brain of you, the gut of you, the heart of you will be wrung dry if you don't open the valve. Let that counter go. Let your forehead go and let the words of you smash the fucking window. Let the words out into the street, into the world, to burst like a flock and head for the river or the harbour or some wooded area between hills. Release the anguish, let it out let it go you fool you fucking poor craytur you fucking maniac stop running your hands through your hair and stop letting that anguish twist you into shapes you aren't stop it… I need to get out and talk to this man, she was thinking. I need to tell him it's going to be okay.

'You've the green light there, Lou,' Tony said, and she released the clutch and let down the handbrake and her foot trembled through the accelerator.

RSWWESWKKWETTOOOOOHADOOPHI
GOWNDAYSWUUSNRBFIEHEHEYDUF
HRJEJWJWKKWLNRNFWGWGWGDUDU
EEEMRKKOORNDNYYYTIEODFDJEJ
ERRRHHEWOOOFFFFYYYJFJSGSIG
OVJYHDHCUIEORNFNDCICGHHJNN
EEPPESJGJEEEJFIIIEENRBWBQR
OOOEEENFDJJTDDDTNYDHEEEBTH
SWHIN T HE STATIC just before

194

she went missing, Tabitha had started this new thing, whereby she went into corners and sort of dug them out. For example, she climbed from the windowsill to the bookshelves, and she started pawing out all the books from the corner of the second shelf. When most of them were out, pawed to the floor below, she jumped down and wandered off with a brief satisfied miaow. Or she climbed onto the bureau's folded-out desk and emptied the cubbyhole where Marta kept her payslips. Just emptied it out and left, as if she were looking for something she'd lost, and wasn't bothered cleaning up after herself.

And nothing more. Nothing else different. She used the litter in the same way, at roughly the same times. She purred when Marta scratched her head, her cheeks, her bony rump. And yet Marta wondered now, there at work, making beds, unable to think of anything else, if that new habit was something to do with Tabby's disappearance. Whether she'd gone looking for something, to empty out some corner somewhere elseaakkfjrjjjje hehdufufidotoooyoyoyjddjddjrhsgcuoofjfhxuisijhth xydiierekdppogirhehjjdysyyigjtjdoofjehthfisosktj tjhyuofjfhridosjfhdhrbrjeebdyvghhyyiiirreiioooo kdshsnssabaaanfikfnrnssiigurheheheosorotjthsyyii tjssjfvootvjrnwwwmtjeokrooouyddhhhejthfidkrfigur hsiroooftfjnndndsee

---

ON-AIR

ALISON
—and so are you back on the sauce then, Jay?

JAY

Well, sort of, y'know. I was doing really well
and I was looking forward to hitting the pints
next month, and not a minute before as we all
agreed, Alison... but then you'd wonder with
all the terrorist attacks in London, like, is it
even worth it? Abstinence or whatever you call
it? Why bother if your time could be up any
minute, y'know? I was thinking I should just
enjoy meself and have a glass of bleedin vino,
y'know? If you were going to go, you'd want to
go out at your local, wouldn't ya?

ALISON
So you're saying the terrorism has driven you
back to the drink and out of our Sober Club,
Jay?

JAY

Well, if you were going to go, you'd want to go
out at your local wouldn't ya? There's a lovely
wine cavern called Diane's just down from me
on the corner, Alison... A glass of rioja and a
small bowl of olives to pick at and they can take
me whenever they bleedin well want!

ALISON
But people don't want to go, Jay, and that's why
they're coming back here in droves. Because the
same threat isn't there in Dublin. So what I'm
saying, Jay, is that I think you're having us on a
little bit!

JAY

Ah, go easy on me, Ally! I'm only human!

ALISON
Tut-tut. Emily, you had a slip-up as well I
believe?

196

EMILY

I did, Ally, unfortunately. Éilis came over to tell
me that she'd passed her module on Ear, Nose
and Throat, and of course next thing I knew
we were at the offie buying naggins of vodka,
and the next thing I know I was out, and the
next thing I know it's the morning and I hate
myself! But I'm trying to sort it all out now.
I'm feeling positive! Feeling like I want to try
this again!

ALISON

Well tut-tut to ye all. Tis just myself and
Georgina left for our sins! Now, coming up
next we have that brand new Mazda to give
away. If you know someone who has moved
back from London amidst the Troubles, or
you've moved back from London yourself, this
could be a very, very good day for you—

OFF-AIR, thanks to Lou's phone, they weren't long
making it to the cordoned-off section of O'Connell Street,
right beneath the Spire, more or less on time. She would later
remember the sound and blur of a small crowd that quickly
gathered to watch, with a couple of people already yelling,
indignant, arms raised, about being first to spot the car. She
would remember, on a bus stop shelter, an image of Ireland
at night, as a map, electricity-lit – no towns, no rivers, only
the traces of electricity, the grid pulsing through darkness.
[static] a ghost in this house...

*

Tony would remember a teenager with a bloody nose, watching on, with a BMX sort of hanging off him. He had one
foot planted on the ground and the other poised on the pedal

of the BMX, seemingly ready to bolt, its handlebars held by one hand.

★

And Lou would remember the aluminium railing around a monument – a statue of a hero whose name she couldn't remember – so that even O'Connell Street seemed part of the endless roadworks and infrastructure.

'It reminds me of the time we did the car giveaway in the shopping centre,' Tony said of the crowd, waving at someone. 'That was *years* ago now.'

'It reminds me of the protests,' Lou replied.

The Dublin radio station team, who all wore emblazoned blue bomber jackets, peppered the crowd with freebies, though a couple still grumbled, protested that they'd seen the Mazda first, one audibly swearing to a poor fella with a clipboard that she'd be complaining to *her* ombudsman. Tony and Lou stood out of the car, and were applauded after Tony's words into a microphone. Lou took a couple of pictures, and stood aside then to prep the winner for the interviews, of which there were two, back in the car, with Alison and Dublin first, then with Tony and Cork. This returned exile – Siobhán – was livelier than her predecessor, and not from Dublin but from Offaly, a ginger woman of about thirty-five, with lovely slender hands, who'd been an artist, or 'photographer in various moulds', and who even brought a quiver to her voice when she considered the conundrum that this violence in London posed to the world – that we in the West were under siege and yet they from the East had been under siege for so long too.

Siobhán said that she had returned to Ireland at the request of her parents, who were elderly, but could only get work in Dublin, so if she won it the car would be so handy for getting back to see them. Because her mother suffered from her nerves now and had to ring Siobhán almost every day. The mother had had a dream that Siobhán was killed in the street and that she couldn't see Siobhán's face anymore, and the mother had not been the same since. She was originally from Cork – the mother – and listened to Tony every day; that was how they'd first heard about the competition.

So you were certainly affected by the violence, Siobhán?

Alison would ask when it was her turn. Oh, of course she was. She planned to explore her reactions through her work. She had taken lots of photographs in London. She hoped to raise the money and to find a space to put on an exhibition. Siobhán said the world was changing now beyond anyone's comprehension, and that she was sad to leave London, and felt she'd left too soon, but was glad to be home all the same. She was polite, and full of smiles, with her slender hand wrapped around the mobile and a long finger rubbing the dash slowly as she spoke thoughtfully to Alison first, then Tony.

★

When the interviews were over, and the gifts and music withdrawn and the crowd dispersed, the radio station staff quickly extracted themselves. The banners, the stand, the cordon, the balloons: all were gone in minutes. Lou was asked to reverse off the pavement and as she complied Tony saw the pillars of the General Post Office across the way, rising out of the movement of passersby.

'I wouldn't be up for living in Dublin,' he said to Lou.

OFF-AIR, as they stopped by the PLEASE WAIT TO BE SEATED sign, Dad said: 'Now, Jada, now Sally, I bet none of your friends are having dinner in such a fancy place this evening.'

He looked around with a rare kind of a smile, kind of dreamy and proud, even though it was a dark sort of empty place, with big plants and dark curtains and black and white tiles, and there wasn't much to see because all the tables were around the corner. He wore a new shirt from TK Maxx – one of those white-shirt-navy-collar-and-cuffs ones. Embarrassing.

'The Italians know their food, see,' he said.

Sally was holding her hand, a bit shy, looking around at the plants and the curtains. Mam was quiet, which was unusual, and didn't seem as jittery as normal either. She was gaping at the wide round lampshades above, which cast pools of light down onto the tiles.

Then a waitress in a white shirt and black trousers came and piped, 'Hello!' and took them to a table around the corner, beyond the curtains.

'Now,' Dad said, when the waitress was gone and they were sitting with big books of menus at a large black table. 'It's our lucky day, so you get whatever you want. Doesn't matter how expensive.'

'Chicken and chips!' Sally sang. 'Chicken and chips! Chicken and chips!'

Mam said, serenely: 'Want me to read the menu for you, Sal?'

'I want Jada to read the menu for me.'

So she began to read the menu for Sally, even though Sally was definitely going to get chicken and chips anyway, while Mam and Dad held hands across the table and looked at their menus thoughtfully. But actually it was a bit of a laugh because there were some very strange words on there, words that none of them knew what they meant. And she had this burning question, so when the waitress had taken their orders and finished making stupid faces at Sally, she just asked them outright: 'Are we moving home?'

'Oh,' Mam said, breaking off from Dad and sitting up straight.

'No, love,' Dad said. 'We just got a bit of luck.'

Their voices were suddenly a bit lower and they looked around and touched their faces even though no one else was there. The place was empty in fact. She felt a sick feeling in her stomach now; she'd been so sure that this was it.

'Why are we celebrating then? What are we celebrating? Have we found a new place?'

'Your dad won some money on a scratch card, love.'

'A scratch card?' She knew what it was with Mam now; she'd gotten her prescription again. For the first time in ages. 'A scratch card?' she said again.

Dad sat up in his seat, grinning. 'A lucky day, Jadey.'

'Why are you buying scratch cards? We can't afford to live in our own home – why are you spending money on scratch cards?'

'Jada, love…' Mam stretched a hand across to her.

'No,' she said, pulling away, her voice suddenly close and tight. Her throat seemed to be closing on her but she went on anyway. 'If we can't afford rent we can't afford scratch cards. Why am I, the *child*, having to tell ye this? This is fucking crazy! We're out spending money on fancy food now when it could be rent!'

'It's not enough for rent, love. Not for a deposit or rent.'

'But it's a start? It's part of it.'

Dad rolled his eyes.

'Sometimes life gives you bad luck and sometimes good luck,' Mam said. 'You have to celebrate the good luck. You have to give yourself relief—'

'Anyway,' Dad interrupted, 'it's *our* money. We're the adults and we decide what to do with it. When you're the adult and you earn money, you get to decide what you do with it.'

And looking over her shoulder he went suddenly smiley and sat up straight again because the food was coming on a big black plastic tray.

She got carbonara; Dad got bolognese; Mam got a Hawaiian pizza, and Sally got chicken and chips. The plates all steamed. Somewhere around the corner a door swung and there was talking for a second and the clattered stacking of plates or bowls or something, and when that unseen door swung closed again there was no talking, because the restaurant was dead, just some kind of quiet European music, and then the waitress stood back and asked: 'Ye all set now?'

'Perfect,' Dad replied.

'Just give me a shout if you need anything.'

'I have eaten one chip,' Sally said, in her robot voice.

'Excellent,' the waitress grinned. 'Plenty more where that came from.'

And then the waitress was gone and the others were all eating. The carbonara steamed in a big bowl under her face, looking congealed – a disgusting mess, like vomit by a drain on a night pavement – and she knew she wouldn't touch it.

'And anyway, Jada,' Dad said, his face over his plate, chopping all his spaghetti with his knife and fork. 'You never, *ever* complain when we give you pocket money, so you can buy your stupid spray paint and go acting the scut around town with your mates. You always get your pocket money, and you never ask about rent then, do you? Never crosses your mind then, funnily enough.'

And he started to wolf down his food.

'Bon appetit, everyone,' Mam said.

'But, Dad,' she started, and failed to finish the first time, the heart squeezing away in her. 'But, Dad, we're homeless.'

'We're not,' Mam said, pulling apart the slices of her pizza, gently blowing on them. 'We're not. We're just between places. Between homes. We're just waiting on a place to come up. We're on a list.'

'I have eaten five chips,' Sally said.

A glug of bolognese fell off Dad's fork and there was a little splat, and there was bolognese on his shirt then and he shouted, 'FUCK,' and then went quiet again and carried on eating.

'Don't ruin this, Jada,' Mam sighed.

CAMDNSNDLFKHJGNTT H R E P P
OOORDSAMDNBEMDNFHRNGBF
NDMFNTHRIPLOAIDJKFMDJH
SHNABDBVEVRHEFMDKSOEDSM
SMSANDBFINTH E STAT IC

two voices:

'Poor Bernice is asleep there, Marta, is she?'

'She is, doc.'

'Ah, maybe I'll come back again at the end of the round then.'

'Sure.'

'She's sleeping well then?'

'Well, we help her with a bit of flurazepam. She's not in great form since she fell.'

'It wasn't a good one.'

'No. By the fireplace… like that…'

'Absolutely awful.'

'Poor thing… but she is fighter. She has years of working hard.'

'What was it she did?'

'She had two jobs, she told me. She said she cleaned hotel rooms six mornings a week and then worked in a chipper by Anglesea Street four evenings a week.'

'Christ, fair play. That's hard work alright. Never let up by the sounds of it.'

'She had five kids too. I mean one woman, doc!'

'And did the husband not work? Was there a husband?'

'There was husband for a while, I think—'

'Long enough for five kids, says you!'

'Yah! But she talks more about him drinking than working.'

'She's turning a little there — the facial scarring looks like it's healing anyway.'

'She's a fighter. She told me they were both drinkers, until she had vision one time… there are some stories there, doc.'

'She told me the first time I examined her — when was that, about eighteen months ago? — she told me that her one true love was bingo.'

'She told me that too! Every Tuesday night, like mass. But she don't play the bingo in here. Not even one time.'

'She doesn't socialise much?'

'No. There was one lady she liked, but she… you know… and no one else since. For what reason I don't know. She chats to us; she's nice woman like.'

'And they're generally a friendly bunch in here too… I suppose she won't be going anywhere for a while now anyway, the state she's in.'

'No.'

'…'

'…'

'And still no visitors?'

'No.'

'The kids? The husband? Siblings?'

'We found them and we notified them, but they haven't come. Not one in eighteen months.'

'That's awful. *Awful*.'

'I wonder what happens. What does a person do that one year and a half in a nursing home and nobody comes.'

'Are you sure she can't hear us?'

'She's *out cold*.'

'…'

'…'

'And she doesn't seem like a bad sort. She's never anything but lovely to me.'

204

'I like her a lot.'

'But no one? In a year and a half?'

'But, you know, it doesn't seem to bother her. She's happy enough. Well, until she fell. She likes having her little radio on, listening in the bed. It keeps her company. I put it on here for her now, to keep her company.'

'It's a great comfort for her I'd say.'

'She's so lovely. What happened must have been bad.'

'Sure who knows what happens in families. Listen, I better get on. I'll see if she's awake when I'm back this way in a bit.'

'No problem. I will turn her and leave her with the radio.'

'Do. Chat to you in a bit, Marta.'

'See you doccccccccccccccccccccccccccccccccccccc ccccccccccccccccccccccccnvbfnghdnsnabsbddkflgomhng jthenadnsbdnfnthrgenansmdmgnfnhdbfbtpflflloooosid kfmngnfbdshdhsbavsdvfnrjhetgrhrnfhgtbrghewgaqsgf fffbbbdfffbmhnghtjrehdgfbfvncbdvsagsndeoimgkfjhn muyytnrjd

---

OFF-AIR, it was getting late, the sky failing at last, the hills blackening on either side as they came back the motorway, cocooned in the Mazda, and counted off kilometres and half-hours.

'How did you get on with the white witch anyway?' Tony asked.

'Oh, it was grand. Nothing too enlightening.' Her voice made a kind of high wobble and she cleared her throat. 'Nothing there for the show I'm afraid – she's not much of a personality.'

'Ah. She didn't give you the lotto numbers?'

'She didn't, no.'

'Ah.'

Hard shoulder, verge, central reservation. She focused on objects. Real things.

'She said a lovely thing about my mam and dad though.'

'Did she?'

'She said they'd an extremely powerful love bond, and that that was why I'd such a strong aura.'

'Ah, lovely! A strong aura, ay?'

'I know sure. They fought a lot, my parents, but I suppose it was true. They did love each other.'

'...'

'I've been thinking about her a lot lately.'

'Your mother?'

'Yea. Don't know why.'

'I only met her the once. What a lovely woman, though. She had a twinkle in her eye, Lou.'

'She did... Do you ever wonder, Tony, do you spend – I mean *you* like *one*, like does *one* spend too much time dwelling on the past?'

'Jesus, all the time. Lately especially. With all this London stuff – or old age maybe – I feel like I'm *living* in the past, never mind dwelling on it.'

[static] the roooooose of traleeeeeeee!

'I'm like... I dunno. I've been watching a lot of Disney movies lately! Thinking about Mam. The trip we took to London, all that.'

'Why do we do it, Lou? Get lost in things like that when they're gone? When they happened years ago?'

'I don't know... I've been wondering the same. To avoid the present maybe? Because the present is frantic? And the future's... unknown?'

hospital bed [static]

'Maybe, Lou. Maybe.'

'Or maybe because the past is always there anyway. It's underneath everything anyway.'

'Aye.' Tony readjusted himself in the seat. 'How long has it been now, since your mam? Ten years?'

'Eleven years. Time flies, doesn't it.'

'God it does. I remember when you came in first – wasn't it transition year you were in? Big thick glasses on you and baggy jeans. How long does that mean you've been with the station?'

'Eighteen years, though obviously I was away minding her for those two years as well.'

'Aye, of course... That was so noble... And where was it your mam was from?'

'A village in Connemara. Tiny place.'

Rapidly, nervously, before he thought better of it, he said: 'You know, I've an old friend in Connemara that I was thinking of maybe trying to get in touch with. Lolly. Lorraine. Maybe after we do the Galway stop next week we could head up there and see your ma's old homeplace and call in to my friend. She runs a pub I think, somewhere up there.'

'*Lorraine*? Tony are you telling me there's been a woman in your life other than *the Dancing Queen*?'

'Ah now!' He fumbled and dropped his phone between his feet and clamoured to retrieve it. 'An old friend is all, Lou. Someone I hung around with in London.'

'I still can't believe what's going on there,' Lou said. 'It feels surreal that we're here doing this competition and that over there, things are falling apart. I mean, London like? We went on a school tour there in second year. Saw Shakespeare in the Globe Theatre. Ate shitloads of sweets, til we felt sick. There was a flagon of cider being passed round the hotel rooms in the middle of the night and all... And it's the only foreign place I ever went on holidays with Mam. London, like?'

'...'

'...'

207

'You know, Lou, there were loads of things I didn't like about London, but I did love living there. I remember we went fishing once, in the Thames estuary – me and a few lads from the hurling team chartered a small boat. We went right out to the mouth of the sea and fished all day. And I caught nothing, only a massive dogfish. Vicious little fella, thrashing on the boat floor. I thought it was a shark! But it was only a dogfish.'

'A dogfish?'

'Aye,' he sighed. 'And I remember thinking the Thames water must have been absolutely riddled with chemicals and sewage and all sorts of filth, but yet there was plenty of life in that fella… It's mad isn't it, Lou? How you remember little moments like that for decades and yet you can't remember your PIN at the bank machine. Mad how things stay with you like that…'

'You know,' Lou said, 'Mam used say that you should think of your life not as a pathway but as a collection of memories. It's not a path from youth to old age with some end goal, she would say, but just moments, all added up… I think she heard an athletics coach say it on the tele or something. That sport wasn't actually about trophy cabinets or medals, but about all those moments you built up in your memory, over time. And that these memories were the things that made life worth something. Because life is only experience. And experience is only layers of moments. Like this journey. The people we're meeting. All those moments are like dots, and when you join up all the dots, that is the experience, the life.'

'Wow,' Tony said. 'Wow.'

'Do you think I'd be a good mam, Tony?'

'A good mam? Jesus!' He put a hand on her shoulder. 'I think you'd be a great mam, Lou. A brilliant mam. Why? Are ye thinking… ?'

'Well, we haven't really spoken about it. I haven't said it to anyone really. Til now. But it's been on my mind.'

'I think you'd be only a brilliant mam. Though now I'm already thinking about mat leave and how I'd survive without you!'

'I wonder would it be me taking the mat leave…'

'God! I didn't even think of that! As if ye didn't have it complicated enough!'

'Ha ha. Well I'm glad you think I'd be good anyway. Marta thinks we've the wrong genes for it. Cancer, alcoholism, all that stuff runs in both families.'

'Genes? Look, I wouldn't worry about anything like that. You've no control over it, and, speaking from experience, you just can't quantify for a young life in the house. You can't dictate how it'll turn out and you can't quantify how it changes your life. For the better, I should say! I mean, we lost Aaron after a couple of days and it made us stronger. And now here we are with two teenagers what feels like ten minutes later and, well, the memories are amazing. The way they light up lives… And nobody's a good parent, Lou. Everyone just learns on the job and gets by. You just roll with it and you'd be brilliant at it I know. That'd be some lucky kid.'

'But what if it's a lucky kid with a predilection for alcohol, or cancer – you know? You're unleashing suffering like? You don't look into a newborn's eyes and see its last hours as a fifty-something-year-old man, gasping for breath, dying in a hospice bed… But I think I would… I wouldn't… I wouldn't want to get sick and have my young fella or young girl having to look after me, like. You're unleashing guaranteed suffering like.'

'Ah, Lou… But you're unleashing love as well. A lifetime of it. And more joy than you can imagine. The happy times are far more frequent – and memorable – than the sad times. Now, look, it's not all sunshine and roses – we're having hell with Sadie at the moment – but that's all part and parcel of the adventure, I hope anyway, God willing she'll be okay, you know? But I suppose my problem is that no one seems to talk anymore about how much craic those early years are.'

'Yea, I suppose.'

'I'm telling you, Lou. My two are the best thing that ever happened me. IMRO awards don't come close!'

'Yea, I suppose. I don't know why I'm so morbid.'

'Arra. It's natural to worry.'

'...'

'So you have asked her?'

'Well, no. But you have random conversations, you know?'

'Well I think ye'd be great. And I'd love to see another little Lou in the world. I've known you eighteen years, Lou, and I can honestly say I don't know a more considerate person.'

'Ah, you're very nice, Tony.'

'Now don't tell the Dancing Queen I said that!'

And then the conversation in the car stuttered a little, and began to repeat itself, and Tony and Lou began to count the kilometres aloud again, repeating distances to each other and speculating about times of arrival, and increasingly retreating into their own thoughts, eyes lost in what seemed like the same road that had taken them everywhere so far, punctuated by the same lines and arrows, the same lanes, the same steel dividers, the same streetlights and hard shoulder and verge, and the same long mystery of the central reservation.

★

As he looked out the window, Tony realised that Nuala would be at home now, already making for the bed probably, her pro-grammes finished now, calling in the two bedroom doors to tell the kids stop playing the computer or get off the phones or whatever, checking that homework was done. And Lolly was – what? – looking at the clock, counting down to last call? Did she still raise her eyebrow in that funny way when she checked the time? As if she didn't believe it? Nothing was as real or true or memorable as that first time being in love. Nothing.

God.

He hoped she was happy. In general, she'd always been of a happy enough disposition. Her calm parting words had gone round his head for years. *Look after yourself, Tony.* A few tears shed alright, after, alone. He had only been able to say, *Good luck. Keep in touch.* It was pathetic, looking back. Probably she'd been glad to be rid of him, and found happiness, free of him, soon after. Ah, Lolly! She stood by a doorway in their Lewisham apartment, sometime in the late eighties, about to say something, and then walked away.

★

And as Lou flicked her awareness between the mirrors, sitting there next to Tony, she was in fact a million miles away, and she wasn't thinking about her mother now at all, but was dying, in her mind, and in dying she was figuring out a way to say goodbye to Marta. She was saying, Marta, from the very first night we met I knew it was you. Or I hoped it was you. Maybe she was bleeding out on the floor of a London theatre or maybe she was dying of a rare bone cancer in a private room in a hospice, or on a ward in the Cork University Hospital, saying, I hoped it was you, Marta, I did. There was just something about the way you opened up to me, the way you saw me, that just arrested me. You arrested me, Marta, there at Val's house party. Or was it James's? And there was never anyone after, Marta. Never anyone close. The white witch thing: nothing. Just a momentary loss of control. Nothing actually happened. I swear to you that nothing did. With the white witch or with Clíona Murphy that time. Or with Helen. They were just moments of error – mini-betrayals maybe, of mind, but bodily I never gave myself to anyone else ever, Marta. I failed you in so many ways, I know. I was never good enough for you, not from that first day, but once I gave myself to you that was it, I swear. I would give myself to you again and again and again for eternity, if only I had it. I tried to make myself the best person I could be for you, I swear it, and I know I failed, I know I did, but I did my best, I swear. We had good times, Marta, didn't we? It was worth it for you, wasn't it? And here it is. My time. The end. I'm nearly gone. And you have this son of ours now as a sign of that love, as an embodiment of it. I'm there in him. My love for you lives on in him. I have no idea where I'm going, if I'm even going anywhere. Part of me hopes it's the latter – that there's nothing and I'm now in for a good long rest. But I got to know you, Marta, and I got to love you, and that made everything else worth it. The sadness, the weirdness, the difficulty sometimes even in breathing. The fucked-up-ness. You know, as long as I can remember, for however many years now, I always felt like a temporary construction, something always on the verge of falling down. Like an excuse I was making up and had to run with. The only thing that ever felt permanent and true and not full of doubt was what I felt for you. So I can say goodbye now to that temporary construction, thank god, and just hold on to *us*. As I go, these last hours, only us. Just us. Oh, I never meant to hurt you, Marta. Anything that ever happened like that – the white witch – that was just a stupid mistake. A moment's stupidity. Getting lulled. Nothing actually happened. I love you. I will always love you. I take that love with me. I leave it with our son too. Nothing actually happened.

MBNVNCBZXNSJKDDKFKGJTHREHE
WNWNAAANEEEEERFFFFFFFFFOOP
GLGKHJUYYTNTHREWAHEEESNDBE
BDBGFBFGMGGMGMYHLLLLLJKKKK
KKINTHES TATIC in his efforts to clear the static the engineer lifted the spectrum tuner from the top of the FM dissipator and went back again to listen to the signal, to check the chosen frequency versus the alternates, the room humming around him. The room itself being a micro-current in the macro. Anywhere in that room you could touch the jack of your headphones to metal – the fuse boxes or the transmitter shelves or anything else – and you would hear the radio, the voices, the transmission of frequency, crystal clear and flowing outward. **If you picked up**

a hearing aid in and around the Winthrop Street area... and were the engineer to touch his headphones now, to the lock of the door say, at a particular angle say, he might hear next an anonymous shortwave station broadcasting a sequence of numbers, numbers transformed to signal, sent away out at the speed of light from a transmitter somewhere, out over the horizon, in from the horizon, signal then turned back into numbers, and the broadcast would then have been received by listeners at various locations in the world. And one scattered group in particular would have been listening out for that broadcast and on receipt would have begun the task of decoding from one-time password sheets, and somewhere amidst the numbers, which had been signal once, were the words: CANAL DOCKKKKKKKSSNDNDJFKFOEWWPPPAAKKKKKKKKDM MFNGBRRBEBEBWNMDMMMDMMDNSNNANNANBBBF FKKTHEEHASMDNGBFNDHEFNNTTBEHFFMDSDSLLLAS WEEEEAREEDDDENNNSALSSMDNNNFFBFKKKGJDJJFNO KOKOKOKOKKKKKOSSSMMSNDB

golgotha

(pequod)

ON-AIR

TONY

So this phrase, the Queen's English, has rightly
annoyed Adrian, who I'm led to believe is a
teacher these last forty years. Is that right,
Adrian?

ADRIAN

Forty years teaching, Tony, and sixty-one years
learning!

TONY

And the Queen's English?

ADRIAN

Well, this phrase – *the Queen's English* – is a load
of old you-know-what!

TONY

Why is that, Adrian? You've got about two
minutes to tell us!

ADRIAN

Well, go back to way, way back. The Romans
are flown from what we now call *Great* Britain,
and who comes in? Germanic tribes. Your
Saxons, your Angles, your Jutes. And they all
bring their own languages. We hear about
counties in England now – cricket teams: West
Sussex? East Anglia? These're all the Saxons
and Angles who settled east and west... So they
bring German into contact with Old English,
a half-Roman thing as it was then, and of
course they all want to trade and so everybody
speaks a little bit of everyone else's language,
a kind of pidgin if you will, so that everyone
can communicate with everyone else. And who
arrives next, Tony?

TONY
You're gonna tell me I bet?

ADRIAN
The Vikings. And they bring their language
into the bargain too. We all know that Thursday
is Thor's day, for example. But sky? Berserk?
Steak? Slaughter? These are all Viking words.
Sky, Tony, is the Viking word for clouds.

TONY
Appropriate today!

ADRIAN
Indeed. And to make a long story boring,
Tony, the Normans come next, with another
new language to add to the mix. The Vikings
brought earthy words – food and violence and
whatnot – and then the Normans bring the
vocabulary of love and organisation, because
they were more organised, structured types. And
next, Tony?

TONY
You're down to about a minute, Adrian!

ADRIAN
The French! And the French come to rule,
and so they bring the language of the court.
Disposition. Legality, force majeure. Rendez-
vous. And so on… And by the time the French
are shoved out, English has ten thousand or
so words added into the mix. The language is
by now a complete and utter pidgin language,
mixing up vocabulary and grammar, robbing
expressions from here, there and everywhere.
There are more exceptions than rules. Nothing
can be explained easily or logically. And we
still have Irish to add into the mix, because we
gave them words like Tory, hooligan, boycott,

brogue... So you see English is basically a
pidgin language or a creole language and the
Queen can do nothing about it. English is alive,
Tony, a living beast, and it belongs as much to
the man who gets off the boat from Gambia as
it does to the fecking Queen!

TONY
Fascinating, Adrian. God, every day is a school
day on this show! Here comes Barry in the
newsroom—

[static] news and advertisements redacted [static]

———

TONY
Now Maura, you've been listening to Adrian's
four-minute history of the English language?

MAURA
I have, Tony.

TONY
And what do you want to add?

MAURA
Well now, I'm not as clever as Adrian, but I
was listening away there and I was thinking to
myself – d'you know the way it all started with
cave paintings? Like hand-prints and finger-
paintings of horses on cave walls in Spain, all
that?

TONY
I do, yea.

MAURA
Well, like, I do be looking at the
granddaughters' messages there. Them
emojis? The smiley faces, d'you know? And

219

I wonder are we actually going backwards?
Back to pictures? Are people actually too
lazy to actually write words anymore? All
these abbreviations and emojis and pictures:
everybody's just googly-eyed looking at them!

TONY
God, 'tis all philosophers we have on the line
this morning!

DDDDEEEAAAASSSMMFNDBNGHRWM
ALKSKFJGNTHYHTOOUUULLGMDNF
NOPUILLLKSMDNFNGGNKKTHAANS
DBFNGHTRNEMAKSMLPOIMENWAHS
NGBTHEMNWPALSKDJFGHTYREIIN
T HESTATIC it started in the kitchen,
where he found her at the end of the table, and
it was all over quite quickly after that.

'Dylan!' she said, looking up from her sudoku,
her cup of tea, the dregs of the fag between her
two fingers. 'You gave me a fright! I didn't know
you were calling in.'

He didn't answer, but went to the kitchen
counter, where on the draining board all the
breakfast dishes were perfectly stacked and
drip-drying.

'Is your mam with you?' she asked, turning in
her seat to watch him. 'Dylan?'

He glanced at her sideways, to see the look
of fear that had always been in her face around
him. He ignored her though. There was no need to
talk to her now. What he was looking for was the
coloured ones, the ones not serrated or anything.
Green yellow pink blue, in the see-through plastic
block. *I got 'em on Groupon!* she'd boasted, a

220

long time ago. There'd been coloured chopping boards to match but there were regular upgrades to things in this house and the chopping boards were gone now, maybe in the Vincent De Paul or maybe in someone else's home already.

'Dylan,' she said, as he began to move some plates around to aid his search. 'Are you—?'

'SHUT UP, GRAN.'

He went quickly back to the table and grabbed her by the sides of the head with his hands and he kind of squeezed her head for a second and growled at her and then wrenched it back and forth — he didn't really know what he wanted to do with it — and she squealed and some spit came out of her mouth and through his fingers and he said SHUT UP again. Then he sort of pushed the head down onto the plastic tablecloth — the grey one with all those European places on it, like the Eiffel Tower and the Colosseum and the London tower — and he was kind of banging the head on the table now, and he could feel her sort of bracing herself each time, her hands struggling feebly with his, and as he banged the head his eye fell on the postcards on the fridge, from all the others, from all sorts of other places, and he was going much harder on the head now and she was making a curious sound, one he'd never heard before.

'Alright?' he said, gasping a bit, and left her now and went back to the kitchen sink. 'Shut up like?'

He caught his reflection in the window above the draining board — his cheeks were so puffy now! And there was a black bird too, in the garden beyond his face's reflection. Maybe she fed it.

Maybe it liked them. He waved at the sorry bird. He began to unstack the plates again so he could look better.

The blue one was under a big saucepan; that's where it was. They made vegetable soup in that big saucepan every single Wednesday morning without fail. The soup wasn't bad.

'Jim!' she was calling now, weakly. 'Jim!' her head resting on the table, one arm hanging down. She had all these smudgy marks around her neck and face — oh, he'd never washed his hands! 'Jim!' but Granddad wouldn't hear her in a million years with the volume he had the racing on at in the front room. Not in a million years!

He went to her in the chair and without pausing or even thinking about it he just jammed the blue one into her back. The blue one was the fat one for chopping big hard things like sweet potato. Going in, it didn't feel that weird at all actually. It just went in. No different to the time with the SuperValu roast chicken. He did it again, and it was the same. And then did it again. And again. He did it a good few times. She didn't say much or give out, there at the table where he still remembered having to say grace when he was a kid. Gary had always made faces at him when they all had their eyes closed, and yet nobody ever believed him that Gary was doing it. Gary was a fucking shit.

And he was still ramming the blue one in and there was quite a lot of blood spraying about when he noticed Granddad was at the door, saying, 'Dylan?'

And Granddad was so dumb that he came further into the kitchen, moved towards them rather than running for the front door, and Dylan wanted to feel it again so he went towards Granddad, who put his hands up, saying something like, *'Calm,'* and the natural move, how Dylan had approached him, was to cut up — it was just happening naturally, he didn't even have to think about it — thrusting up into the stomach area, or thereabouts, and then when Granddad was doubled over and coughing, or choking, or both, just sort of holding on to Dylan, hugging him around the waist almost, then Dylan moved around the back and jammed the blue one in there a few more times. Granddad was so weak, and the incisions were so soft and pure, like morning light, so easy. How did a heart beat for seventy-odd years and yet the body be so weak? And yet there must have been some kind of struggle, because he realised now that there were splayed cookbooks all over the floor, in the blood, and there was smashed porcelain all over too — all the ornaments they'd collected. And yet that stupid dog-in-a-suit one had survived smashing, somehow.

The blue one was actually pretty clean, but he washed it anyway. Put it back to drip-dry and patted his hands on a tea towel that hung neatly from a drawer handle. His fingernails were still pretty filthy — probably because they were so long these days and caught on everything — but he had a brush thing at home for those; he'd clean those later.

He walked around the two bodies on the way out and tried not to step in blood, to not get it all over the hallway carpet. He was a big stupid oaf who did things like that sometimes. His acne had been quiet the whole time but it was already driving him crazy again now, but he really didn't want to scratch it with his dirty fingernails, and but it was doing that thing where it was beginning to itch so bad that he wanted to peel the skin off his face, off his back, so that he wanted to peel every layer of himself away, and of course now this was going to be the start of another panic attack, yet another panic attack, and so before he could even get out of the house he had to sit down on the carpet by the telephone in the hallway, his breath coming hard and piercing, something still moving in the corner of his eye. A thump somewhere. And what he did was he sat with his back as straight as possible against the wall. In through the nose, out through the mouth, just like Clare taught him. Control the breathing. Breathe away the itching, the skin crawling, the desire to scratch. He zoned in on the buzzing of the fridge in the kitchen, and the radio. And back to his breathing. He picked up the telephone and listened to the dial tone. That started to helplplppppppamsnfgbfnsppplleeeehhlm nsnnnakakakknenenenoteenotdddllsaaaammslslsldfmf gnghtjealamsddmdngbgyo

---

OFF-AIR, a phone call:

'Hello?'

'Hello, Ann?'

'This is she.'

'Ann, it's Lou. From *Talk To Tony*? On the radio?'

'Ah, Lou! How are you, my love?'

'I'm good, girl, good. And how are you keeping? Battling away there?'

'I am, girl. Sure you know yourself. Taking each day as it comes.'

'Yea… I… And how are the offspring?'

'Ah, great. She's here, annoying me about vitamins, and he's gone back up to the tech til Friday.'

'That's great, girl… Listen, I'm only ringing ahead of your call with Tony on the radio in a little bit, to make sure that everything's okay and you're still on for it?'

'Ah, you're very good. I'm looking forward to it.'

'Great. So Tony will just ask you how you are, and how treatment is going. How is treatment going? You'd a setback, did you?'

'Yea. Well, you know me, Lou, I'm used to them by now. I had a procedure recently and I'm back on the chemo for another six months. But lookit, I'm coping. There's plenty worse off. But listen, I've some good news too for a change.'

'Oh, we love good news! Go on?'

ON-AIR

LARRY

Tony, I'll put it to ya this way: there'd be an awful lot more bad things happening if there weren't these fine women providing a service to men who… y'know… might be a bit *lonely*… See, us men, we're poorly made, right. Sure anyone can tell ya that. We're poorly made from a psychological point of view, like. We've no pressure release and so we act the idiot. We bottle things up and we explode then. War, abuse, that's all in us, Tony. Toxic is the word for us, Tony, but it's like a toxic pressure cooker, a man's body. And certain bodily functions, Tony… Well, getting that bit of release is essential, whether a fella has an auld doll or not…

TONY

So you're in favour of legalisation, Larry?

LARRY

Oh I am, Tony.

TONY

And are you speaking from personal experience, Larry?

LARRY

Wha?

TONY

Have you used a prostitute before is what I'm saying. You seem very opinionated on the matter.

LARRY

Arra yea, I have, Tony.

TONY

You have?!

LARRY

Arra, I'm hardly the pillars of society, Tone!

TONY

Well fair play to you for your honesty, Larry, if nothing else.

LARRY

Sure that's the way it goes...

TONY

James says by text that some of these women are very dear. Shelly says that Larry would want to get his head checked. Now, Larry, I've Deirdre on the line here with a question, if you don't mind?

LARRY

Fire away!

TONY

Are you on the line, Deirdre? You're on *Talk To Tony* and Larry is waiting for your question.

DEIRDRE

Hi Tony, love the show! Hi, Larry!

LARRY

How're you getting on, Deirdre?

DEIRDRE

Larry, if you don't mind my saying, you don't sound like a spring chicken. If you don't mind my saying!

LARRY

Not at all. I'm sixty-three years young, Deirdre girl.

DEIRDRE

So how d'you make it with these women of the night? At that age? Is there something you can tell my husband that he doesn't know about please?!

LARRY

Aha! See Deirdre, I'm great pals with this little blue pill...

DEIRDRE

Doubt ya, Larry boy! I knew it!

LARRY

Sure I've been taking it years.

TONY

And have you any advice for interested listeners,
Larry?

LARRY

Well, Tony, I'll put it like this. Don't be doing
the dog on the pints with it, because it doesn't
work then. What happens then is you get
nothing on the night in question and you wake
up then in the morning with a huge *búdán* on
you—

TONY

Larry we better leave it right there! That's what
my kids call *too much information*. More after
these—

[static] jingles and advertisements redacted [static]

———

TONY

Now, she shouldn't be here. Stage four ovarian
cancer. Diagnosed three years ago. She
shouldn't be here. And yet – this is just making
my day, to have her on the line – here she is.
Ann, love, are you there?

ANN

I am, Tony boy.

TONY

Now that's just made my day. How are you,
Ann?

ANN

Surviving, Tony! Given til Christmas this time!

228

TONY

Ann, if it's not too intrusive a question – and
you know me, I'm just not like that – you've
been through the wringer with cancers for years
now; are you surprised to still be here?

ANN

I suppose in a way I am. But sure, Tony, who'd
cook dinner only for me? There'd be no dinner
only for me!

TONY

You're gas, Ann! But remind us. Given six
months all those years ago, you fought and
fought, and you've been checking in with us
regularly enough since you first moved listeners'
hearts that first time, and they've been asking
for you ever since and here you are still…

ANN

Well, I am I suppose. But what else would
anyone do? I'm not ready to go, I suppose…

TONY

And what kind of a… of a mental toll does that
take on a person – that struggle? Fighting for so
long?

ANN

Ah, you know yourself, Tony…

TONY

Do you know what I mean, Ann? Like, how do
you keep going?

ANN

… Yea, I know what you mean. Sure you know
yourself. I suppose, Tony, life has always been a
struggle for me. To find work, to find a home,
to raise kids, to pay the rent… I mean, Tony,
when our two were only in nappies I was going

to Vincent De Paul with the hand out, looking
for every little bit of help I could get. We slept
on my sister's couch for a number of weeks.
Life has always been a struggle that way. Cancer
is just another thing to deal with, you know?
I mean, who said life was supposed to be easy
anyway?

TONY

I hear you, Ann... So what are the doctors
saying now?

ANN

Well, I stopped responding to the last thing so
it's chemo again. I'm in the middle of that now
and then it's watch and wait again.

TONY

And how do you *feel*, Ann?

ANN

Well, I don't feel great, Tony, being honest, but
I'm not one for complaining... Especially when
I see the children who are going through the
same thing. It's much worse for them like. I say
private prayers for those children, Tony.

TONY

God, yea. And how are your own children? Well,
they're not children anymore I suppose—

ANN

They're great. They're a great support. Very
positive, very helpful. And sure they're sick of
me too, as always...

TONY

Hah! And are you yourself positive, Ann? About
everything?

ANN

Of course, Tony. You have to be. Sure you have
to be. There's no point being here if you're

230

going to be moping around feeling sorry for
yourself.

TONY

You're great gas, girl. And tell me, do you spend
time like this taking stock of your life? Like,
y'know, thinking about decisions and regrets
and things like that?

ANN

Not for one second, Tony. A) I don't have time
for stuff like that. I'm still caught up in all the
daily stuff: the appointments, the procedures,
the group meetings, keeping fit and healthy,
filling the fridge with food, getting the rent
paid, the dinner made, all that stuff. And B),
maybe the thing we never realise is that –
regrets, decisions, all that stuff in the past –
none of that really matters. Whatever you did at
the time, you did it for a reason, and it's gone
now. You can't change it, and really it doesn't
matter a damn whether it was the right thing
or not. What you come to realise, what I've
come to realise, is that life itself is the thing;
living – that's all that matters. Life is to be
cherished in whatever form you have it. That's
the thing.

TONY

...

ANN

...

TONY

... You're an amazing human being, Ann. Jeez,
I'm lost for words... And so, look, tell us about
life since we last spoke. I hear you don't hang
about?

ANN

Ahyea like, I knew you'd ask! Well, yes, I remarried.

TONY

Congratulations! Who's the lucky fella?

ANN

Arra, Jerry's been about years. It was just nice to celebrate it, you know?

TONY

I do, girl. We're all delighted for you here. Well, go easy, Ann, look after yourself, and we'll check in with you again soon.

ANN

Thanks, Tony. Mind yourself!

TONY

Amazing woman, that. God. Now, Ann mentioned her experience sleeping on her sister's couch, and we're going to go back to the topic of homelessness next. It took up a lot of our time yesterday, *and rightly so* – but there's more to be said. The calls, texts and emails have been flying in, so don't go anywhere or you might—

———

ANDY

Look, Tony, someone has to be the one to say it, right, but all these people who are homeless – someone has to say it, how did you get here?
I mean, Tony, I can promise you it'd never happen to me because I'd never let it happen. I made my mortgage repayments for thirty years. Never missed one because I made it a priority. I put it before the nights out, before the holidays, before fancy clothes. Before the second homes. These people who are homeless – they put something else before rent. I'm certain of

232

it. Before the mortgage. It might have been
drink or it might've been drugs, or holidays or
holiday homes or clothes or *whatever*, right, but
this is what you get when you live beyond your
means. I'm sorry to say it but it's true. They've
only themselves to blame, Tony.

TONY

But, Andy, hold on, right. A lot of these people
are *normal people*. We're not talking about addicts
here; we're talking about people who bought
houses at the height of the boom and now just
can't afford the mortgages. They bought beyond
their means perhaps, but—

ANDY

Exactly, Tony. They bought beyond their means.
Who's to blame for that? No one put a gun to
their heads like...

TONY

So you feel no sympathy for them at all? People
who were perhaps encouraged to take out loans
or mortgages, or second mortgages, or one
hundred per cent mortgages? Or people who
were simply priced out of renting? Or given
eviction notices by greedy landlords and can't
now afford the rental market as it is?

ANDY

None. They should have read the terms and
conditions. They should have worked and saved
for that rainy day like the rest of us. Because it's
always coming, Tony. And look, there are way
sadder cases out there, Tony. People who can do
nothing at all about what happens to them. In
Africa, for example. And in the countries where
Americans and Russians fight out their mockea
wars.

TONY
Right, well, I can tell you that Debbie feels
differently. She's on line two. Debbie?

DEBBIE
That caller there has no sympathy for the
homeless; I wonder does he have sympathy for
all the millionaires, billionaires, politicians and
bankers who caused all this? The people who
we – *the citizens of this country* – had to bail out?
Does he factor that into his sums? The people
who walked away scot free and who we now
pay increased taxes for?

TONY
Well said, Debbie. And, look, for anyone who
wasn't listening earlier, Alchemy up on Barrack
Street are offering free teas, coffees, soups and
sandwiches to people who are experiencing
homelessness *all day today*. And they're
encouraging people who aren't sleeping rough
to head up along there too, take advantage of
a discounted tea, and just share their stories.
Experiences. Just listen. Be sound, they're
saying. You don't have to prove anything, or
explain yourself, just head up there and avail
yourselves of their hospitality and have a bloody
chat. That's all. Reach across the boundary. I
think it's a lovely idea, and a good local business
there too, Alchemy...

———

A VOICE
And what are they building, Tony? Hotels.
Hotels.

———

A VOICE
And like, what use is a bloody car with tens of

234

thousands of our own homeless? Are yeer heads
screwed on right or what?

———

A VOICE
And, like, Tony, I was in a WhatsApp group with
that man!

———

TINNNNADMDFMFLFLGMHNTHEDKA
SSLFPFGOTIGHNENFBFBFBSN IN
THESTATIC the worst thing was that Tabitha
was out there somewhere, in the city that very
day. And maybe she was injured or maybe she was
just lost. Searching the air for a familiar scent,
or on a high wall somewhere, looking out for some
place or thing she recognised, or trying to sleep
behind some wheelie bin, or just hiding, afraid
and uncertain. Maybe she was trapped in a shed,
starving, or crouched by the back window of a
house, off an unfamiliar street, scavenging for
food with a broken body. If she were lost, or hurt,
would she have the same habits? Would she want
to smell the underside of people's shoes? Would
she look to each side suspiciously as she ate?
Cover her eyes with a paw as she slept? And were
the other cats of the city helping her, or not?
   Or maybe she was just dead. Hit by a car and
flung into the river or a bin. Or caught and torn
apart by dogs.
   Yes — the worst thing was that she was out
in the city, somewhere, but might be alive or
dead, breathing or starving or decomposing. Well,
actually — the worst thing was not knowingggggggg
gmmmhngntnthehjjjjjjjjjjjjjjjjjjjjjafnfbdnandppoe
errllmdnandbffff

235

ON-AIR

TONY
—because when the history books look back
it'll be seen as one of the biggest blights on
our society in these decades. But we're going
to sidestep homelessness now for a moment
because we think we have some breaking news.
We think we've made a breakthrough in a case
we've been trying to solve on *Talk To Tony* for a
while now, the case of AERO, a *so-called* graffiti
artist, a gurrier basically, ruining the walls of
our city with his tag. Scrawling it on walls,
doorways, shop shutters, bollards, hoardings...
You name it, basically. And never getting
caught. Well, we've a caller now – she doesn't
want to give her name, so we're going to call
her Sarah – and she says that she knows who
AERO is. So... *Sarah*... you're very brave for
calling in. Tell us what you know.

                                        'SARAH'
                                           ...

TONY
Sarah, are you there?

                                        'SARAH'
                                          Yea.

TONY
What do you know about AERO, Sarah?

                                        'SARAH'
        Emm, just... Look, it's not what you think.
        Everyone thinks this is some scumbag wanting
                 to... [audible sigh; a struggle to
                                    articulate]

236

TONY
Well what is he then, Sarah, if he's not a
scumbag?

'SARAH'
Eh... It's, like... eh... [a long silence]... It's
just... [further silence] You... ah, fuck it.
Fuck off. Fuck ye. [a click]
TONY
... Sarah? She's gone without so much as a
goodbye or a thank you, but plenty of effs and
jays. Pretty rude if you ask me. But look, never
mind her, what do *you* think? Give us a call,
send us a text, or daub your opinion on the
comments section of our various social *meeja*
pages...

OFF-AIR, she stood there with the phone in her hand,
shaking like a leaf.

OFF-AIR, they had achieved the countryside within
minutes – the second last week of the road trips – rising up out of
Blackpool into the hills and wide fields, where the turbines and
pylons rose, where the hidden rivers coursed and the soil shifted
and the ditches marked human boundaries. On the radio came a
report of an elderly couple murdered in their home in Montenotte.
Neighbours had raised the alarm and a man in his twenties had
been detained. Tony picked his nose. Lou was thinking about her
mother – things coming back to her like helping Mam into the
toilet, onto it, off of it, out of it. Once she was in constant pain
she had unravelled completely. Weeping, struggling for breath,
delirious, she had said to Lou that last day, from her hospital bed:
'Society still has use for the dignified man. The watch. The suit.'
That was as profound as it got that last day.

237

What it had meant, Lou had no idea. Maybe it was something Granddaddy had said to her, way back, a morphine echo as her life flickered before her eyes.

'Tell me,' Tony suddenly asked the passing scenery. 'Is Marta your first love?'

'Jesus, Tony! I dunno. Probably not, no… But she's probably the first love I had who loved me in return. Probably? I mean, what even is love?'

'Aye,' he agreed, suddenly sullen.

'Buttevant,' he read as they passed another country town's welcome sign. 'Twinned with Plourivo, France.'

'What *is* the twinning of towns?' Lou asked, yawning.

'Don't know. A business arrangement, maybe?'

'Or maybe a cultural thing? Like student exchanges in schools or something?'

'Maybe.'

By now they were crawling through the main thoroughfare of Buttevant in a line of heavy traffic that had appeared out of nowhere. Houses and local businesses gave a guard of honour on both sides of the street.

'These one-street towns,' Tony said. 'I love them. Everything about them is familiar to me.'

'…'

'*You* wouldn't know,' he said. 'You're from the *burbs*. You wouldn't know the feeling of living in a town. Knowing everyone. And even if you didn't *know* the person, you knew the face. You'd have seen them around. And if you hadn't seen them around, they were a stranger. A blow-in.'

Lou eased them over the speed bumps, and Tony nodded towards the young woman in activewear pushing a buggy on the left-hand pavement.

'See her now. And see him on the other side of the road? Him wiping the bird shit from his windscreen? They might or might not know each other by name, but even if they don't, she'll recognise him, and he her. She'll know something of his

238

routine – "Oh, he's usually off to work by now," or something like that. And he'll know whether it's her first child or second or whatever. He'll have some observation or comment on the father of that child. Everyone in a town like this is a detective, you see. The curtains in these places twitch, the windows squint, and that's how the soul of the town keeps going, how the heart of it keeps pumping. Completely different to the burbs or the city, where most are anonymous. In a town like this, everyone notices the change of colour if a house is painted, and everyone has an opinion on it. They're all woven into the town's history that way... Opinions...

'And moods get picked up on the breeze, Lou. I remember days where everyone in Passage seemed to be in the same glum mood, as if it was a cold going round.'

'Wasn't there a book with that name? *The Squinting Windows* or something?'

'Probably.'Tony yawned now, holding on to the handle above his window. 'Yerra, I suppose all that means is that every langer in the place thinks they own every other langer.'

Lou nearly laughed out loud. 'I was thinking that exactly, and you making your grand speech!'

'Aye. I suppose there's nothing so special about it after all!' He barked a laugh. 'Jesus... first love, hah! What kind of a mood am I in at all?'

ON-AIR

KEITH
So it's National Dog Fouling Awareness Week, Nathan. Can you tell us why this is an important week for dog owners?

NATHAN
Well the idea, Keith, is to improve awareness of the damage that indiscriminate dog fouling

> does to our towns and cities. I mean, I don't
> know about you guys, but, I mean, is there
> anything worse? You're walking along, and you
> feel something strange underfoot – you don't
> quite land right – and you look down and… *oh
> Jaysus…*

OFF-AIR, Galway drew closer, and relentlessly the calls came in. One caller wouldn't be seen dead picking up after a dog. Another said stepping in dog doo was worse than a dig in the face. Lou pointed out a sparrow-hawk perched atop a mound of sand on a construction site, but Tony missed it. With the windows open they heard the rush of wind and the flat grind of the Mazda's wheels on the road.

> **A VOICE**
> **The yellow weather warning that has been in**
> **place for the west coast has been upgraded to**
> **orange—**

'I was walking our dog, years ago,' Lou grinned. 'Now, Mosca always had a bit of a grá for eating other dogs' shit, you know the way they do…'

'Jaysus…'

'I know! You'd be roaring at her to stop. So we're walking through the park and Mosca's off the lead, and up ahead there's this woman with her child, a little toddler, probably two or less. And I didn't really get it at the time but it's clear to me now that either the woman was in the middle of potty-training the child, or she'd forgotten to bring spare nappies. Or something like that. Because all of a sudden, in the distance, I see her pulling down the child's pants and airlifting the child to the side of the path. Holding her out over the grass, you know? The child then started shitting, held out from her mammy's arms like that, knees all bent and all. Sound. No problem. It happens. But then I see Mosca cantering up to them and she's very interested in them, Tony. Head up, tail wagging.'

Tony's hand clenched the handle above him in the doorway.

'And she gets to them, Tony, and her tail is going ninety and she does that little sniff, and then, very politely positions herself so that she can catch the child's shit in her mouth as it falls from the child's arse—'

His hand came up to his face: 'Fucking hell…'

'Tongue out, Tony. Happy as Larry.'

'Jesus Christ.'

'I was fucking mortified.'

'Jesus Christ. That is the most disgusting thing I've ever heard.'

Tony started laughing then, because what else could he do, and Lou started laughing as well, explaining how the child's mother had laughed too, thank god. Embarrassment never killed anyone yet, her mother had often said to her. And then, on the radio, word emerged that British police had shot and killed two US backpackers on the steps of a West End tube station. The end was nigh, a texter said.

PAPQLWKDMSNDJGHFTNEBDJSKA SLAPWOEMTNRHENDBFGRHFMDMS LAPWEDSLKEMDNGHTEMANDHWEKS PEOEMDNFGOOOOANMDNSBENHI N THEST ATIC the interviewer leaned forward over her plastic bottle of water. 'Darren, look, thanks a million for coming in and for your time — we appreciate that it was short notice.'

'Oh, it's no bother at all, girl. I'm mad to get back to work so any notice at all was fine by me.'

'Appreciate that… so that's one of the ques- tions actually. It looks from your CV like you've

241

the experience to do the job — look, it's pallet assembly, it's not rocket science — but there is a big gap in the CV which, I suppose, you know… we have to ask about that.'

'Yah, I get that. I totally understand.'

'…'

'…'

'So… was it a period of illness? Or education that's maybe missing off the CV? I just can't see anything there filling in that eighteen months?'

'Oh, yah. Well, look. Look… look, I suppose the thing is…'

'Do you want some water there?'

'Yea, thanks… thanks… sorry. It's not easy. I suppose the thing is there was a bit of a wobble. We let things go. I let myself go. A bit of a mental health wobble. Some personal stuff, and look, we lost the gaff then. The house. And the money wasn't there to get ourselves sorted. I don't know what to say to you. I don't want to make excuses. Except to say that things got bad, and it was all my own fault. And then they got worse. And here I am now with two daughters and a partner and the four of us are in the one room in a guesthouse and we're completely helpless. Completely at the mercy of the state. Unless I can get this job. My daughters are six and fourteen. They… you know, they don't deserve this. If I can get a start, get some money together, and get us back in a house, then we can find a way back. I'm really not meaning to guilt-trip you or anything — believe me. I'm the one who should feel guilty. My own life choices got me here, where my own daughter doesn't even… I let this happen. It's nobody's fault but my own. We're homeless. But

242

trust me I have been crucifying myself. I am up
here on the cross and I put myself here. My whole
family here... but, you know, fresh start and all
that... this job would be the first step back for
me. Honestly, not trying to guilt-trip you, girl,
I'm just trying to be honest. I know I can do
this job; I know I'm able. I have good references
from... before... you know, before the last one. That
was a shitty... but all my fault. But a fresh start
here... I can promise you I won't let you down. I
can guarantee you there's no one out there needs
this job more than me. Will cherish it more than
me. I've let people down before — sure, I won't
lie to you — but that's how I know I won't do it
this time. I need this more than I've ever needed
anything. Do you know what I mean????neammmmnsbdb
ndsdkfkgthenamsmsmddnfbdjfjgjawawwwweasdcmgnfhrm
elloiismmdnebssnammma

OFF-AIR, looking out the window of the hotel room onto
Galway Bay, he called her.
'Lorraine?'
'Speaking?'
'Lorraine, it's Tony? Tony Cooney?'
'Tony!'
'Lolly? Is that you?'
'It is! God, Tony. It's so strange to hear your voice on the
phone, after all these years. Mad. How are you? Where are you?
Thanks so much for your messages.'
'Lolly, we're in Galway believe it or not. Salthill tonight.
Myself and my producer are on Galway radio in the morning.'
'Wow. You're that close, after all these years. You sound the
exact same now as you did then, Tony. The very same.'
'How are you? How are things in the pub?'

'Grand, Tony. All good. It's very quiet here – it's a tiny place. Very quiet. Not like Lewisham you know! It was strange at first, but it's *so* beautiful. And the punters are lovely, like a family.'

'God, I can imagine.'

Flattening his hair, combing it with his free hand, pulling at it, looking out the window. Sitting down, standing up, kneeling on the soft seat of the chair. Wanting to say that while their bodies might age their voices didn't, because she sounded the very same too.

'God, it's really your voice, Tony.'

'What are you doing in Ireland, Loll?'

'I came home three years ago. To run a pub for Daddy.'

'Three years! Are you serious?'

'Yep. Mad, isn't it?'

'Where's this pub? We might call out to you after we've done our bit on the radio tomorrow. Myself and Lou. She wants to visit her mother's homeplace.'

'Lou?'

'My producer.'

'Ah. It's... I'll message you the directions. It's a bit complicated. A townland called Lochán.'

'Do. Great. God, it'll be great to see you.'

'...'

'And how is your father, Lolly?'

'Alive and well. Too old to leave London but he wanted me to come back before I got too old. The pub was a sort of gift I suppose.'

'Are you not worried about him now?'

'Sure what would terrorists want with an eighty-seven-year-old Paddy sitting in a dark pub in Catford?'

The girl reared in the same pub. The daughter of every punter, well used to the cushion of every knee in the place.

'...'

'Tony, I'd love to see you. To meet you again. It'd be great to chat.'

244

'It would, Loll… It'd be great, I mean. But we're on a tight schedule here. Tomorrow look, we'll call in. Before we head back to Cork.'

'That'd be perfect. Stop in for lunch… We do a great toastie – on me of course!'

'We'll do that so! Jesus, it's been a long time, Lolly.'

'It has. Twenty-six years I think.'

'And your voice hasn't changed. Not one bit.'

'Yours neither, despite your bigshot radio career.'

'Hah! What's the name of your pub?'

'The Silver Branch. On the main road as you pass through the town. I'll message you the directions, and if you've any trouble just ring me.'

'Right. Well, we'll see you tomorrow so, Lolly?'

Just to say her name aloud…

'I can't wait, Tony.'

'Me neither. Til then, Lolly.'

'Good luck with the radio.'

'Thanks, Lolly.'

'Bye, Tony.'

'Bye, now.'

'Bye, bye.'

'Bye.'

'Bye.'

'Bye.'

'Take care now.'

'…'

'…'

MMLLLDJKGKKFINNNNDDDERNNDH
HSSSAKSMDNFBGHRALAPWPEOREO
TIYTUNGMSNDFMWWMAPAKLFKGMH
NGFHEERHERHEHRERHERHSDNDND
KKKFDL I NT HESTAT IC Lou's father

245

was sat on the couch, with a glass of red resting on its arm and a shoebox full of photographs in his lap. Photos of Áine and himself before the kids, on holidays in Dublin, or in the early days of the first house in Mahon, when he still worked for the post office. Then, photo by photo, Deb and Lou started to appear, as babies first, then little girls, and the rooms changed and the tents from the camping holidays changed, green to blue, and Mosca appeared, and the faces went from young, chubby and dirty to thin and made up, and the graininess of the photos sharpened and the hairdos changed, and then at a certain point Áine was gone from them, and only a few after that he got to the bottom of the box. Had they stopped taking pictures when she died? He flipped back through them all slowly, pulling each one from the shoebox up to his gaze, and then down into his lap, and when he got to the end again he put them all back in the shoebox and started once moreeee eeeeeeeeeeedddddddddffffffffffffffffuuuuuuuuuuukkkmj hhhhhhalapslalheeeeelllllllpppmmmmmmnnndddkkkffmgn gnhbfkakfmdsappwedkdkdnsbweebdbs

---

OFF-AIR, the following morning, Tony and Lou were directed in through the gates of a city centre primary school yard by the waving arms of the woman from the Galway radio station.

'The heroes arrive!' she cried, leaning a curly head of hair in Tony's open window. 'Fáilte romhaibh a Gaillimhe! How is the day treating ye?'

'Howdy!' Tony said, surveying the yard. 'All good so far! What's the plan?'

'Well I'm feeling borderline perky now, Tony!' she beamed. 'We've it all set up. No one knows yet – they only know it's

the city. The phones are on fire. The school's in on it, and we're going to get the kids to line the yard. They're gonna sing for the crowd – they're in there now practising away. The principal's a good friend of mine – fine singer himself actually. We'll call it in then in about ten minutes.'

'Where should we park up?'

'Right here in the yard is grand. Right where you are; we'll set up around you.'

Lou noticed for the first time that a posse of young people were assembling things in the corner across the coloured bright swirling lines of the schoolyard.

'Is there a toilet I can quickly use?' she asked.

The woman pointed. 'Straight on through to the school reception there.'

'Is there a toilet I can use?' she asked a receptionist inside, who lifted a dour hand from his work to point the way of double glass doors.

'Through there on the left.'

Stepping into the corridor of a primary school was like suddenly being in a dream of the past: twisted and strange, but somehow so familiar to her as a space. The sound of the children's singing practice somewhere was faint but true, and she stopped to admire some of the children's artwork on the wall. It was, of course, Dog Fouling Awareness week in the Galway school too, and pencilled and painted pictures of dogs on A4 paper ran the length of the corridor. Age ranges and qualities varied, but she was taken in particular by a work of great skill, done by a ten-year-old named Grace, depicting a red setter taking a shit. There was no background, only white paper, but the colouring and posture of the animal was perfect, the positioning of the forepaws and hind quarters, the tongue hanging out, the dog half smiling, looking west off the page in a moment's contemplation. The artwork was so good that she could almost see the dog's flanks quivering as its bowels processed excrement. She thought of Mosca, her best friend so many years. She wondered about herself and Marta having a ten-year-old named Grace walking the halls of their apartment with a picture she'd drawn, calling her two mams to show them. She thought of the white witch's house. Of sleeping with the white witch in her filthy house. Could the brain never stop fucking things up?

'The principal is a good friend,' the radio station woman was saying to Tony again when Lou returned to the car. 'Fine singer too. Great man for a blast of Sinatra.'

In those few minutes the yard had been transformed, with an area cordoned off with maroon ribbon and the pullup banners of sponsors. These were set up in a line leading directly to the car. Passersby lingered at the wall to see what was going on. Every second person seemed to be on their mobile phone. And then a woman came screeching through the gate, making for the car until one of the radio people snagged her and took her aside and began to ask her questions while she stared with a child's gape at the Mazda.

Presently, a mild, grey-suited principal emerged from the double doors to cross that yard and to welcome Lou and Tony to the school. Shallow of face and pale of skin, he reminded Lou of someone: a face, a memory. It would come back to her.

The principal was proud of the kids. He was childhood friends with Michelle, he informed them, laying a friendly hand on the radio woman's shoulder. Michelle was a great guitarist, he informed them.

'This is going to be very special,' he said, as the teachers began to lead troops of children out the double doors to line up in the yard. Lou gasped performatively, and as they stood out of the car they were enveloped in the footfall and breath and giddiness of children, chatter and laughter and squealing and then hush, and then perfect smiling and perfect posture and perfect lines, and all of a sudden, a soft drizzle materialised across all their shoulders.

Memories of school flitted, fell like tiny drops on the fresh, wet air. The excitement of the line in the morning. Copy books. Windows with green and grey wonders beyond, and the freedom of the sky. Snot wiped in the hand and spread then across the

248

back of the skirt. Tennis ball games. Chessies. Life was made up of moments, but were moments not made up of things? Buck teeth. Loose ties. A broken pair of glasses. A warm bath to ease the worms. Deb with whooping cough, and the fear of Deb dying. An argument in the wall. A rat out the back of the swimming pool. Dad lifting her up on his shoulders so she could change the light bulb. A broken terracotta plant pot placed carefully back together. The Galway schoolchildren began to sing: '*Dirty old river, must you keep rolling, flowing into the night? / People so busy, make me feel dizzy, taxi light shines so bright…*'

And there were hand actions suddenly.

'*But I doooooooon't feel afraid! / As long as I gaze on Waterloo sunset, I am in paradise…*'

Tony and Lou stood and listened with their hands at their sides and vague smiles on their faces, poses usually reserved for the national anthem.

ON-AIR

GARY
Well, it's the moment we've been talking about all morning, all week in fact – a brand new car to be given away to anyone who's come back from London because of the attacks. The great Tony Cooney and his producer Lou have been driving this brand new Mazda 2 around the country the last three weeks, from Cork to Waterford to Dublin to here, and it's no longer a secret that they're now, as we speak, nestled in the yard there at St Pat's. And the kids provided the song we just heard, and there's already a fine crowd there, and I'm joined on the line now by the great man himself. Tony?! Such

249

an honourable competition, this – a car for a
returned exile, and a year's free petrol too...

TONY

Well, it's great, isn't it? Of course it's all down
to Jerry Collins at Jerry Collins Motors in Cork.
He told me he just wants to do his bit to help
connect people, Gary, amidst all the chaos. I
wish we could sort them out with homes and
jobs too, but we can't...

GARY

And tell me now, Tony, more importantly, who
is the bauld winner of the Galway leg of the
journey?

TONY

Well, Gary, I've a feisty woman here in the
passenger seat by the name of Lorna White and
I'll put her on to you now.

GARY

Hello, Lorna?

LORNA

Hello, Gary! Oh my god!

GARY

Oh my indeed! You caught us out good and
early I hear, Lorna?

LORNA

I've been following the story on the internet
all week and I was only passing through town
getting some messages when I saw the car!

GARY

Tell me, Lorna, where are you from?

                              LORNA

      I'm from Oughterard, but I only came back
      from London three weeks ago. When they hit
                  Stockwell, well, enough was enough.
GARY

Were you living near there?

                              LORNA

      I was, Gary. Living *right there*. I was working in
      a pub there called The Crown and we heard the
                        gunfire and the sirens—
GARY

My god. You were working at the time?

                              LORNA

      I was working at the time, Gary. I was on the
      day shift and one of the lads, Davey, he came
      in from a shmoke and he said to me that he
      thought he heard popping from the direction of
      the Swan. He said to me, Gary, he said, Lorna,
      don't be surprised if it's all kicking off down
      there. Well I didn't believe it of course. But
      we all like shpeculating and telling shtories of
      course, but so I went out anyway to have a look
      and I just saw people running in all directions,
      Gary, and I swear I saw a man with a machete
      as well, walking down the middle of the road
                        talking to himself—
GARY

[radio silence; expert, audible intake
of breath] And what did ye do, Lorna?

                              LORNA

      Well, Podge was there having a pint with his
      Daily Star, and Podge used be a London county
      hurler, a big strong buck, so I just asked him to
      come help me quick and we pulled the shutters

most of the way down and closed the door, and
I didn't know then whether to close it or not
because maybe we could help people who were
running away from it all. So we did that then.
We started trying to get a few people in and
Podge was holding the shutter up himself so
that he could drop it if they came for us... And,
well, we got a few in, but then the popping
noises got louder so we just dropped the
shutters and locked the doors inside and pulled
the curtains—

GARY

And how long were ye locked in the pub there?

LORNA

Chrisht, Gary, a good couple of hours. We'd a
couple of brandies to settle the nerves, then
said some prayers, and then by and by we had a
little sing-song!

GARY

You're joking me...

LORNA

Well some of us were singing and some of
us watched what was going on on the news.
Horses for courses I suppose.

GARY

And so, Lorna, tell me, you didn't stay long in
London after that?

LORNA

Only long enough to sub-let our flat and try to
persuade everyone that it was the right thing to
do. And then of course you've to drum up the
money to get everyone home. It wasn't easy but
we got back eventually.

GARY
And did you get everyone home?

LORNA
...

GARY
Lorna?

LORNA
[sobbing] ... My aunt... my beloved aunt...

GARY
Lorna?

LORNA
Oh my aunt, Gary, I miss her! [sobbing]

GARY
I'm sorry, Lorna...

LORNA
[sobbing]

GARY
I hate to ask, Lorna, but is she a victim of the
London Troubles?

LORNA
She's refusing to come home, Gary. She won't
budge!

GARY
Right. God. I wish there was something more I
could say...

LORNA
She says she's too old to change.

GARY
... I suppose you'd love to have her home
today?

LORNA
I would. More than anything, Gary. She was like
a mother to me over there. She went to

253

London as a midwife in the seventies. Delivered
thousands of English babies.

GARY

Tell me, Lorna, what would the car mean to you?

LORNA

Everything, Gary, everything. Maybe I'd even
drive the car over, if I won it, to get her. Right
through all the chaos, and I'd get my aunt
back...

GARY

Well, Lorna, your name is in Friday's draw and I
hope for Galway's sake and your aunt's sake that
you're the winner...

OFF-AIR, as if they were diplomats, Tony and Lou shook
the small hands of children who squinted up at them through
spectacles and freckles and bruises. One child fainted; another
child handed them each a small scrap of paper with a pencil-
drawn smiley face on it.

Then Lorna came over and gave both of them big hugs as the
place emptied around them like a football ground after a game.
Shaking Tony's hand, she said, 'Is it you I have to suck off to make
sure my name comes out of the hat next Friday?'

She screeched laughter at the horror in his face, and then
turned utterly serious. 'Honestly though, I can't thank ye enough,
lads. I was in London fifteen years. From the age of nineteen. I
don't know myself being back here.'

She went in for hugs again then, gave them big wet kisses on
the cheek, and was soon dragged away to provide personal details
to the station.

Shut back into the car, back on their own, Tony sighed and
said, 'Will we strike out for Connemara so?'

'Are you sure you want to?' Lou asked. 'That weather warning
looks dodgy.'

254

'I've an idea,' Tony said. 'Why don't you drop me off at my friend's place in Lochán, then go visit your mother's homeplace, and we'll stay the night in Connemara then and drive home in the morning. With this storm due it's no weather to be driving long distances in anyway, and we're both off tomorrow and sure we could do with a bit of a relax in a beautiful place.'

Lou thought about it. 'Fuck it. Why not.'

ON-AIR

> **JUDY**
> **Gary, it's not that I've any problem with these people. Don't get me wrong. They are our own people and they are in a time of need. My problem is with these junked-up media terms.** *Displaced people.* **Like, in my personal** *OED,* **that's a person forced to flee from home. Well, unless I'm mistaken, are we not Irish? Are these people not returning home? Albeit in terrible circumstances, fair enough...**

GARY
'Tis a fair point, Judy. I've heard them referred to as returned exiles too, to be fair.

> **JUDY**
> **I mean** *displaced.* **Displaced? Aren't we all displaced in one way or another? I'm displaced. You're displaced. Everyone's displaced! I don't have to be shot at to be displaced, for god's sake!**

GARY
They're only words, Judy!

> **JUDY**
> **I know! It just annoys me when the media get their hands on them!**

255

OFF-AIR, his text to Nuala said:
Weather shocking. Meself + Lou gonna stay in Galway + drive back when the storm has past.

*

Her text to Marta said:
Luv we're going to stay in Connemara. Storm looking bad & Tony has a friend he wants to visit. Ring you in a bit but just to let you know you're cooking for yourself tonight! Xxxx

---

OFF-AIR, they drove north in the Mazda. Whole, momentary geographies and journeys were described by rainfall on the water-beaded windscreen, wiped clean each second by the mechanism, only for new, jittery droplets to begin traversing the glass again. Bitter rain drove down across the car and the coast road, fell so hard that the shoreline shimmered darkly, as if corrugated. He could just about make out the seaweed and plastic-strewn strands at the water's edge, and the odd wooden pallet shouldering wet green rock. His palms were drenched in sweat and he kept wiping them on the backs of his knees. What if he were to have a heart attack getting out of the car in Lochán? How would he explain that away?

Bold veil of rain that darkened the greens and greys and pale peaches of rural homes, fishermen's cottages and farmers' yards. It sounded like Lorna had arrived in London not long after he'd left, as if the place was exchanging captive Irish souls one for the other. How different was Stockwell to Lewisham? The Crown to The Joiner's? He remembered a drunk woman calling him a cunt one time because he hadn't stood up for the national anthem. He remembered looking at Lolly, who was doing a shift behind the bar as a favour, and thinking he could spend the rest of his days with her and want for nothing else. Despite being a cunt.

His belly felt tender now, also his heart. Or, the spaces around and beneath his heart. Was he, in actual fact, going to have a heart attack? The wind in the ditches along the road suddenly made him want to cry. His eye and chest trembled, the half-crumpled smiley face beaming up at him from the small damp scrap of paper in his hand.

'When we were in college,' Lou said. 'We studied this fella – a philosopher, or a mystic – and apparently he quit academia to work as a gardener in a house hotel – some kind of castle – up around here. Maybe we could stay there? Sure no one gives a shit how much the expense claims are anyway. Maybe we could even meet him?'

'Sounds like a great idea,' Tony said. 'I'm not worried about the dosh anyway.'

'Remember movement essential versus movement local? He's the movement guy.'

As they turned inland and wound into the country, the road itself became a dark, unnerving spectre, skinless, washed raw of grit, rippling water. He had no idea where that road was taking them, but Lou had the maps up. GPS co-ordinates, she informed him, were based on twelve satellites in space. Orbiting the earth, she said, pinpointing them and their world down to the nearest cubic metre. Pinning them to a grid that was the world. And yet here we are, Tony thought, going deeper and deeper into the country, with no idea what is water and what is road.

'I don't know whether we're even in Ireland anymore,' he grumbled, shoulders hunching forward into the dash, 'or under the fucking sea.'

'Try driving in it, Tone,' Lou said drily.

Feeling completely nervous then, utterly rattled, he turned up the radio.

ON-AIR

CORNELIUS

Gary, listen to me. It boggles the mind. There
we were in 2004, fields turned into lakes.
Homes washed out. Lives lost. Livestock lost.
Livelihoods lost. Memories destroyed. Photo
albums, Gary. Family heirlooms. Items of
furniture hundreds of years old. And these
gangsters from Leinster House... I'm very close
to using unbroadcastable language here, Gary...

GARY

I understand where you're coming from,
Cornelius, but please don't!

CORNELIUS

Well, these, shall we say *charlatans*, in
government... they *say* it's an outrage. They
say that something must be done about the
flooding. They announce figures. Budget plans.
They cut red tape. They get their pictures
taken in welly boots and high-vises, next to
boats and sandbags, Gary. As if they're doing
something. They make empty promises and
they get elected by desperate people based
on their empty promises. And I mean people
who are *desperate*, Gary. Desperate for hope...
Desperate for a chance to live their lives... The
flooding of 2009, five years later. Was anything
different? No. Was any of their great promises
and policies and plans put into action? No.
Were we flooded yet again to within an inch
of our lives? Yes. Insurance companies? Won't
come near us. Won't touch it. I live between
two great pillars, Gary: nature and finance. And

258

one after the other they fall in on top of me.
And government do nothing. Those gangsters
in the Dáil are only finance yes-men. They think
Ireland is an economy; they forget it's a country.
A nation. I mean – Direct
Provision, homelessness, the way we treat our
native Travelling community? Like what the
actual *FUCK* is going on, Gary?

GARY
But—

CORNELIUS
THE POLITICIANS IN THIS COUNTRY
DO NOTHING, NOTHING TO HELP. WHEN
HELPING THE PEOPLE IS SUPPOSED TO
BE THE *SOLE* REASON THEY EXIST—

OFF-AIR, rain swept over and across the car as if there was
nothing else out there in that land only the voices they heard on
the radio. Tony's heart, at this stage, was pounding in his chest. It
was giving out on him altogether. It'd be less than an hour before
he saw her again. Mere minutes, after all these years. All this.

'I've lost the GPS signal again,' Lou said. 'Fuck's sake. The
reception is shocking.'

'The road has narrowed somewhat,' Tony informed her.

She gave him the side-eye.

But it had! The emerald smudges of ditches encroached upon
both sides of the car.

'We must be near Lochán,' Lou concluded, again. 'It must be
here somewhere?'

'Are my old eyes deceiving me,' Tony said, 'or is that grass
growing up the middle of the road?'

Then the radio began to flicker and—

ON-AIR

INDECIPHERABLE
—drone warfare has been illegal since *TSKDK*
FAKSKSDNDNFBGHREALSKDJDJFNFF **be**
using the technology the UN could*TIIDDKKFJ*
GGMHNFFFFFFFFFFFFFFFFFFFFFFFFFFFFFFF
FFFFFFFFFFFFFFFFFFFFFFFFFFFTFFFFFFFFF
FFFtact with some old*TFFFFFFFFFFFFFFFFFF*
FFFFFFFFFFFFFFFFFFFFFFFFFFFFFFFFFFFFF
FFFFFFFFrade in your car now*TFFFFFFFFFFFF*
FFFFFFFFFFFFFFFFFFFFFFFFFFFFFFFFFFFFF
FFFFFFFFFFFFFFFFFFFFFFFFFFFFFFFFFFFFF
FFFFFFFFat we're putting int*TFFFFFFFFFFFFFF*
FFFFFFFFFFFFFFFFFFFFFFFFFFFFFFFFFFFFF
FFtext only when saFe to do so*TFFFFFFFFFFFF*
FFFFFFFFFFFFFFFFFFFFFFFFFFFFFFFFFFFFF
FFFFFFFFFFFFFFFFFFFFFFFFFFFFFFFFFFFFF
FFFFFFFFFFFFFFFFFFFFFFFFFFFFFFFFFFFFF
FFFFFFFFFFFFFFFFFFFFFFFFFFFFF **all we really**
are*TFFFFFFFFFFFFFFFFFFFFFFFFFFFFFFFFFFFF*
FFFFFFFFFFFFFFFFFFFFFFFFFFFFFFFFFFFFF
FFFFFFFFFFFFFFFFFFFFFFFFFFFFFFFFFFFFF
FFFFFFFFFFF –

[hmmm... tricky business this... struggling here...]

[static, indecipherable]

OFF-AIR, then, all of a sudden, the two of them were leaning forward to peer through the windscreen, because, as if by magic or in a fairy tale, it appeared that the road ended in a gate. The journey ended.

In the split seconds of clarity between the drenching and clearing of the windscreen, what they saw beyond the gate was a long bungalow, whitewash evident beneath flurried ivy, and a black tiled roof that streamed. In front of the house was a sculpted garden – shrubs neither could name, small trees warped by country weather, neat lawn.

'Where in the fuck are we?' Lou complained to her phone. 'Sorry, Tony. Your pal will be waiting.'

Then out of the deluge a small grey thing caught Tony's eye – squarish, but rounded, like a toastie-maker on wheels.

'Do you see that thing?' he said to Lou, pointing.

Lou pressed forward. 'What thing?'

'A grey thing. Burrowing around in the grass there. A machine?'

And it was too. Zipping back and forth as if on important errands.

'D'you know what?' Lou smiled. 'I know what it is! I've heard about these. It's a robot lawnmower!'

Tony wiped the fog of his own breath from the windscreen, and cupping his hands had an uninterrupted vision of the robot. Like a remote-control car, or a moon voyager, it roamed back and forth across the lawn, in the rain.

'By Christ,' he said.

Here we are, he was thinking. Her looking for her dead mam's homeplace, me looking for god knows what, and the two of us at the end of a lane to nowhere, in the armpit of Ireland – with literally nowhere left to turn – and we are watching a robot mow a lawn in the pouring rain.

ON-AIR

OFF-AIR, through the rain, the car in reverse, Tony with his head out one window, watching the ditch, Lou with her head out the other, cursing and reversing. Fog and rain filled the rear-view and the back window. Leaving London in fog and rain, on the train to Brighton with Lolly, and somewhere outside the city sprawl the sky cleared and they saw pristine fields from the carriage window. London by the sea, some called Brighton. Beneath the red-brick arch of the railway line they held hands, relaxed now, released from some unspoken mental strain now that they were out of the capital. In a laneway bookshop Lolly showed him strange science-fiction covers: giant worms with crowns on their heads, fish men with guns, huge green birds locked in battles with spaceships. One book he remembered still was called *A Stainless Steel Rat for President.* They laughed. He ran his hand through his hair dramatically. He felt the dust of the bookshop in his lungs.

Tony with his head out into the rain, saying, 'You're okay on my side!' He felt his comb-over raised in the wind. Rain on his skull, his face. It felt like they'd been reversing for hours, with no space enough for a three-point turn anywhere. On the beach in Brighton, Lolly had gathered pebbles and was placing them on her broad denim thigh. The pebbles were various colours, bone white and earthy terracotta, and beautifully fossilised with streaks, spots, swirls, stripes and dashes. He began to help and it became serious work, and all the while they were chatting, finding ways into the future, into babies and returns to Ireland and gardens. No child of his would have an English accent, he insisted. He apologised. City was set against small town – she for one, he for the other – as the gulls swooped on ketchup-smeared chip paper. Her thigh soon hosted an assembly of pebbles. The sky was so blue now, and that was the same sky that was over Cork, she said. And beyond, he added. In fact, it went places they couldn't even fathom. Then they slept in the warmth of the sun; he could still feel the stones under his back now, and the heat on his closed eyelids, and her head in the nook of his armpit. They were not displaced then.

The gulls gathered. A few pigeons ventured amidst. People took their rubbish with them when they left, mostly. The seafront hotels and guesthouses faced that sky like it was oblivion. As he waited for her to come back from the toilets, he stared at the skeletal underside of Brighton Pier on the water. The lights of the arcade on the pier came on strong against the sky. He felt as if his life could be contained in that moment, as if captured in a photograph. While he would move on and she would move on, that moment was stamped in coin, and would last forever, rocking horses hanging from the ceiling of white plaster, and weak canteen tea and a stack of crumpling cardboard and the echoing voices of the arcade's glass dome; and her voice coming back to him, and the glorious triumph of her body eclipsing space, walking through the Brighton evening alongside him. And now himself and Lou reversing, through some wilderness, with rain falling all around them and grass up the middle of the road and cursing and readjusting and reversing again. Most of the time you think things and they are not real. Then sometimes you think something and it is real. You're in Brighton with someone you love, and it is a wonder how – with all the workings of logic and geography and history and the world and time – it is a wonder how it could actually be happening. And they finally reversed onto a crossroads and were able to turn the car the right way around.

'Listen,' Tony sighed. 'Never mind me visiting my pal. I'll catch her tomorrow. This is disastrous weather to be out in, and we don't have a fucking clue where we are.'

'Well,' Lou said agreeably, 'don't look now, but believe it or not there's our hotel.'

ON-AIR

[static, indecipherable]

BROADCASTING SIMULTANEOUSLY on 5264 kHz + 1420 MHz…

playback: the pale moon was rising above the green mountain / the sun was declining beneath the blue sea…

first voice: *[static] three… five… nine… two… they do say your life flashes before your eyes… but what if it was just a moment that did? some random few minutes or hours or days of your life? this, for example? or what if it was all already over? what if all these voices were already gone, wiped out by a noiseless light or a global virus or some digital or environmental catastrophe? or just your heart's last beating? what if the voices were just being broadcast on loop, via moss-covered masts? what if the last guy out of the building hit the REPEAT button, and what if that was years ago? what if the broadcast went out to an empty city? an empty world?*

second voice: *or just two lonely listeners… the reception coming and going…*

first voice: *listeners and speakers both, perhaps.*

264

second voice: *long-time listeners!*

first voice: *long-distance listeners!*

second voice: *jaypers. would that i had earlids like i have eyelids…*

[static, indecipherable]

EVOKE

aero

ZEL

nep

RANCID

DONT STEP ON MA MUTHAFUCKIN SHOES BIZO

MANIC SMOKE!

BOKEH

Yo EZZO

I ♥ CHIARA

SW7I

$7I

MERMAN

KAZ

MAUS

0894382137
4 A GUD TIME
SUCKY
SUCKEEEEEEEEEEEEE

FERRERO

ON-AIR

OFF-AIR, there it was, the Castle Hotel, or manor as it really was, ivy-clung, squat amidst the foliage, a forgotten monument from the colonial intrusion. And yet there was something of the fairy tale to it all, a huge mysterious house by a river in the woods. They came over a narrow humpback bridge, stopping to observe through the rain the rushing river beneath, and the hedged gardens around, and what looked like a lake beyond.

'Some spot,' Lou said.

'Wait,' Tony said. 'I feel bad now. Do you not want to go and find your mam's village?'

'Sure same as you,' Lou said, pulling up. 'We can have a look tomorrow, once the weather clears and we've some local knowledge to guide us. We're in no rush home sure.'

Rain and wind hurried them from the car to the hotel entrance, a pair of old oak doors, and once inside they were transported back entirely. Dustyframed and cobwebbed pictures hung crooked on wood-panelled walls: photographs, paintings and sketches of exotic animals and Indian princes, and old Irish people in woollen jumpers, with rods or caught fish or guns or musical instruments or baskets or pipes. Lou did the check-in business while Tony stumbled up and down steps and through corridors in search of someone from whom he could order tea and sandwiches. Then, once he'd found a young lad in uniform, he sank into a leather armchair in the lobby, stretching and yawning in front of the brightglowing hearth.

'The philosopher is dead,' Lou announced, coming down the three steps into the lobby.

'Your philosopher?'

266

'Yep.'

'Who worked here?'

'The very man.'

'Christ. Recently, like?'

'Is fifteen years recent?'

'… Ah well. It's a beautiful old place anyway, Lou, and I'm glad we found it. I realised there I'm bloody knackered.'

Lou collapsed into an armchair beside him, the two of them looking into the fire. 'There's a nice picture of him behind reception. And the lady told me a good story about a crooked floor.'

They had their tea, and a sandwich each, and sleepwalked their way through a conversation, increasingly exhausted, drawing out each other's yawns, and soon their minds were on other places and times and things, so much so that to Lou the hearth suddenly felt like a place that their bodies were taking shelter while their minds were out wandering the storm-ragged hills and fields of the west.

'I think I need a nap,' she eventually admitted. 'And I must ring Marta and fill her in.'

'I can never sleep during the day,' Tony told his colleague. 'But I must ring the Dancing Queen myself.'

And they did drag their feet from the hearth up to their separate rooms, and Lou found short strands of clipped black hair in her bathroom sink and washed them down the plughole, and slipping the hotel receipt into her purse, ordered neatly for expenses, she found the scrap of paper the white witch had given her, which she'd forgotten all about. The witch's scrawl was barely readable, full of spelling errors and mistaken affirmations about Lou's life, but then at the bottom she'd written something she hadn't said to Lou:

The tremblin is gud. It means your living your life.

267

She turned it over to see if she had missed something on the back, a continuation or some other missed explanation, but there was nothing else. She read it again. Now how could the trembling be good? The trembling was pure fucking agony, it was the thing vibrating her all over the place, scattering all her thoughts and plans and decisions. The trembling was *stopping* her from living her life. It was disrupting her life. What kind of advice was that? She crushed the note and dropped it in the empty bin beneath the desk. Fuck the trembling. And fuck the white witch. She chewed her back teeth, sat on the bed, squeezed her temples, stood again, this wave of intensity pouring through her, through whatever it meant to *be* her. Then took her phone from her pocket and pushed call.

'Hey? Hey Marta?'

'Hey love. How are you? You on your way home?'

'No. Did you not get my message?'

'What message?'

'Oh. I sent you a message. We're staying up here. The weather's atrocious for driving. The storm—'

'Ahhhh. Okay! No problem.'

'...'

'...'

'What are you up to anyway?'

'I was clipping the nails. Until you called.'

'Ah. Sorry.'

'How's it going there?'

'Grand. Hey, Marta?'

'Yea?'

'Let's have a baby?'

'...'

'...'

'Say again?'

'A baby. Let's have a baby together. You and me.'

'...'

'What do you think?'

'Have you been drinking, Lou?'

'No! Jesus! I'm not— Eh, I'm serious?'

'How would we even? I don't know. Lou, that's a big thing.'

'I know, I know. And it's not for the phone. But I've been thinking about it for ages and now I'm just saying it. I'm just saying it. I love you. You love me, as far as I know! We're together years. We're happy. I'd love to have a family with you.'

'Wow, okay. I don't know. I mean—'

'Well you don't have to say anything now. We can talk about it. I know what you think but, I dunno… And if we want to, there are loads of options.'

'Is this something from the radio?'

'The radio? What? No. Mar, I love you and I… It makes sense, I think? It's like, the next step? And I want it. I want it, okay? I think I want to be a mother. To be a parent myself and not someone's kid anymore.'

'…'

'But look, let's talk tomorrow. Or some time. I shouldn't have said it over the phone, sorry. Go clip your nails. I—'

'Yea. Let's talk. Maybe we just need to have a talk. I think there are some things too… There are things. I— '

'What things?'

'…'

'Marta?'

'Yes? You're breaking up. Let's talk tomorrow.'

'What things? Is everything okay?'

'Everything is fine. I miss Tabby. It's hard—'

'Marta?'

'Lou? Lou, I can't barely hear you. I'm going now. Let me know what time you're home tomorrow.'

'Okay, okay. Love you, Mar.'

'Okay, bye now.'

And like that, all her resolve was gone and the only thing left again was the worry, the squirming and the sickening, the great ever-present twist in her gut. The fucking trembling. She had a mind to go back and ask the witch how exactly *this* was her in any way living her life.

*

On the other side of the wall, Tony found himself looking at her number. Lolly had found him. Lolly wanted to meet. And here he was, mere miles from her still.

'Some people,' a caller said to him once upon a time, 'are afraid to pick up the phone. I'm not joking, Tony. I swear it. There is a type of person who is afraid of what's on the other end of the line. Afraid, Tony, of what might happen to them if they pick it up.'

There were all sorts of people walking the earth, with all sorts of hopes and problems and distractions. He sent her a message to say that he couldn't make it today, but that they might try again in the morning, and then he tried Nuala but couldn't get through, and he was trying to figure it all out for the millionth time when he fell asleep in his clothes, on the bed, not to dream.

ON-AIR

[static indecipherable]

RUUNNINNPLSKDMFNGHTEEMDNFH
RTUIOSKDUTHDOPLASMSMSNDFMG
NRHTHEAASSKDMFNGBRHEMSMMIN
THESTATIC running was good. It always had been. Nuala didn't know whether it was a way of coping or forgetting or just tiring out the body and therefore the mind, but in any case it always helped: these nights at the gym; those mornings and evenings years ago on the country roads around Carrigaline, keeping close to the ditch, trying

not to think about that man, those times. All
three therapists over the years had recommended
exercise; exercise that wasn't swimming of course.

Now, swimming, that's my thing—

All these echoes. So Tony took the kids swimming because she couldn't stomach it. Swimming
was *his arena*. Blah blah blah. All these voices
and moments that rippled through a life. The
treadmill rolled; Nuala ran. She ran to no music,
to no distraction other than the sounds of the
gym, the mechanics and the soft thuds and exhaled
exertions. She wasn't one for talking, or for
whinging, but it had been on her mind recently
that maybe she could write a book about her experiences. About overcoming these horrible things
that can happen to a person. About trauma. About
how life was a work in progress. About running.
She'd been listening to a lot of podcasts recently
and it seemed from those like normal people could
write books too, and have them published. That
having something worth sharing was the key to it.
And she had so much worth sharing: the swimming
thing, the grief around Aaron. Tony would surely
know a book publisher or two — they'd surely look
favourably on this kind of project. And even if
they didn't she would write the thing anyway. For
herself. For the kids. She didn't need anyone's
permission to write a book; she could fucking
well do it if she wanted to!

There was, she knew, that writing group down
the library who helped each other along. Angie
was in that writing group. And there was of course
that stocky young man from the city who came to

facilitate a writing workshop with them once a month, he who was broad and square-chinned and, well, who she definitely would…

So but now what would it be like to go through all that again? To bring that stuff up again? What would it be like to write it down? She could call it *The Running Book*, a cheeky little double entendre about running as a reaction and running as a cure… running as reclaiming her body, reclaiming space, reclaiming rhythm. Yes, this was exciting. This was going to be a thing. The treadmill rolled; Nuala ran onnnnnbbbovvodme nfbghrederedkskalaifigighoumfmfngnutterdsdndndbf mtmtlsslasksjmdmdbsbaifmdnghftekwellweeessssfnnng bfhdjsutkemsndhfkglddcassmandbfgrheecausedmfngth endklummmnueydldldksjsnfdnbfbfhdewpalaksdhfgjgtn rheamamans

---

OFF-AIR, evening bedroom window like a porthole. The rain no longer beat against it but through it lay a dim fog of drizzle. A wetmisty glow somewhere beyond, a streetlight perhaps, shining enough to give him some sense of his room: a mahogany-looking dressing table with a mirror, a chair, a dark vase of flowers. He felt a knot in his stomach when he saw no new messages on his phone.

The stairs creaked and groaned as he wound his way down past the galleries of old pictures and along a crooked corridor. He stopped to admire an old newspaper photograph of Michael Collins talking to a hurling team by the side of a pitch. The players wore caps; the crowd looked on. Life was all moments; not trophies, but moments.

And he chuckled then, and found himself singing: '*Maaaaagic… moooooooments, when two hearts are caring. Maaaaagic… moooooooments, mem'ries we've been sharing… I'll never forget… da da da da dah... do do do do deeee deee...'*

Thus, Tony arrived into the hotel bar whistling like a maniac, and on seeing him, Lou, who was at a table with eight or nine strangers, gesticulated, stood and drunkenly cried, 'Players!'

Tony approached the table of grinning faces of different ages, hands held softly in his pockets. 'What's that now?'

'I'm after meeting a bone fide group of travelling players here, Tony. We're in exalted company!'

'Very good. Playing what, lads?'

'Actors, Tony! Travelling actors!'

'We're trying to bring Shakespeare to the small Irish towns,' a short-haired girl said.

'In different styles and lengths,' a grey-bearded gentleman added. 'However they like it.'

'Very good!' Tony beamed. 'Can I get any of ye a drink?'

And they began to drink together, and by and by a scattering of wild locals came in out of the shivery evening, and theatre ensued.

[static, indecipherable]

'Tickets for the mate raffle! Anyone else want tickets for the mate raffle?'

A small, roundy spectacled man in a shell tracksuit who had been doing the rounds plodded to their table the last. There wasn't a hair on him that Lou could see. 'Tickets, lads?'

'What's first prize?' Lou asked.

'An absolute hape of mate, my love. Beef, pork, chicken, sausages, red mate, white mate.'

'And how much are the tickets?'

The roundy man held up a hand full of ragged stubs: 'For the contents of your left pocket, phones not included, you can have three tickets.'

'Well let me see what I have here.'

'Don't mind the phone. No need of phones in this place.'

273

'Not in a fit!' someone across the room yelled. Or was it, 'Talk in a bit!'?

'Cancerous bastards!'

Tickets were purchased; pockets were emptied. Stubs were stuffed into pockets, or left to soak on tables. While they waited on a hearty meal, Lou asked the players to perform something short.

'What do you want?' one of them asked.

'Anything,' she said.

'*Hamlet!*' someone called from the bar.

'Ham sandwich!' someone else cried.

'Ham-fisted!'

'Tickets for the mate raffle!'

'Hambolic!'

'Alcoholic!'

'This same skull, sir,' one of the players suddenly announced in a grave, posh accent, standing up tall, 'was Yorick's skull, the king's jester.'

'Let me see it,' another at the table replied, standing.

In place of a hollow skull, an empty pint glass was held aloft and handed over.

'Alas, poor Yorick!' yet another player started up. They spoke their lines seemingly at random, in various strange timbres.

'I knew him, Horatio. A fellow in infinite jest, of most excellent fancy. He hath borne me on his back a thousand times, and how, how hateful to my imagination it is! My gaze rims at it.'

The voice at the table changed again; a wondrous turn: 'Here... hung those lips that I have kissed I know not how oft.'

Fingers were draped down the sudsy glass. The whole place had fallen quiet.

'Where be your gibes now, Yorick? Your songs? Your flashes of merriment, that were wont to set the table on a roar? Not one now to mock your own grinning? Quite chap-fallen?'

'And all these moments,' someone slurred from the bar, their eyes closed as if singing a dirge, 'will be lost, in time, like tears in rain...'

274

'Why dost thou grin at me, hollow skull?'

'I have lived in important places! Times when great events were decided. Who owned that half a rood of rock, a no man's land!'

'We'll teach you to drink deep, ere you depart!'

'I could count myself the king of infinite space, were it not that I had bad dreams...'

'*A Thiarna, déan Trócaire! A Chríost, déan Trócaire!*'

'What are these lunatics on about?' a woman's voice above the table asked Lou over her shoulder.

'Full moon has them caught,' someone not Lou answered.

'Is there a full moon?'

'Sure there is, somewhere out there.'

'Beyond the cold window...'

'And the sterile promontory...'

'*All colours of the night turn every darkness into light!*'

'What?'

'What is the meaning of all that? Yorick and skulls and that?' Tony asked her after a round of cheers and applause, and a sort of resumption of pub chatter, surrounded by shrugs, teeth and large noses; silhouettes big and small; ringlets of soft hair; reddened profiles; pale moonfaces and smiles.

'What's the meaning of anything?' someone replied on her behalf.

'Shame your philosopher isn't around to tell us,' Tony said.

'What philosopher?'

'Lou here wanted to meet some fella that worked here as a gardener. He was a philosopher, but he's dead now.'

'Arra! They're all philosophers in this place.'

'Serve 'em enough porter and they are.'

It was as if the whole bar were having the one conversation, each listening and contributing from their own stool or perch or table, calling out to all other souls at sea.

'You stay in the one place long enough, you get to thinking...'

'You think too much, nothing good happens.'

'I came to the end of thinking once.'

'And?'

'I still didn't have the answer.'

'Some lives are one completely avoidable disaster after another.'

'Some nights are typhoons. They catch you and lift you and when you touch your feet to the ground again you are somewhere else.'

'Some nights around here are magical. You can feel the magic around you in the air, like electricity. Like a frequency, it changes everyone it touches.'

'So you studied philosophy did you? Now what kind of a job would you get out of that?'

'We work in radio.'

'In ray-jo, is it?'

'The only way out of the magic is through it.'

'What about the magnetic?'

'Some nights are for laughing.'

'Some nights are for crying.'

'What art thou that usurp'st this time of night?'

'Here comes the night now – how now, Johnny?'

'How are ye, lads?'

'Where've you been, John?'

'Fuckit lads, I've had some cold on me the last week. I swear to god – I think I might have the fuckin COVID again. Or fuckin HIV or something.'

'HIV?'

'I nearly blew the nose clean off meself yesterday.'

'Jesus Christ! Get this man a hot whiskey!'

'The only way out is through, Johnny.'

'By god and it is… Some crowd here!'

'Actors. Ray-jo people. Philosophers.'

'Suppressed souls all.'

'Aye, Johnny.'

'Did ya hear the fuckin COVID is back?'

'That and the fuckin 5G.'

'Where is the philosopher?'

'Over there, lah.'

'There!'

'Have I something on my face, lads?'

'No, no! I was telling Johnny here you're a philosopher. Louise, isn't it?'

'Well—'

'Listen, Louise, would you know a psychopath if there was one in the room?'

'I don't know! Probably not?'

'Are you not a philosopher?'

'I studied philosophy. I think you're looking for a psychologist though.'

'Same thing, isn't it?'

'Not exactly.'

'Fuck. See – I've a deadly fear of psychopaths. A deadly fear. I'm stone cold terrified of being caught by one of the fuckers. You see them on the tele. Have you any tips for spotting them? Could you lamp one from across the street would you reckon?'

'Jesus, I don't know. Probably not.'

'Is that Johnny, hai?'

'Fondu!'

'Johnny, you're back in the land of the living.'

'Barely. I've HIV I'm sure.'

'Have a blast of this ta fuck.'

'What is that under your oxter?'

'Plum poitín. I brought it down from the farm. The magic is in the air tonight. Do you feel it?'

'By god'n it is and by god'n I do. Look at all the lads from out of town! This lassie's a psychologist!'

'A radio producer actually. I studied *philosophy* though.'

'Same fuckin thing!'

And the plum poitín was rested upon the counter, and waited.

'So, Tony, who's this pal of yours you're going to see? Some blast from the past? From your London days?'

'Who's that now?'

'This publican you're supposed to visit?'

'Ah! Yes. Lorraine. Lolly. An old flame. From my own time in London actually.'

'An old flame, ay?'

'Indeed.'

'How long ago was this then?'

Headscratching. Counting. Hair combed through fingers. 'Twenty-six years ago?'

'...'

'It didn't end well.'

'...'

'I'm a bit nervous about going to see her, to be honest, Lou.'

'I can imagine. An old flame. Twenty-six years.'

'I came back out of London and she stopped there. To this day I regret leaving. I think. God, it's nearly impossible to know what you think isn't it?'

'And she's in Ireland now?'

'She lives here now.'

'Jesus! Coincidence! Returned exile? Displaced – whatever!'

'She moved here in the last couple of years to run a pub for her father, so I suppose not. They're an Irish family, though she's second generation.'

'Married?'

'You know, I didn't even ask... Lou, do you think it's possible to love two people at the same time, even if you haven't seen one of them for decades?'

'Jesus, Tony. We're talking romantic love here?'

'We are, I'm afraid. I abandoned that woman twenty-six years ago now and I don't know why.'

'... Hmmm. It's possible I'm sure. But I'm the wrong person to ask, Tony. I'm fuckin useless when it comes to this stuff. I don't know whether I'm coming or going myself... Why, Tony, can't we get our heads around ourselves?'

'God, Lou, I don't know... God I don't know what to do.'

'... Well... Dad always says to me that if you don't know what to do, do *nathing*.'

'...'

'...'

'And that's all?'

'...'

'...'

'That's all, Tony. But I suppose a problem shared is a problem halved either way.'

'We're all fucking displaced!' came a woman's voice.

'What?'

'We are all of us displaced. We are all homesick. Living is homesickness.'

'This woman here is homesick. Get her a hot whiskey!'

'Wait! I've plum poitín here. Just down from the farm!'

'The only way out of it is to ask the right question. That's how you get the pure country back. 'Tis all a wasteland til then.'

'And what's the question?'

'If I knew that I'd have the grail and we'd all be in paradise!'

'Oh.'

'But he's a radio man. Him there. He asks questions for a living – maybe he knows?'

'I don't know about that. I've been asking questions my whole life and I don't think I've done a thing right yet.'

[static, indecipherable]

Tracing the walls with her hands, to steady, yes, but to touch. To touch walls in the world. Crooked walls. To close the cubicle door behind her and purge herself of a piss.

To herself: 'A problem shared is a problem halved.'

From beyond the cubicle door: 'A good piss is a problem solved!'

'Who's that?'

'Just another soul in another cubicle, passing the time in

urination.'

'...'

'Though with the ashtrays out and the plum poitín being rationed about, I don't profess to know who or where I am with any actual certainty.'

'It's a magical night, someone said.'

'There are plenty of magnetic nights up this way.'

'...'

'Do you have a problem you need to share? I couldn't help overhearing you there?'.

'...'

'I could hear a confession – no bother.'

'Are you a priest?'

'... I might be one day... Or might be now in a parallel universe, where there are women priests...'

'...'

'I'm in no rush anyway. It's cooler out here. They're after cooking the air with their dancing inside.'

'...'

'Go on. Unfold yourself.'

'Well, what can I tell you. I was going to ask my partner of six years if she wanted to start a family and now I think she's going to leave me.'

'Yikes!'

'And god knows I deserve it because I nearly cheated on her the other week. I deserve every bad thing that happens to me.'

'...'

'...'

'And why are you sure she wants to leave you?'

'... I dunno. A vibe I got on the phone earlier.'

'A vibe?'

'But even if I'm being paranoid, to have children would be so irresponsible. With the world the way it is, with all the mad shit in our family ancestry... With the way I am...'

'Up here you'd get a gorse fire every few years, and the whole place is blackened after them. But then when the new shoots come up they are absolutely glorious.'

'… What's that supposed to mean?'

'Look, whether I'm a lady priest or just another human in the storm, I think that the human soul is glorious. And I would say that no matter what you do – no matter what happens to you in your love life or your family's past or whatever – don't suppress your soul.'

Through the cubicle partition she heard the other pulling at the toilet paper roll and remembered to do the same.

'Jesus, I can't think straight anymore.'

'Well there are no straight lines in nature, as we say up here.'

'So ye keep telling me!'

'…'

'… And our cat is missing too… Well, her cat – the cat came with the relationship.'

'Ah, they do do that, cats. After months away then they waltz in the door like they were gone ten minutes… But, look, seriously, suppressing your soul is the worst. Don't suppress your soul, whatever you do. Never.'

'Right-o.'

'Feel better?'

'Haven't a clue.'

'Good.' After the flush: 'Now, your penance. Return to the bar. Drink a half a glass of the plum poitín and belt out the national anthem without even a pause for breath. Don't wait for others to follow. Just do it. Don't stop singing til it's sung.'

'… Consider it done.'

'Now, a confessor should never see the face of the clergy that has cleansed her, so I'll go first and you follow when you hear the toilet door close behind me.'

'Thank you. And good luck.'

'The same to you, comrade.'

Rattle of lock. Bang of cubicle door. Hard-heeled footsteps. Squeal of toilet door.

OFF-AIR, Ann, living, in her front room, in her chair, a wealth of cushions propping her up and a wealth of tablets taken to ease the pain and sharpen the mind. But the pain was bad, the nausea worse, and the mind remained foggy. The kids were both home for the evening and the plan was to watch a movie. Jerry was around the house somewhere too, doing something – she couldn't remember what. Making something? And the two kids were on their phones on the couch and they weren't kids anymore, they were adults. Big lumps of things with slumped shoulders on her couch, both in their own worlds on their phones. The son looked up and smiled at her.

'What are we watching then, Mam?'

'God,' she said. 'I haven't a clue. I... no... Sorry!'

'It's grand. If Jerry's had his way it's going to be one of those shitty car chase things.'

How much time had passed? The door swung open and Jerry came in with two cups of tea in each hand. It was as if he had walked into her life again after years away. She smiled at him. 'Hello, Jerry, my love.'

'Hello, Antoinette, my darling. I've a cup of chamomile here for the patient, and three real cuppas for the rest of us.'

And another wave of pain came. Wave of pain, wave of nausea, and then they were saying something else, talking about someone else, some man in the next bed over, and then it seemed they were watching a movie.

OFF-AIR, Lou returned to the bar and stood, rocking, at the glowing hearth, resting her elbow on the antique mantel, and saw from the corner of her eye the shadow of a woman lean into the fire, and heard her say to the flame, 'You are so fucking beautiful...'

And Lou closed her eyes as she began to sing: '*Sinne Fianna Fáil...*'

And wasn't she lifted on the voices of the people around

her, as everyone joined in, and sang on, and weren't their voices transported through the oak doors and through the gravel car park and across the humpback bridge and away over wet blustery darkness in search of the moon.

Laughter and roars of applause echoed from the distant bar.

'Well sung!'

'Beautifully delivered!'

'The only way out is through!'

'There are no straight lines in nature!'

'We are but transformed groceries!'

'Tis pure fucking e-lec-tricity!'

'Hot whiskey for everyone sick or home from London!'

'I fucking built that city!'

'We're all still alive. We have our health and be glad for that.'

'Who's there?'

'Well there's this thing, Declan, called *emotional proximity*—'

'Don't tell me that!'

Exalted, a young figure was tap-dancing on a table and the women and the men still with their feet on the floor threw their bodies up onto the rhythm and into some primal moment.

All turned.

Did a suited man whisper to Lou in conversation, 'There is still a place on Earth for the dignified man...'?

And did Tony smile tearfully and give her a hug, saying, 'You're a great singer, Lou, and you'll make a great mother. A great mother!'

And did the night not end there?

OFF-AIR, she was finally caught writing on a Friday turning Saturday. It was an easy spot off the South Mall, a cul-de-sac away from the pubs, and she was in the middle of a huge O, and she was in the middle of having the same projected argument with her parents – *again* – and she was telling Dad to JUST FUCK OFF YOU FUCKING CUNT, and she was saying to herself, why go back to the guesthouse at all? when she heard voices on the lane and it was too late to run.

Three tall lads in hoodies blocked off the alley. She could see the streetlight of the South Mall through them, beyond them.

'Holy fuck,' the guy on the left said, looking from her to the piece-in-progress and back. 'Look what we've found for ourselves, lads.'

She began to back away, the shock of fear collapsing through her.

'Well fucking well!' the one on the right crowed. 'Fucking AERO.'

The first one slung off his backpack, barely looking at her as he crouched nearby and opened the zip. The middle lad stared at her, unblinking, a can of cider hanging from his hand.

Her arms hung by her sides; there was no easy way past them. She wouldn't get away. 'I've just got one question for you,' the first guy said. 'Why in the name of god do you waste so much time on the easy ones? Fair enough bomb away like, but some of your spot selections are fuckin *wild* – but why waste time on railings and stupid shit like that? Isn't it just a pure waste of time?'

'Well—'

'Like, don't get me wrong. You're *all city*, I get it. But like, it's petty or something… and technically? I dunno – it's clear from some of your throw-ups that you've got potential—'

'And fuckin brave, too,' the second guy said.

'But I mean… like… I dunno, I just wouldn't be wasting my time on railings and bins and all that shit.'

'Em, yea. I dunno.' She was still wildly aware of the distance to the road, but yet the rebuke felt… good somehow? 'I, eh…'

'Here, don't listen to that gowl,' the middle guy finally said. 'He thinks he's the professor of graffiti or something. We all start somewhere. Go on, don't let us stop ya.'

She grinned nervously, heart still pounding, and she went back to work, slowly, trembling even, still ready to sprint, to flee, still waiting for it to be a ruse, for some attack, for some horrible turn, as the three lads started their own work along the wall – MANIC, FERRERO, FLY – and eventually they introduced themselves and told her where they came from and which forums they were on, and she didn't talk much, just stood quietly beside them, all four doing their own work.

When Manic finished a nice loud throw-up, he came and appraised Aero's. She'd been able to relax a little, safer knowing that she had three other people listening out for the sound of anyone coming. It gave her the time to really focus on the flaring. Manic nodded slowly, arms folded like a professor in a gallery. Fly came and joined them, hands bunched in the pockets of his hoodie.

'Ah, yea,' he said, to no question she'd heard. 'Here, d'you fancy coming painting trains with us Tuesday night?'

OFF-AIR, she played him, and he played her.

'We've Lou on line one, do we?'

'Where are you, Tony?'

'Out here, Lou, in the dark, with you.'

'Are we all in the dark, Tony?'

'Don't get me started on how many of us are stuck out here in the dark, Lou.'

'I'm hopping mad, *bai*.'

'I'm livid myself. Tell me, Lou.'

By god but Lou did a great Tony Cooney.

'Well, Tony, I'll tell you. It's a disgrace what happened here tonight.'

'Tell me, Lou. What happened?'

'Well, these two *crayturs* – *ray-jo* people, one of them a *psychologist* – were supposed to be in bed good and early, and now it's god knows what hour of the night or morning, and the two of them, two *gurriers*, Tony, are out wondering the black roads of Connemara in the dark. Total dark, Tony. And they don't know what's their arse and what's their elbow and what's the ditch.'

'God. Disgraceful. They are far too old to be carrying on like that. They're supposed to be running a national competition, for the love of Jay.'

'You're telling me, Tony. They've come down out of a house party on a farm now and they don't know where it was or where they are.'

'Blaggards. That's just not on, is it?'

'Christ, no.'

'Well, from that to something completely different. I'm joined now by a horrendously crippled individual – a boy with no legs and no arms, and only one ear – whose dog has been trained to dress him. Timmy, can you bark for me, please?'

And Tony barked into the dark, and laughed so hard then that he fell through the darkness into what became a ditch.

As ditches went, this would have been a fine one to rest in, more fern than bramble by his estimation. Lou had to feel around and call his name to get in there and pull him out again with a strong arm.

'The dog also empties the dishwasher,' she said as he rose and they struggled across the dark together. 'And takes the boy's nappies out to the bin.'

'Deasy's Home Appliances! Thanking you for two decades of support in our efforts to provide the best deals in… home appliances.'

'That's just not on, is it.'

'I'm gobsmacked at the fact, to be honest.'

'I'm hopping mad!'

'I mean, would you go back to London now?'

'Not in a fit!'

'I'm dying of cancer you know.'

'Tell us all about it. Every last detail. I want you to particularly dwell on your deep sense of mortality, and fear, and yet wonder. If you could also describe every aspect of the pain, and the constitution of your chemo-vomit… Tell us how you made your peace with your dear old sister after decades not talking, and tell us how, in fact, you made your peace with the world. Tell us live on air, if you don't mind, and make us all feel that bit more poignant while we fill up our cars with petrol and do our grocery shopping and fold our laundry. And while we're at it, did your own mother die of cancer? And is your own father an alcoholic?'

'Cancer – now sponsored by DELL computers.'

'Why die, when you can surf the internet on a brand new DELL laptop?'

'Four-thousand-euro scrappage bonus! Just drop your carcass in the yard there and we'll give a friend or relative four thousand euro for your decomposing corpse!'

'Yea!'

Voices fell to a co-ordinated whisper, the word muttered in penitence amidst sharp intakes of breath, and unseen tears: 'Yea.'

'Yea.'

'Hmmm.'

'Yea.'

'Yea.'

'Yea, yea, yea.'

The wind blew from a direction that did not know itself.

'It's not the first sewage leak on that road, I believe.'

'It's disgusting, Tony. Nappies. Tampons. Shite. Blood…'

'See, what happened was—'

HDHFJGNTHRBEBDFHJFJFFFFFFF
FFFFFFFFFMGNGNDHJSAJAWEERRP
POTUIYIUHFKNSNDBFGJRHRINTH
ESTATI C what happened was Marta woke to
the alarm at half three in the morning, and the
rain and wind were harassing the windows of the
terrace house, and it felt so warm in the bed, and
Marta said to herself through the fug of sleep,
*It's lashing with rain. Wherever she is, she won't
be out in this weather. She'll be sheltering in
some nook, or a warehouse or something. I'll
never find her in this weather.*

And she turned in the dark, reached over her
head to the windowsill to silence the alarm on
her phone.

And then only the nightsounds were left again,
the clicks and whirs and breezes and tappings,
the house stretching and groaning in its own
rain-addled slumber, and then she was awake
again, what seemed like an hour later but wasn't,
realising again that Lou wasn't there, and saying
that she couldn't sleep now anyway. That she'd
go and look even if it was just for her own peace
of mind. And so, with sleep still crusting her
eyes, and that film of waxy slumber on the skin
of her face, in the stiffness of her hair under
her raincoat's hood, she was out in the night,
the wet wind rattling wheelie bins and gates,
the sharp rain bothering her hood and the pale
skin of her hands as she clinked the food bowls,
calling softly, 'Taaaabby, Taaaabby,' while she
kissed her lips and whistled the special whistle,
and called, softly, 'Taaaabitha? Taaaabby?'

She walked down the quay beyond the North Gate

Bridge, stopping in behind the Bierhaus on her way, calling, seeing no cat, falling quiet and embarrassed when hooded figures came along the pavement towards her, plodding home, or to work, or wherever.

She made a figure of eight, crossing the Shandon footbridge and walking as far as the opera house, and then back to the north side of the river, to the mouth of the N20 — where the road widened and poured north, through Blackpool in the direction of Charleville, Limerick and Galway — where she turned back towards St Mary's, and her voice echoed up the wide limestone steps of the church and in around the arcade and the front doors, and when she'd finished one figure of eight around the river she did another, in case Tabby had heard her once but she'd moved on too quickly — all the time clinking those bowls and calling her name softly, into the city night, where a hundred thousand slept in rooms behind windows — calling, whistling softly, kissing her lips over and over.

And she went in then around the back streets of the Bridewell and the Paul Street car park, emerging again onto the river by the traffic lights, and crouching to peer in beneath the lip of a huge blue warehouse door, to clink and call again, lowly, into the dark of another hidden city space, on her knees there by a couple of busted sandbags. And it was there the wet, warm blustery air of the city night was suddenly filled by the coarse *wooeeerrrr* of a cat, like a bawling newborn, barely even pausing to draw breath before it wailed again in desperation.

wooeeerrrrr
wooeeerrrrr
wooeeerrrrr.

Marta jumped up and for a moment she just looked at the warehouse door, before calling back, 'Tabby? Tabitha?' and clinking the bowls while the wailing continued to scrape against the night.

wooeeerrrrr
wooeeerrrrr
wooeeerrrrr.

Where was it coming from? She looked up at the warehouse door, around, down. The wail was everywhere. 'Tabby? *Taaabbbyy?'*

The rain heaved down on the city, blurring the outlines of the buildings up and down the river. Her cat cried out, unseen, as if from another dimension, while she gaped around the windowsills and rooftops of the building, trying to see her.

wooeeerrrrr
wooeeerrrrr
wooeeerrrrr.

Was it coming from the roof?

She stood back into the puddles of the road to look up to the roof, with no sign of Tabby's little white face, her bewildered green eyes.

But the caterwaul went on, so urgent, pleading for life.

The warehouse?

No.

She started to stride across the road. It was coming from the other side of the river, from the church!

Marta rushed against the glistening limestone river wall to hear better. The church? The river itself? Was she in the suck and swirl of the river, clinging somewhere, to a gape in the wall where a block was missing, or some overhanging ledge? The tide was high and sweeping. Marta became aware of her jeans and socks and docs. She was ready, she realised, to jump in for Tabitha.

'Tabby!' she called, and the cat continued to respond. *wooeeerrrrr wooeeerrrrr wooeeerrrrr.*

'You're not in the river!' she said, suddenly calm, almost smiling. 'You're under me.'

She turned on the spot, looked downwards, around her, searching the pavement, and then ran to a manhole cover a few feet away on the riverside pavement by a skinny young birch.

'Tabby?' she said. 'Tabitha! Tabby? It's okay, I'm here. I'm here, Tabby!'

wooeeerrrrr wooeeerrrrr wooeeerrrrr.

The manhole cover was set heavily in place, slick and dirty; grime came off on her hands when she tried to get a grip on its edges. The caterwaul beneath went on like an air-raid siren.

'It won't open, Tabby,' she gasped.

What would Lou do? She would ring the guards or the council.

'Okay, Tabitha, okay,' she said to the manhole. 'I'm coming.' She drew her phone, searched for the council emergency number, but then put the phone away again. They would never come, not at this hour. 'Okay, Tabby — I'm gonna get you out.'

She was already thinking forward then, frantically — through violence against the manhole cover, through hammering and smashing, through scraping pain and sirens and embarrassment — to wrapping a blanket around her cat, a blanket or a coat, and in thinking forward, she was also thinking backwards from some further future, thinking about how she'd tell the story to their friends in the Friary, to her mother, to Lou's father, on the radio with *Talk To Tony*, how she would explain that she was utterly unable to calculate or rationalise the odds of her finding their cat in a sewer at four in the morning on a Saturday, in the rain, and while she crouched and thought and tried to soothe the unseen screaming cat, her free hand had begun to work on the edges and the corners of the manhole cover, finding a corner that was just a little out of joint with its slot, meaning that it was sticking up, jarred just a few millimetres from flush. Meaning that she could almost get a finger under it, though not quite enough to get any purchase. She stopped then, held her hand out under the rain to clean it, wiped it on her jeans and started again.

Meanwhile, Tabitha continued to *wooeeerrrrr wooeeerrrrrwooeeerrrrrwooeeerrrrrwooeeerrrrr wooeeerrrrr* and what happened — 'between the jigs and the reels,' as Lou would always say, a phrase Marta could use now in her telling of it — was that while she went on reassuring Tabby, saying her name over and over, she eventually worked her fingers under the broken corner but couldn't quite lift it, though now it wriggled a bit, and

292

so she wriggled the lid and clawed at it and pulled at it harder and harder.

wooeeerrrrrwooeeerrrrrwooeeerrrrr.

She was thinking of running home for a hammer, when that corner came loose to about an inch, so that she could get her fingers under it properly, and she did, and she began to pull hard — **wooeeerrrrr wooeeerrrrr wooeeerrrrr** — and then the manhole seemed to fracture from one square into two triangles, like a cut sandwich, and though the two halves were still locked into each other somehow, it gave her the space and momentum to yank harder at the corner — 'Okay Tabby, okay Tabby!' — and to rip at it — *wooeeerrrrr wooeeerrrrr wooeeerrrrr* — to go from crouching over it to standing over it, levering her whole body against it til the gap in that corner was three inches, then almost five, then she ceased pulling and knelt with her head on the pavement to see under — **wooeeerrrrr wooeeerrrrr wooeeerrrrr** — and said, by the light of her trembling phone's torch, 'I can see you, I can see you!'

It really was Tabby, there on the top rung of an underground ladder and there was water up to that top rung and she was soaking, the poor thing. She was so skinny she was rattling like a leaf.

wooeeerrrrr

wooeeerrrrr

wooeeerrrrr

Still straining with the manhole lid, almost propping it on her head to keep it open, Marta

reached for her bag with her free hand and pulled
out some of the wet food she'd brought in a
Tupperware container. And she squeezed the bowl
into the space beneath the lid and yes, Tabby was
tasting it, and eating it, a little, but then
Tabby fell in the water and shit it was deep, it
was deep, she was gone and Marta reached in but
couldn't find her in the water and then Tabby was
back on the ladder somehow, but Marta couldn't
reach her, she couldn't reach her yet, and so she
rose again and started pulling harder and harder
on the manhole lid and parts of her back seemed to
be coming apart between her shoulder blades and —
wooeeerrrrr wooeeerrrrr wooeeerrrrr — and okay Tabby,
okay Tabby, okay, it's okay, I'm nearly there —
and she worked her fingers along the ridge of the
lid so that she was now lifting the corner nearer
to the ladder, nearer to Tabby, where she clung on
to the ladder, shivering in the watery dark, and
Marta was waiting to hear her fall in again, that
light splash, and soon, soon, she had that corner
up four or so inches and she kept pulling at it
and Tabby seemed to be wailing a little less,
and as she pulled, yanked, hauled away she saw a
bloody paw emerging from beneath the lid to test
the dark drenched pavement, just a paw, first one
bloodied paw, then, after it had disappeared, the
other appeared, bloodier, drenched in blood, to
test too, and then both paws were there together,
and then Tabitha's head was out, and somehow then
Marta had Tabby in her arms, and the manhole lid
clattered shut, and Tabby, ragged and skinny and
drenched and stinking of sewage, was wrapped in
the blanket she'd brought from the couch, the
one she often napped on, and now she wailed and

294

purred in intervals, and then ate ravenously from the Tupperware Marta held up to her and Marta was saying, 'You only seem to be bleeding from the paws,' and 'You're fine; you're fine,' and she might have been crying, only then, at the last, when Tabby was found and no longer lost, and a garda car came along the road and slowed by them, and then took off again, and she was laughing and crying and saying she couldn't believe it, over and over for dayssshhhhhhhhhhhhhhhhhhhhhhhhhhhhhhhh hhhhhhhhhhhhhhh

leaves

   turning

   into

    birds

HHHHSSSSSSSHKKOOOOOOOOOUU
UUUUEEEEMMMNNNOOMMNNNFHHH
DJSSASNSNDBFVCGSAHENB I N
T H E S T A T I C the engineer took
a last look around: the broom, the empty cardboard
boxes, the fans, the Jesus stick, the transformer,
the capacitor, the dodgy filter coil, the cages and
cabinets of the place, the hum and whir and click
of the place that never stopped. It was sorted
now until the next glitch, and then he'd be back
with his tools, looking for light switches again,
looking for the spectrum tuner again, repeating
the process again, seeking the pure frequency… but
for now, he could turn out the light, and go and
quickly check on the generators, and get home in
time forrrrrrrrrrrrrrrrrrrrrrrrrrrrrrrrrrrrrrrrrr
rrrrrrrrrrrrrrrrrrrrrrrrrlllllllaaaaaassppddllkcjf
ghtnendndnndmmattchhhhhanndnnddbfbtreesaatteaaa
aadddmdmdmmzzzznnddnsnemdmmdmdmdmmxxmxmxmxmmmmmm
maaaaaaaaachchhuuuuhhhhhhhccchuuucchhhhhhhhhhhhh

BROADCASTING SIMULTANEOUSLY on 5264 kHz + 1420 MHz…

playback: the pale moon was rising above the
green mountain / the sun was declining
beneath the blue sea…

first voice: *see the engineer finishing his repairs
there? he is in many ways like god
in nature: everywhere present, but
nowhere visible.*

second voice: *except that we can see him of course…
trudging to the transmitter, rustling
around in there for a bit, squeezing
back out the gate…*

first voice: *naturally. but i must say i prefer the poet to the engineer… [static] take, for example, the story of the japanese poet who was said to have walked out of his home and travelled thousands of miles with little interest in provisions or possessions. just journey for journey's sake…*

second voice: *he just cast himself out into the world so that he could be in it. but the poems he wrote were broadcasts too, in their own way…*

first voice: *and i imagine his travelling as a sort of investigation…*

second voice: *all our travelling, all our thinking, all our living is an investigation…*

first voice: *and our listening! and our seeing! drifting across frequencies and bandwidths and bearing witness…*

second voice: *well, y—*

first voice: *but i like to imagine that this poet had a particular lining to his rough road coat, and stitched into that lining was a special piece of parchment, onto which he would write the answer when he found it… or maybe the question… maybe finding the right question is more important than the right answer.*

second voice: *you are losing me a bit now. what question?*

first voice: *i dunno… THE question…*

second voice: *right. i can't say i follow you, but say what you must.*

first voice: *oh, shit. i don't know. something about living and dying. but i suppose at the end of it all, we only have our heads to live in. the world is out there.*

300

second voice:	*[static]*
first voice:	*and the world is all that is the case…*
second voice:	*and yet leaves turn into birds… go on, give us another one… there can't be many left now, i imagine…*
first voice:	*i hear it, therefore i see it… six… one… four… eight…*

[static] the hum of electricity [static]

OFF-AIR, lemongrey morning light shone through the windscreen.

'I need to pull over,' Lou coughed, and as soon as she'd pulled into the motorway's hard shoulder she pushed her door open and began to vomit onto the asphalt.

Tony could say said nothing.

That sky's light filtered over the wet ditches and fields. The two of them had been stunned to silence by the night's drinking. Somehow they had woken up, fully clothed, in the same hotel room in the same bed, wrapped in each other's arms, and now they were headed south, barely able to talk, their mobile phones dead.

'We never called to your ex,' Lou croaked, after a few minutes nursing herself.

'We never found your mam's homeplace either.'

'We're in no state to be going on soul adventures I suppose.' Her legs had fallen out of the car and she was collapsed sideways against the seat. 'I shouldn't even be driving in this state. If we're pulled over, I'm goosed.'

Tony sighed a curse, cradled his bottle of Lucozade.

'Come on then,' she said, turning in and pulling the door shut again. 'Away home.'

★

They crossed the country in addled silence, a country where bus fares were increasing and people would be ever-reliant on cars; a country that pitied the terrorist attacks on its old neighbour; a country that could never settle on its feelings about its old neighbour; a country with a history of blood, a country of terrorists; a country where we were only ten per cent human, and ninety per cent alien microbe and transformed groceries; and yet an electrified country, where airports were adding new transatlantic routes, and the future was bright; an economy that was fast-growing again; a road network and infrastructure that was ever-burgeoning, where the voices of folk told tales of passed and failed NCTs; where a woman was jailed for not allowing her home to be repossessed; a country that was flooded, where unseen voices made fraudulent calls; where a fast-food restaurant worker had a heart condition that meant she could faint at any moment; where they were thinking of tolling a decades' old link road; where cancer lurked in sausages, in microplastics; where people suffered from damp; where a man was known as the Unofficial King of Ballybricken; where a troubled young man killed his grandparents in their kitchen; where a woman told how her childhood dentist had been a dwarf named Bill Shakespeare; where sewage leaked out onto the road's surface; where, for the first time, an eighty-two-year-old lady found a letter her husband had written to her twenty years before his death; where a caller from London looked for a man he'd known through site work in Finsbury Park forty years earlier; where citizens died on roadsides; where meat was murder; where a doctor was imprisoned for indecently assaulting the teenage daughter of a cancer patient; where you could get four-thousand-euro scrappage for your old car; where a group of teens raised seventy-one thousand euro for charity; where we suffered from a prescription culture, were a **highly medicated tribe**; where the **deargleach** was the red glow in the sky; where one-way systems were on the rise; where people supposedly flooded home from London; where, of an evening, you might hear the hoarse rumbleroll and crack of a skatepark nearby; where foreign companies paid little tax and pumped their waste into the rivers and lakes and seas; where you might feel constant physical pain without medical or scientific explanation; where they'd been trying to build an incinerator on one patch of land for over twenty years but still the people resisted; where towns disappeared behind flyovers and bypasses and the signposts to them were like gravestones; where people tried to stay sober for the month of November; where you could win a car just by turning up at a particular place, at a particular time; where on that very day, two people were parking up at Grand Canal Dock in Dublin, readying to denotate a huge car bomb as commuters gathered at a tram stop, and 'the Troubles' would be said to have arrived on our shores again.

And now, at the last, there was only road before Tony and Lou. No towns, no people. Road and car and ditch and field and sky. Yoohoo, Road! Lou was blasting the cold air and Tony's feet felt like ice blocks. His feet were in the car frozen present, while his mind wandered an empty vessel where the ghosts of bad thoughts stood and rubbed their faces. He could never have gone to Lolly in this state anyway, with this mind on him. There was no point in regretting it. What could he have said anyway?

Hi Lolly, how have you been? Me? I'm a broken man.

Hi Lolly, I have been a broken man since I came back to Ireland.

You know, Lolly, what we had was very special to me. Very dear. But I've been happily married these last eighteen years. I don't know how it happened, Loll. How I found happiness after you. I don't know what happiness is, Loll. I don't even know what I am.

How are you, Lolly? You look as beautiful as ever.

Lolly, I am so sorry I left you like that.

Would you take me back, Loll?

One more time for old times' sake, Loll?

The years have been kind to you, Loll. I wish I could say the same for meself.

Do you remember, Loll, when you cornered me at Ruislip, after Monaghan beat Cavan in an Ulster Championship semi-final? Some say, Lolly, that sport is about moments and not trophies. Do you think life is like that?

I've never loved anyone else like I loved you. And yet is that enough?

★

As she drove, Lou was thinking of an unspoken argument. Maybe one of the first. Marta had mentioned a trip somewhere, to Donegal maybe, and Lou had baulked at the idea. Baulked at the idea of the drive, of picking some random guesthouse and being checked in by some weirdo, picking some list of things to see, pubs to visit that were probably terrible. The idea of going to a place because there was some deal going, and not because either of them actually wanted to go there. She'd added up all these arguments against the idea of the trip and lined them up against Marta without ever mentioning them aloud to her. She'd said nothing; Marta had said nothing, and yet all those unspoken words grew up into a wall in the air between them. Whether Marta had her own unspoken accusations Lou couldn't know, but she probably did, and so probably Lou's 'maybe' and Marta's 'sure' were the culmination of thousands of negative words stacked against the other, the culmination of unbirthed tirades attributing desperate things each to the other. Why would a simple suggestion of a trip somewhere lead to something so toxic like that? What trauma or badness did Lou have in her that she could turn a positive into a negative like that? What did she have against Marta, the love of her life, that she could mess her around, flirt with others? And then of course, when they lay together that night, because of this unspoken thing, it felt like they'd fought to exhaustion even though they'd barely said two words to each other. It was ridiculous, she knew even then, at the time, but there she was in the dark, watching the curtains' shadow, railing against this trip to Donegal and everything that had come before. Thinking, fuck you Marta and your stupid notions. Sad woman that she was, determined to cause herself pain. And worse, too self-centred to think of Marta's feelings.

And now Marta wanted to 'talk'. Did she know somehow about the white witch? About something else? Was it the end?

Well – she would be saying nothing to Marta about kids now. She would only try now to be as good to Marta as she could, to try and keep her. As if a person could be kept...

The car trembled as she rolled over cat's eyes.

'I'm dying,' Tony said. 'I'm actually dying.'

'I'm fucking dying myself,' she said.

She drifted and found the cat's eyes again.

'Sorry,' she said. 'Jesus Christ.'

'Actually, can we pull over?' Tony asked. 'I think I'm gonna gawk here.'

She pulled in again and Tony got out and stumbled away from the car.

★

The mid-morning was fresh. Cold. The fields rolled out and rose into the distance, and in some way it all felt familiar. From the car, Tony stumbled down off the road to a field gate and leaned on it, groaning. The grass was soft under his shoes. Where are we? he wondered, holding his belly. He felt a sinking of himself, from his head down through his veins – probably the lack of sugar in the blood. He felt as though, were he to turn, he would see someone in the back seat of the car, but he didn't know who.

Four noble ditches framed the near field, in a blurred, crooked rectangle of dark green. From the centre of the field a great big antenna rose, a transmitter station of all things, and he saw that some bright thing hung from one of the lower braces of the structure. Lifting a mucky shoe from the grass, he climbed the gate and traversed it.

He crossed the soft field and stood at its heart, by the ragged wire fence that surrounded the antenna and the tiny breezeblock transmitter station. He placed his hands on the rusted wire of the fence, where a DANGER sign dangled from one last cable tie. The way he looked up, the antenna framed the pale sky, a sort of grid upon infinity that crackled with electricity, receiving and transmitting at the same time. The sky's close magnitude made him dizzy, and so he cast his gaze back down, where he found the object he had first seen from the distance.

It was a faded yellow balloon, the size of a child's fist, hanging limply by a thin string from the lattice steel of the antenna. It just hung there. He couldn't tell whether it was swinging gently in the breeze, or whether he was the one swaying. He had brought a yellow balloon to the hospital once, for his son that had died. Enfolded in that memory was an old Irish song – what was it? He held on to the wire fence.

Then, from what felt like a great distance, Lou was suddenly alongside him, looking at the balloon too, clearing her voice and saying, 'Will we go?'

She had come to join him. To see, perhaps, what he saw.

*

As they walked back, a wood pigeon hurtled past overhead, freeing itself unto the sky, and then Lou heard the creaking of a branch in the ditch. She turned and saw leaves of green grass and the heads of white clover waving and bowing and rising in the breeze. She heard the trickle of a streamlet somewhere. Heard the windchime through the grass and through the ditch, and the swishing of her own trainers in the grass. Wind that'd ease the soul of her, that lifted her hair and brought it down over her face. The four ditches of the field chiming. A crow hopping through the long grass. A little skylark hopping on a crumbled chunk of wall. Ferns and nettles fanning. Everything trembling, sort of. Everything chiming. Clusters of wildflowers and curled dock rising in parts of the field like towers in distant towns. Dried clumps of cut grass. Gorse, cobweb, hawthorn, bramble, fern, nettle, dock. The windchime in the antenna behind them, and no longer the electricity. In the distant sky, bird flocks shattered into brilliant shapes. Actually, there were fields all round them.

BROADCASTING SIMULTANEOUSLY on 5264 kHz + 1420 MHz…

playback: the pale moon was rising above the green mountain / the sun was declining beneath the blue sea…

first voice: *[static] … and i feel as though i am there in the field with them, listening, seeing. the birds, the grass, the electricity, the wind. they say your life flashes before your eyes… i like to think that LOU visited TONY at the end of his life, in the cork university hospital. and that maybe she had to leave then so that she could pick up her and MARTA's teenage boy from a pal's house. or perhaps the boy mooched around the wilton shopping centre while she visited TONY — 'an old work friend'… and maybe even the boy would have seen NUALA, going into or out of the shopping centre toilets, patting her hands together to dry them, and maybe she was vaguely familiar to him, somehow. who even knows…*

second voice: *ha. or maybe MARTA dumped her the moment she walked in the door [static] dropped down dead on the road there and then [static] or everything… everything…*

first voice: *[static]… is lost in the light. who even knows. who ever knows? nine… five… seven… two… [static]*

OFF-AIR, they were back on the road and Tony asked:

'Do you mind if I put the radio on again? I need some distraction.'

'Not at all,' Lou said. 'Could do with it myself.'

ON-AIR

A VOICE
—lost a wedding ring. Nine carat gold, three diamonds. A priceless object by anyone's estimation. She was visiting her husband in the Cork University Hospital... and lost it between the visit to him and a trip to the Wilton Shopping Centre across the road—

OFF-AIR, Lou saw the shopping centre in her mind's eye: squat red brick surrounded by a lake of shimmering parked cars and landscaped verges. She'd spent so much time there when Mam was ill.

★

Tony was able to visualise the shopping centre from a window by a hospital bed, some echo of a previous visit maybe? He could smell antiseptic, and almost feel the coarse rub of the three diamonds under his thumb, in a hand held.

ON-AIR

A VOICE

She's thinking that maybe she lost the ring when she washed her hands in the shopping centre toilets. She didn't take it off – she never has, in *TFFFFF* of marriage – but it's possible that it slipped off. This woman is heartbroken. She's distraught. Her husband, in the CUH, is suffering *TFFFFFFF*. He isn't doing well. The ring again is nine carat gold, thr *TFFFFFFFFFFFFFFF*—

OFF-AIR then, radio silence. Dead air.

'Nine carat gold,' Tony repeated.

'That's strange,' Lou said, as Tony began to press the buttons, looking for signal.

'Nothing.'

Lou kept her eyes on the road. 'No signal?'

'Nothing. For any frequency.'

'Try turning it off and on again?'

Tony did so, to no avail. 'Nothing at all. No signal.'

Radio transmission – it seemed – had ceased, and the endless sky glared through the windscreen at them, as if the sun was about to emerge.

Then the road before them darkened.

'Now that's strange,' Tony said.

OFF-AIR

acknowledgments

The author could not have discovered, compiled, improved and presented this manuscript without the care, generosity, wisdom, time and belief of the following wondrous people:

Tracy Bohan   James Roxburgh

Cal Doyle   Tom Morris

Ciarán Dowd   Max Porter   Adrian Scally

Gavin Corbett   Lisa McInerney

Bobby Mostyn-Owen   Amber Burlinson   Liz Hatherell

Rich Carr   Jon Gray

Will Atkinson   Emma Heyworth-Dunn

Jamie Forrest (& team)

Kirsty Doole (& team)   Gemma Davis (& team)

Alice Latham (& team)   Niccolò De Bianchi (& team)

John Sprinks (& team)

Comrades at the *Stinging Fly*

Comrades at University College Cork

Mam and Dad   Emily, Rosie, Ben

Cora & Yuki

Luan & *little fig*

and of course Rachel, who makes *everything* possible, never mind the bloody books.